EBURY PRESS

THE GIRL WHO DISAPPEARED

Vikrant Khanna is a ship captain and the bestselling author of *The Girl Who Knew Too Much* and *Secretly Yours*. He lives and works in Singapore. You can contact him here:

www.twitter.com/_VikrantKhanna
www.instagram.com/vikrantkhanna/
www.facebook.com/writervikrant/

ALSO BY THE AUTHOR

The Girl Who Knew Too Much
Secretly Yours

THE
GIRL
WHO
DISAPPEARED

VIKRANT
KHANNA

EBURY
PRESS

An imprint of Penguin Random House

EBURY PRESS

USA | Canada | UK | Ireland | Australia
New Zealand | India | South Africa | China | Singapore

Ebury Press is part of the Penguin Random House group of companies
whose addresses can be found at global.penguinrandomhouse.com

Published by Penguin Random House India Pvt. Ltd
4th Floor, Capital Tower 1, MG Road,
Gurugram 122 002, Haryana, India

First published in Ebury Press by Penguin Random House India 2020

10 9 8 7 6 5 4 3 2

ISBN 9780143449188

Typeset in Adobe Garamond Pro by Manipal Technologies Limited, Manipal

Printed at Manipal Technologies Limited, India

www.penguin.co.in

To my daughter Amyra.
You teach me to love and live.
Everyday.

A Note on the Book

I've always hankered to write a story about a missing person. But I didn't for the longest time, simply because I couldn't think of a sound premise. Then Nisha (the character in the book who goes missing) appeared in my head, and well, almost literally, hand-held me through the story. The plot weaved nicely around her and the secondary characters, and the writing was mostly effortless, except for the ending.

The ending—the last three chapters that is—took me the same amount of time to write as the rest of the book. It was the most brain-racking job I've done in a long time. I had a heap of resolutions to the story, but after a lot of rewriting and much thought (and a nod from Nisha), I chose what you will now read. I sincerely hope you like it, and that the ending catches you by surprise. There's nothing more disappointing to a writer than knowing the readers have predicted the story's end before getting there.

A Note on the Book

The story is set in Writer's Hill, a beautiful retreat in Himachal Pradesh. It's a real place, and a few years back, I had the pleasure of visiting it with a few friends. I loved it so much that I knew I would set one of my future stories here. Everything else in the story is fictional of course.

Well, without further ado, I welcome you to Writer's Hill. Hope you have an enjoyable stay here.

PART 1

The events leading to the mysterious disappearance of Nisha Dastur

1

A car cruises along National Highway 44. The weather is nice and balmy, and the traffic is mild. The man behind the wheel is humming to the sound of a Bollywood track.

His companion, Nisha, doesn't appear as relaxed as him; in fact, she looks nervous, scared. She peers at him, watching him for a minute or two. He continues humming and drumming the steering wheel with his thumbs.

Finally, she says, 'Rishi, are you acting calm, or are you really so at ease?'

The drumming stops. Rishi looks sideways at Nisha. 'To be honest, I'm trying.' He looks back at the road and takes a deep breath. 'I . . . I know what happened is very unsettling—my ex-girlfriend threatening to kill my present girlfriend . . .' He shakes his head. 'Except she wasn't my girlfriend at all. Ha!' He lets out a short laugh.

'She's a psycho!' Nisha spits out. 'Why does she say she is your ex-girlfriend?'

Rishi raises his arms in despair. 'She's just my neighbour. Alright, we went out for movies, coffee occasionally, but that's it! There was never anything between us.'

'And she feels I'm responsible for'—she makes quotation marks with her fingers—'coming between you guys?'

Rishi lets a short hiss escape through his lips. 'I'm sorry for what happened, for what she said to you.' He gives her hand a tight squeeze.

Nisha, looking out the window, doesn't reply. They are passing Ambala. There is a row of *dhaba*s to her left and she contemplates asking Rishi to stop for a quick bite. They'd left Delhi in the wee hours of the morning and she hasn't eaten anything. And now her stomach is grumbling. But she ignores the hunger pangs and decides to eat lunch at their destination.

They are headed to Writer's Hill, a quaint, secluded tourist spot in the mountains of Himachal Pradesh. This isn't a planned vacation, but a last-minute, get-your-stuff-together getaway. They want some peaceful time together, but primarily, they want to be away from Avni—Rishi's ex-girlfriend, or whoever she is.

Suddenly, Nisha feels a chill rising in her spine at a memory. She shivers.

'The way she . . . she *screamed* at me!' she says, horrified anew. 'How she pounced on me like a rabid animal . . .' She trails off, her face contorting as she relives the episode. 'We need to stay far away from her.'

When Rishi turns to her, he sees the fear in her eyes. She still looks frightened after almost twelve hours of the incident.

Justified to an extent, he thinks. Avni has been a revelation. He had known her for more than three years but saw the real Avni only yesterday. How difficult it is to truly know someone! Nisha is right, he agrees—Avni *is* a psycho.

'I get a strong feeling that something horrible is going to happen on this trip,' Nisha's voice is shaking when she speaks again.

'Ah, come on now, Nisha,' Rishi says, waving a careless arm. 'You're thinking way too much about it.'

'Am I really? What if—' She lets the sentence hang.

Alright, last evening's events were . . . unnerving, even frightening, Rishi admits, but they don't warrant the stress Nisha seems to be suffering. It's over now. He knows it wasn't the best decision to invite Nisha to his place last evening—*that* had been the catalyst. They had their entire lives ahead of them for intimacies.

Rishi and Nisha have been dating for a few months. Rishi works in a prominent IT company in Gurgaon. One day, Rishi had a bad toothache. It was a Sunday and he stayed in bed until noon. When the pain got too much to bear, he went to the nearest dental clinic, his left hand firmly pressing the jaw.

It was the dentist's assistant, Nisha, who had told Rishi that a root canal therapy was required. He remembers how scared he was at the prospect, and the subtle, reassuring way

Nisha calmed him down. She explained to him that it is the discomfort experienced before one seeks dental care that is truly painful, not the procedure itself.

In the end, he thought Nisha was right. It was no more painful than having a filling placed. He'd been avoiding a root canal for a long time despite occasional bouts of pain, and now he knew the reason. It was how everything in the world worked out.

Destiny.

He was destined to meet Nisha. To be cured by her. And then fall in love with her.

They kept in touch, went out on weekends, and laughed about his mild panic attack when he'd spotted the surgical tools during his treatment. He remembers that look on her face well, how she'd smiled first and then laughed, covering her mouth. She'd enjoyed torturing him a bit, and then calmed him. Through the pain, his subconscious mind told him she was pretty, and that he should ask her out if he managed to make it out of the treatment alive.

He did, and he knew it was the best thing he would do in his life.

And now, a few months later, he had done a stupid thing, inviting her to his place when he knew full well Avni would be watching.

Stupid. Stupid.

2

Rishi knows two things about Avni—that she loves him obsessively and that she is a little nuts. Avni lives next door to him and is always keen on going out for a movie or coffee with him, coming to his flat, inviting him to her flat, any activity that involves only the two of them.

Out of politeness, Rishi has obliged on a few occasions but lately he has started avoiding her. Simply because she is crazy. She doesn't seem to have family or any other friends— he has never seen her with anyone else. Sometimes when he returns from his office, he spots Avni furtively watching him in the hallway through the chink in her apartment's door. He watches her from the corner of his eye and ignores her. But sometimes he makes it obvious that he knows she is spying on him by suddenly appearing at her door. She only smiles coyly—it doesn't deter her. Avni does what she wants to, and Rishi knows better than to confront her.

He wonders why she is attracted to him. He never thinks of himself as attractive—alright, he's a decent-looking guy, of medium height and medium built, but definitely not handsome in the classic sense of the word. He's not rich either; he doesn't drive fancy cars or live in a fancy house—hell, half the time he finds it difficult to pay the rent for his flat. His parents live in Kanpur, and he hasn't taken any money from them ever since he turned eighteen.

A few months earlier, he had casually asked her, 'Avni, listen, it's flattering, really it is, but why do you like me so much?'

'*Love* you,' she corrected him. 'Rishi, you are such a cool guy, you have such a nice beard! What's not to love about you?'

Beard? Doesn't everyone have a beard these days? Outright nonsense—the girl is insane.

When he walked into the hallway with Nisha yesterday, Avni was peering through the door as usual and slammed out of her apartment at once, showing up before them like an apparition.

'Who is this girl?' she demanded.

'Nisha,' he replied.

'Yeah, but *who* is she? Why is she here?'

'She's my girlfriend.'

Avni was already fuming by then and her nostrils flared at his reply. She fixed Nisha with an icy glare. Her fists tightened, and even from that distance, Rishi could feel her nails burrowing into her palms. Then her breathing became fast and shallow. She muttered something to herself to calm down, he thought, and started pacing up and down the hallway in front of them. Rishi and Nisha watched her with unease for a minute. Rishi then stepped towards his flat, took out the keys from the pocket of his trousers, and began unlocking the door. Avni jumped between them and the keys jingled in his hand in shock.

'You are not taking this slut inside!' she commanded.

'Excuse me?' said Nisha.

Avni wagged an admonitory forefinger at her. '*Do not interrupt*!' Then she turned to Rishi and said in a calmer tone, 'You never let *me* in. How does she get a chance?'

Rishi took a deep breath. He considered the words in his mind first.

'Avni, look,' he began cautiously, 'you are a very good friend of mine. You've done a lot for me, I know, and I am very thankful for it. But I don't love you—'

'You love this bitch?' Avni interjected, nodding towards Nisha.

'Please, Avni, mind your language.'

'Yes or no?'

'I do.'

That set her off. She launched herself at Nisha, and taken unawares, Nisha staggered backwards, lost her balance, and fell on the floor. Her head hit the floor and she winced from the sharp pain radiating in all directions from the point of impact. But there was no time to assess the injury; the next moment Avni was on top of her, her pudgy hands pressing down her neck, choking her.

'I'll kill you, bitch!' Avni screamed. 'I'll kill you!'

Nisha started to feel dizzy. Where was Rishi? she thought. Why wasn't he helping? As her vision slowly cleared, she saw Rishi's arms around Avni's waist, trying to drag her away.

'Let me kill her, Rishi!' Avni continued screaming. 'Then we'll be together!'

Rishi continued to pull at Avni but failed to get her to move even a little. She was short but stout and Rishi realized he would have to change his strategy. He saw Nisha was trying to wrench herself free from Avni's grip but Avni's arms were steadfast. All Nisha managed was to move her head from side to side.

Rishi could see the colour draining from Nisha's face. Panic clawed at his throat and he felt beads of sweat beginning to form on his forehead. He shook his head vigorously and positioned himself in front of Avni now. He placed his hands on Avni's forearms, and with all the energy he could muster, tried to dislodge her hold on Nisha's neck. He could see it was beginning to work; Avni's grip was loosening.

Just as he braced himself to apply more force, help arrived in the form of two men crossing the hallway. Finally, the three men jerked away Avni's hold, and with the sudden impact, Avni was propelled backwards. But before she fell back, Avni's right hand, intentionally or inadvertently, Rishi would wonder later, connected with the collar of Nisha's cream top, tearing off a thin strip of cloth right to the bottom.

Embarrassed with her bra on display, Nisha rolled over, away from Avni, coughing and gagging. Rishi dropped to her side and rubbed her back.

'I'm so sorry, baby,' he cried. 'Are you okay?'

Nisha clung to him, coughing and crying in turns.

Avni gathered herself, clearly not done, and began storming towards them but the two men grabbed her from behind.

'Lady, calm down,' one of them said. 'What the hell do you think you are doing?'

'Let me go!' screamed Avni, twisting and turning as she tried to free herself. 'I'll kill her today!'

'You guys go,' the other man offered. 'We'll take care of her.'

'Go, go, go,' agreed the first.

'*NO!*' Avni screamed again. '*She has to die! She has to die!*'

Nisha opens her eyes when the car jerks suddenly. She thinks she had been asleep and dreaming about an incident that hadn't happened. But reality soon sinks in and she feels her throat constrict. The screeching sound of the brakes seems sinister to her. And when she sees what is in front of the car, she freezes.

She looks at Rishi in horror.

Rishi shrugs. 'The cat just jumped in front of the car from nowhere!'

'You realize what this means?'

'Nothing,' Rishi replies. 'It means nothing. Don't make a big deal out of this.'

'It's a bad omen.'

Nisha glances at the black cat that has now wandered towards her side. The cat gazes back at Nisha. She doesn't like the cat's deep yellow eyes. Its stare is intimidating. Nisha swears there is malice in the eyes. Bile rises in her throat. Finally, she has to drop her gaze as the cat doesn't concede.

Rishi puts the engine in first gear and drives away.

'Something bad is going to happen,' Nisha whispers. 'I feel it. Something bad is going to happen on this trip.'

3

Writing a book isn't easy. Hell, sometimes framing a single sentence seems so daunting. And then, when you manage to complete the book and send it out to uppity publishers, they all reject it with a single, apathetic line: *'Thank you for sending us your submission, but unfortunately it does not fit our publishing programme.'*

If I find the person who first came up with this line, I swear he or she will experience a lot of pain in a lot of places. That person will not write such a complacent sentence ever.

Please don't get me wrong. I'm not a violent person but when I get angry, I can lose my head. Hey, come on! This is the twelfth rejection I've got in as many months; what do you expect me to feel? I am beginning to wonder if the work I've been sending out is even read at all. Because it simply can't be that all the twelve publishers tell me the same thing.

Ugh, I need a break.

I pick the cigarette pack from the bedside table and walk out to the veranda. It's a pleasant, sunny afternoon, and even though it's October, winter seems far away. I light up and take a long, satisfying drag. I exhale the smoke slowly out of my nostrils. Gazing around, I take another drag.

Thank God this place is so peaceful. With dense trees all around, the soothing trill of the birds overhead, and the vast expanse of green as far as the eyes can see, you are safely in the lap of nature, and I badly needed a place like this as a writing retreat. I smoke till the cigarette burns out and toss it in the garden in front.

I mull over my story and its rejection. It's a mystery—the story of a man who obsessively loves this beautiful woman, stalks her, and is torn between hurting her or letting her go when it turns out she doesn't love him back.

I leave the ending open for the readers to decide how they want to conclude it. Love is complicated, after all, and everyone views it differently. There cannot be a single conclusion. Love can mean happiness to some, but pain to others. Everyone connects with this universal emotion differently.

So how can I give the story an end?

Maybe that's the reason for its rejection. But I won't change it. Love is the most complex emotion there is and that should be reflected in the story.

Over the next hour, I pace back and forth on the veranda and think about it. And as I expected, I think about Maira and how much I loved her. My heart sinks even as my lips form her name. God, how I loved her!

Her face, those beautiful eyes, flash in my mind and I get this huge lump in my throat. I hear the sound of her laughter, the gentle, reassuring way she would look at me. My eyes well up.

In the end, I know it wasn't her fault. It was mine. She was right when she said she couldn't understand me. I don't blame her. I wish her well wherever she is.

Right, back to my book.

When I was a small boy, my mother would read out stories to me at night. I loved listening to them. There was magic in them. And so much life and hope. Subconsciously, I'd dreamt of writing my own stories someday—to live my life through them, be the character I want to become. Experience love, hatred, anger, jealousy, passion. Real life is so dull.

Maybe when my book gets published one day, I'll dedicate it to my mother. It'll be a surprise. I haven't told her yet that I have finished writing a book. There's no point. She'll be so disappointed that no one wants to publish it. And I can't disappoint her. She deserves to be happy now, with the life that she has led. My asshole father left us. She has brought me up all by herself with two jobs, working sixteen hours a day.

This car ahead distracts me. It's entering this resort, isn't it? I think I saw it at a distance just a few minutes earlier, winding up the hill but didn't realize it was headed this way. It's an old blue sedan, looking as though it's straight out of a scrapyard. The driver parks the car next to mine and honks. He steps out . . . no, they step out; there's a woman with him. The man removes his sunglasses and looks around. I don't think he'll find anyone. He needs to take the stairs to his left and walk up to the buildings. The parking space is a bit cut off from up here.

I see him dialling a number now. A few seconds later, Babu, the caretaker of this place, scrambles out of his small cottage, hurriedly pulling on a white kurta. He looks down and waves towards the stairs. There are just about twenty of them, but they can tire you out as they are very high.

Each step has an artefact or a flowerpot or an embellishment of some sort. In fact, the entire resort is very tastefully done. Anywhere you look, you'll see a beautiful artefact, a showpiece, lilies and roses in all their glory. There's a 40-inch sitting Buddha statue to the right once you come up the stairs, a huge flowerpot to the left. The garden, which starts at the top of the steps, is a blaze of yellow and orange and pink with generous touches of purple; the cottages are arrayed around this beautiful space.

In all there are eight cottages in the resort, not too many, as the owner never intended this place to be big. A sensible idea. I met the guy once, last week. He's a Sikh—a tall, enterprising guy. I told him I'll visit this place regularly as it's so beautifully maintained and he thanked me.

I walk out of my cottage towards the new arrivals. They are headed towards the tiny reception area next to the kitchen, Babu guiding them.

'Hey, new guests?'

Babu spins around. 'Oh yes, Anandji, they've just arrived.'

I walk towards them. They seem quite young, early twenties perhaps. The girl is fair and attractive, a little plump and short. But it's her eyes that attract my attention. They are big but red and sore. What happened? Has she been crying? The guy is medium built, bearded and good-looking.

'Hi.' I throw out my hand. 'I'm Anand.'

The guy takes it. 'I'm Rishi.' He has a firm handshake. We look at the girl; she doesn't look up and refuses to acknowledge my presence. 'And she's Nisha.'

'Hi Nisha,' I say.

Nothing.

There's an awkward moment. Rishi gently nudges her. She looks up ever so slowly and gives a slight shake of her head before walking away. Babu walks them to the reception. I light another cigarette, gazing at their retreating backs. Rishi turns around and catches me staring at them. I don't look away. We look at each other for a few moments before he turns to Nisha and mutters something.

What's their story?

4

Little Meena moves cautiously. She adjusts her dark glasses that are too big for her face. Her mother Moni holds her hand and they slowly walk from their tiny cottage on the extreme left of the resort over to the kitchen. Meena can hear the crickets chirping. She knows dawn isn't far away.

Inside the kitchen, Moni switches on the light and pulls out a big pan from the basket of utensils she had left yesterday to dry out. She fills it with water from the purifier and puts it on the stove.

As the water begins to boil, she asks Meena, 'Will you make it today?'

Meena nods. She lifts her right arm and stands on tiptoes to grope for the jar of tea leaves on the shelf. She opens the jar and puts several spoonfuls of tea leaves in the water. Next, she reaches for the jar of sugar.

'No, no.' Her mother stops her. 'You've forgotten, Meena! We serve the sugar separately for guests. Some don't take sugar with their tea.'

Meena nods. She waits for the hissing sound of the boiling water. When she hears it, she reduces the flame to simmer and covers the pan with a steel plate.

Meena is twelve years old and blind from birth. She has been living in these hills with her parents ever since, helping her parents with the cooking, cleaning, and serving. Her parents cannot afford education for her—well, even if they could, where is the nearest school? Forty-five kilometres down the hill in Basra. And how would she manage to study with the 'normal' kids there? Her parents have had this discussion enough times in the past to come to the conclusion that education is pointless for Meena. It would be better for her to help her parents in the daily chores around this place.

'Enough,' her mother says.

Meena turns off the flame. Holding a cloth, she removes the plate from the top of the pan. Her mother pours tea into three cups and empties out the remaining in a large steel kettle for the guests.

'Here, can you take this cup for your father?'

Meena nods and takes the cup. She walks out of the kitchen, one arm outstretched, across the garden towards their cottage, where Babu is making the bed. In all, there are twenty-three steps.

'Good morning, Meena,' he says. 'Did you make the tea today?'

'Yes.' Meena feels pleased with herself. She hands over the cup to her father.

Babu takes a sip. 'Very good.'

Over the next two hours, the three of them go about their daily morning routine. Meena helps her mother cook the breakfast—upma, aloo parathas, boiled eggs. Babu prepares orange juice in the juicer and readies two big jugs of it. They ready the al fresco dining table that overlooks the valley, offering breathtaking views of the hills. In winter, the hills are shrouded by the mist but still offer a stunning panorama. They set the table with plates, cutlery, glasses, cups, and place the food on another long table behind it.

After the breakfast prep, they clean the common areas, water the plants, sort out the garbage, and wait for the guests to emerge from their cottages.

They are pleased the resort isn't crowded this time of the year. Most years, around Diwali season, the place is packed as people from neighbouring states—many from Delhi—visit to enjoy its tranquility. Presently, there is just the writer sahib, the couple who came yesterday, and another young couple.

Babu doesn't like the writer. He can't put his finger on it, but he feels in his bones that something is wrong with the guy. He smokes two packs of cigarettes in a day, paces up and down his veranda—at least six hours a day, Babu swears—constantly muttering under his breath. His cottage is a tip, cigarette butts strewn all over the floor. And he will always—

Babu feels a sudden rush of blood when he turns and finds Anand standing behind him.

'Go-good morning, sir.'

Anand nods. 'Morning, what's going on?'

'Nothing, sir. Breakfast is ready.'

Anand glances towards the cottage of yesterday's new arrivals. 'Where are they?'

Babu shakes his head. 'They haven't come out of the cottage yet.'

'Go, call them.'

Babu hesitates. 'They . . . they'll come out when they have to, sir. I don't want to disturb them.'

Anand gives him an icy glare and retrieves a cigarette from his jacket. 'Is that so?'

Babu nods sheepishly and excuses himself. Anand sits on a chair that gives him a view of Nisha and Rishi's room. He fixes his gaze in that direction.

Why was the girl looking so sad yesterday?

5

Anand's excessive curiosity about the new couple does not escape Babu who is peering at him from a distance. Anand's gaze does not drop.

Moni walks over with the teapot and places it on the dining table.

'Tea is ready, sir.'

It takes a moment for Anand to realize she's talking to him. 'Ah . . . okay. Can you please pour some for me?'

'Yes, sir.'

From the other side of the garden, the couple from Cottage 1, Roy and Monica, walk out.

'Morning, aunty,' the girl greets Moni.

'Good morning, madam, breakfast is ready.'

'Thank you.'

Anand abhors them, especially the girl. For one, she is always chewing gum, and two, God, he hates her tattoos. Both her arms are inked all the way to her wrists.

Miss Pretentious, he likes to call her.

All cool people have tattoos, so let's get a tattoo! And how to ensure people see it? Wear sleeveless tees! Tattoos are not for ourselves—they are for other people to see. To show them how cool we are.

And always chew gum—it makes you seem cooler.

The guy is a tad better; he's got just one arm tattooed and at least he doesn't masticate gum first thing in the morning.

Monica pulls her phone out and takes a couple of selfies on her own, then with Roy, and finally some pictures of the breakfast spread. She checks the pictures, taps the screen of her phone a few times, and settles down, satisfied.

'Morning, Mr Writer,' says Monica. *Asshole!* she thinks. She pours tea into two cups and offers one to Roy.

'You don't want to throw that out?' Anand gestures to her lips.

Monica doesn't reply; she cocks her head to her right and chews slowly and deliberately. She doesn't like Anand at all. He's tall like a giraffe, thin like a straw, with unkempt hair and, God, that messy beard. *Does he even take a shower?*

Roy butts in. 'How's your writing going? Killed anyone lately in your book?'

Anand throws his head back and laughs.

'You write mysteries, right?'

Anand nods. 'So? Every mystery story doesn't always involve a murder.' He rises, takes a *paratha* from the casserole, slathers it with butter and settles back. He surveys it before taking a bite. 'Do you guys even read books?'

'Only all the time,' Monica replies loftily.

'What are you reading now?'

Monica doesn't hide her annoyance. 'I like to read non-fiction.'

'Name the book.'

'Umm . . .' she glances at Roy.

'I thought so.'

'I don't have time for stupid books.'

Anand chuckles. 'Of course. Clicking pictures and uploading them on social media would take up most of your time. That's *such* an important task of life.'

'What's your problem, man?' Roy says, irritated. 'Stop troubling my girlfriend.'

Anand waves a casual hand. 'Yeah, I'm done for today.'

Nisha and Rishi emerge from their cottage. Monica does a quick survey, her eyes running up and down the couple.

'Oh, pretty girl,' says Monica.

'Not prettier than you, baby,' says Roy.

They follow this exchange with a kiss. That's another of their traits Anand hates—public display of affection.

Shouldn't love be subtle? If you love someone, just be content with their presence in your life. In a world driven by hatred and lies, how many people are fortunate enough to be with the person they love anyway? I'm not of those lucky ones.

Babu comes forward and offers tea to the newcomers. Nisha still looks tense and is silent after the initial pleasantries. The guys do most of the talking. Rishi finds out that Anand is a writer.

When Anand asks him the reason for their visit, Rishi replies casually, 'Just a last-minute getaway.' Anand probes further: he wants to know where Rishi works, how did he meet Nisha, about his family. Rishi answers all the questions patiently.

Meanwhile, Monica has decided to join the conversational fray. 'What do you do?' she asks Nisha, her eyes still sizing her up.

'I'm a dentist.' She sips some tea. 'What about you?'

'Nothing,' Monica replies. 'I go on vacations. My family's pretty rich so . . .' She lets the sentence hang.

Anand rolls his eyes. *I'm talking about love all the time, but what about hate? Isn't that a powerful emotion too? How I hate this tattooed woman! Bloody Miss Pretentious.*

Silence falls as the five of them focus on breakfast before retiring to their respective cottages.

Over the next hour, Babu and family clean the table, wash the dishes, and begin the preparations for lunch.

In the kitchen, Moni is kneading the dough for chapattis and Babu is cutting the salad. Meena is getting the vegetables out for the sabzi when she stops short as a sudden bolt of electricity courses through her. Her body starts trembling. Suddenly, she gets a searing headache. She closes her eyes.

She hears someone screaming and the howls of an animal. The sky turns dark and gloomy. There is a loud rumble of thunder and lightning crackles across the sky in bright, wide arcs. Suddenly, the wind picks up into a strong breeze, which morphs into a storm. The trees bend to the power of the storm, branches are yanked out and fly some distance. The screaming becomes shriller, the howls louder.

Now Meena sees herself in the middle of nowhere. She tries to concentrate hard—the place smells familiar but she can't identify it. Then, in the distance, she sees the silhouette of a person approaching. No . . . there is more than one . . . there are more than half a dozen people approaching. Only they don't look like *people* . . . they don't look like people *at all* . . . They don't have faces, or maybe the faces are mutilated? She doesn't know. She can't see their faces clearly. But they look strange, scary. *Who are they?*

Suddenly, her eyes fly open, and she feels a knot tightening her stomach so hard she recoils and hits the earthen pot behind her. It rocks on the table for a bit before crashing to the floor.

'What happened?' Babu wheels around at the sound. The pot is in fragments.

'They are coming!'

6

'I just hate that guy so much,' cries Monica the moment they enter the cottage, banging the door behind her.

'Who, Anand?' Roy asks with no particular interest as he jumps on to the bed and stretches.

Monica shrugs. 'Why is he always such a …' She struggles to find the right word and settles with 'asshole'. 'Who is *he* to tell me anything?'

'What? About reading?'

Monica waves a hand. 'Forget it.'

Their cottage is compact and elegant, with all the necessities. There is a queen-sized bed with a comfortable and high mattress, air conditioner which is too strong for comfort, a 42-inch television but sadly with not very good reception, an electric kettle with ample tea bags, and a fairly luxurious bathroom. To the right of the bed, a window opens to the garden. Unfortunately, Anand's cottage is on the other side of the garden. Monica swears she has seen Anand peeking into their cottage on more than one occasion. He has a pair of binoculars, she always tells Roy, but Roy doesn't believe it.

Now, Monica has something else on her mind. 'I need you to do something for me.'

'Anything, darling.' Roy is still stretching himself on the bed. Although he says that, he knows he's in trouble.

Monica moves closer to him. 'Did you see that bitch's watch?' When the question does not elicit any interest from Roy, she starts again. 'Nisha was wearing a Cartier Tank Solo, the 18K pink gold model. That's like'—she mulls it over—'at least two lakh rupees.'

'So?'

'So? What do you mean so?' She bashes him on the leg. 'I want you to steal it for me.'

Roy snaps upright. 'Shhhh . . . can you be a little quiet?' He takes a deep breath before resuming, 'We can't let anyone know who we really are.'

'Yeah whatever, you're always so scared. Did you just shit your pants when I said that?'

Monica always does that. It is part of the reason he loves her and, well . . . hates her. She wants to possess everything she likes, never mind if it belongs to someone else. But isn't it justified? he sometimes asks himself.

Monica had a troubled childhood. Both her parents found better life partners, so they abandoned their only child. Monica was eight years old then. She lived on the streets for a few months before finding refuge in an orphanage.

Five years later, she met Roy, a deft pickpocket also dumped by his drunkard father.

With similar life stories, Monica and Roy quickly became friends. In their early teens, friendship blossomed into love, and since then, they've been inseparable. Their lack of education left them with few career options, and they turned to stealing full-time.

They started with minor thefts, stealing from the local *kirana* stores in and around their neighbourhood. The modus operandi was simple. One of them would strike up a conversation with the shop owner and the other, at the opportune moment, would snatch whatever they could lay their hands on and escape. Slowly, they graduated to shoplifting in shopping malls. Here they would mostly steal clothes. They targeted smaller malls where shops did not have a sophisticated security system. They'd enter a shop, pick up a few clothes, and proceed to the trial room on the pretext of trying them out. They'd then hand over some of them to a shop employee and coolly walk out of the shop. Due to their lean bodies, it was very hard for anyone to detect that they were wearing two, sometimes three, layers of clothes inside. They found an unscrupulous garment exporter and sold him the stolen clothes. It was an easy way to make money, they thought.

Another technique they regularly deployed was to carry an umbrella into shops. One of them would hang the closed umbrella on their elbow and the other would pick up small objects and drop them into the umbrella. It was amazing how many small items could be pilfered this way. They would pay for one or two small items to evade any suspicion and then, cool as a cucumber, stroll out of the store.

Sometimes they also used folded newspapers with the same effect although they could steal fewer items this way. The best weapon in their armour was a baby stroller. Now, that was the easiest way to steal. For a baby stroller, you need a baby to ward off suspicion, so . . . well, they even bought a dummy baby. They would cover it with a blanket, put in a few soft toys, a feeding bottle, a diaper bag (all stolen), and enter a store. It was just so easy. There's so much space in a stroller, any number of small items could be quietly dropped in.

Lately, they have become bored of these baby robberies (that's what Monica calls them) and started contemplating bigger gigs where the spoils would be far greater—perhaps a jewellery store, an ATM, a bank. They know they can do it, but they've realized they need some accomplices, and also some money to swing it. Money begets money, after all.

They'd zeroed in on robbing a bank as their mission for next year. For now, they concentrated their efforts on building up a fund for that 'project'. The trip to Writer's Hill was to relax and organize their thoughts, but surely Monica wouldn't let a good opportunity slip by.

Roy rolls his eyes. 'Monica, please, I don't think—'

'Yes or no?'

'What, are you saying stealing a watch is that easy?'

'Yes or no?'

Roy tuts and shakes his head. 'Every watch has a clasp, every clasp has a pin, every pin has a—'

'Yes or no?'

'Alright.'

7

I put down the binoculars. I could see Roy and Monica were having a very intense discussion. Monica, as usual, seemed to be overpowering Roy—something I've seen her do often by now.

But what could they be talking about right after breakfast? Weren't they with each other before breakfast? And before that? So, they found something very pressing to discuss immediately after they enter the cottage. Immediately after meeting the new couple.

Hmm . . . interesting.

I can sense that they are not who they claim to be. If you are rich, would you just be happy about it or would you keep proclaiming it to the world? I'll do the former. Monica always does the latter.

See, of the two classes of rich people—new money and old money—the new money lot have an overarching desire to show the world: *Oh yeah, baby, we have the money!* They buy this, that and what not, splurge to their heart's content. Then they turn to social media to show their conspicuous consumption to the world. That's what they're buying for, after all. The old money folk—who've always had money—don't splurge when they don't have to and certainly don't scream about their possessions from the rooftops.

Now my problem is that Miss Pretentious, going by her actions, is certainly new money, but her story of her family being rich seems to suggest that she is old money.

Doesn't add up, right?

That's what I figured. So why is she lying?

Okay, here's another thing. Why are they here? Babu tells me they've been here for more than a month now.

A month? Who stays a month in such an isolated place? Especially young go-getters like them. I wouldn't deny this is a great place to relax, but a month? Sorry, I'm not buying it.

You must be thinking that I am overthinking this. Of course, I am. I'm a mystery writer. What do you expect?

Anyway, yesterday, I decided to write a short story or a series of short stories. I want to hone my writing and storytelling skills, and especially perfect the art of a satisfying ending. I want to write a good climax. Maybe then I'll rewrite my book and re-pitch it to publishers.

And for any story, you need strong, well-developed characters. I've already decided on my protagonists—who better than our Nisha and Rishi? A protagonist has to have a nemesis—the antagonist. I don't even need to put my brain to work for this—they must be Roy and Monica. Then we need a conflict in the story. Which is again very clear. There must be a conflict between these two couples.

The first couple—Nisha and Rishi—must be hounded in some way by the second couple—Roy and Monica (who wouldn't?)—so much that *something* happens. The rest of the story would revolve around the resolution of the problem. Towards the end, the problem would be resolved—I like happy endings.

So, first, I have decided to come up with a problem, and second, I need to research more on my characters. Oooh, this will be interesting.

Okay, smoke time. I grab the cigarette pack and lighter from my desk and venture outside.

The day, as usual, is beautiful. A gentle breeze is blowing and everything around me looks so green. I light a cigarette and take a drag. I look to my left at the new couple's cottage. I see them by the window . . . wait, is Nisha crying? I'm too far away to see clearly but the way her back is bent, shoulders drooping, she doesn't appear to be in the brightest of moods.

I drop the cigarette and stub it out with my foot. Glancing around, I move quietly towards their cottage. Standing with my back to the wall of their cottage, I slowly slide towards the window. I want to hear what they are talking about. I glance around again. No one. Good.

I reach the window and cautiously take a quick peek inside. Nisha is sitting on the bed now and Rishi is hunkered on his knees near her. Nisha's head is bent, and she is crying. I strain to hear what they're saying.

'Don't be so scared, Nisha, you're safe now.'

Nisha doesn't respond. I can hear her soft sobs. Then she says something, but it is not audible to me.

'So, what will she do? Does she even know we are here?' Rishi replies loudly. I can hear anger creeping into his voice.

What are they talking about? Who is this 'she'? Why is Nisha so scared?

Interesting. Very interesting.

Nisha continues sobbing and I hear Rishi repeating the same words. What is the reason for Nisha's fear? Maybe I'll ask him the next time we meet. Nah, not a good idea.

And just as I think of getting out of here, I stop dead in my tracks. Someone's standing outside my cottage and looking at me. It's the girl—what's her name?—Meena, staring at me impassively. My heart pounds in my chest and my throat suddenly feels dry. What will she be thinking now? Oh wait . . . she's blind.

Ha!

She hasn't seen me eavesdropping. She can't see anything. What a relief! For a moment there, I felt paralyzed with embarrassment.

I continue listening.

I want to know their story.

8

An hour earlier, her parents were staring at Meena and the broken pot in confusion. Despite the cool weather, Meena was sweating. The colour had drained from her face. Babu and Moni exchanged apprehensive glances.

'What happened, Meena?' her mother asked. 'Who's coming?'

Meena doesn't reply. She looked like she was in shock. Babu noticed she was shivering. He walked towards her, held her arms, and gave her a gentle shake.

'What's happening, Meena?' he asked. 'Where are you lost?'

Meena relaxed slightly on realizing it was a dream. *But such a vivid dream.* She ran a hand over her face and was surprised at its wetness. *How long was I dreaming?*

'Sorry, Baba,' she managed to find her voice. 'I don't know.'

Babu shot a puzzled glance at Moni. She shook her head.

'Come now,' she said to Meena. 'Come with me. Help me with cleaning the cottages.'

As usual they start with the writer's cottage as it is the filthiest. When they step inside, they are overcome with an intense wave of nausea. *God, the stink.* The cottage is in a complete mess. Cigarette butts and ash are strewn all over the floor, clothes are lying on the bed, on the floor, everywhere, and the mattress . . . even the mattress is on the floor. *Where does he sleep?*

The desk appears to have a million items thrown on it. Moni walks to the bathroom and cringes. There's water all over the bathroom floor, muddy footprints across it, and it reeks of urine. The pot . . . oh, she doesn't even look at it. She knows.

'Meena, don't come inside,' she tells her daughter. 'I'll manage this.'

Moni starts with the bathroom floor. She has to use a detergent and a strong brush to get rid of the footprints. *How does he manage to make it so dirty?* Next, she targets the pot, scrubbing with the toilet brush with one hand and holding her nose with the other. She cleans it for what seems like a lifetime and flushes.

'Maharaja Anand!' she scoffs.

She has to spend thirty minutes cleaning the cottage itself. The toughest part is removing the ash from the carpet. How many times has she told the writer not to throw ash on the floor? She has put three ashtrays in the cottage—on the desk, bedside table and even in the bathroom—but he ignores them all.

Sodhiji, the owner of the place and her boss, is very finicky about cleanliness, and he expects them to keep all the cottages spotless. But she likes him. He is a generous employer, giving them a good bonus when the place is fully occupied. Now their work seems very light with just three cottages occupied. But this alone feels like three cottages.

At the door, she spends a final minute surveying it and is amazed at the difference she has made in the last forty-five minutes. She shakes her head and steps out. Meena has been standing there, not uttering a word. She feels that Meena has been relatively quiet since yesterday; in fact, she hasn't spoken at all. But she dismisses the thought quickly—kids are mercurial. As she closes the door and turns to leave, her jaw drops.

What is writer sahib doing outside the new guests' cottage? Is he eavesdropping? What is wrong with him?

She watches as he casually walks away. Moni looks after him until he's out of sight and, not for the first time since he moved here last week, feels something is terribly wrong with the fellow.

9

Inside the cottage, the atmosphere is still tense. Rishi feels more and more that Nisha is taking the incident with Avni far too seriously. They are here now, and Avni doesn't even know about it.

'And how long before she finds out?' Nisha asks, her voice shaking. 'We do have to leave this place in a week. Don't you think she'll be waiting for us once we get back?'

'So what? What will she do? Why are you so scared of her?' He rubs his hand over the back of his neck. He's still on his knees with his arms on Nisha's lap. Shaking his head, he rises. 'I shouldn't have—I shouldn't have called you to my place.'

'But that's not the point.' Nisha rises too. She fixes her gaze on Rishi. 'That's really not the point. Someday she would have known, someday she would have done what she did. She's an animal. We *need* to do something about it.'

'But what?'

Nisha shrugs.

'Hey!' Rishi's voice brightens. 'Why don't you tell your dad about it?'

What's wrong with him? Nisha thinks. Alright, her father is a Member of Parliament (MP) from a north-west constituency in Delhi and a prominent politician, but what's that got to do with dealing with a psychopath? Sure, he knows the right people but what would she tell her father?

Listen, Daddy, I had plans to sleep with my boyfriend in his apartment the other day, but just before stepping in, I was attacked by his psycho ex-girlfriend, or whoever she is, who also happens to be his neighbour. Could you please do something about it because I'm dying to sleep with my boyfriend in his flat, and I'm afraid the next time I go there, she'll attack me again.

Oh, and did I tell you, she wanted to kill me?

'What do I tell my dad?' she says, putting the brakes on her thoughts.

Since yesterday, she has imagined the thousand ways, if not more, Avni will kill her the next time she sees her. The creepiest of them is the one triggered by the memory of a scene from an old Hindi movie, where someone is buried alive behind a wall.

The thought of it sends a chill down her spine again.

Rishi is aware it isn't so easy. She can't tell her father she'd come to spend the night at his place. 'Just tell him you came to visit a friend. You don't have to say it was me. And then tell him how, out of nowhere, this girl attacked you.'

Nisha raises her eyebrows. 'You know my dad, don't you? He knows all my friends, he knows where they live, their names, what they do, etcetera. It was damn difficult to convince him that I'll be spending a couple of days in solitude and that he should leave me alone for this trip. He's very protective.' She shrugs. 'Well, every father in Delhi is overprotective of his daughter these days considering the crime rates against women. If I tell my dad, he's going to send his men there and then he'll find out it was you I was meeting.' She walks to the small fridge, pulls out a bottle of water and takes a few sips. Putting it back, she turns around. 'Don't get me wrong ... my dad is very cool, but I don't want to embarrass him, you know?'

Rishi nods. 'Yeah, I understand.'

'So, I don't want to involve him at this stage. What would he tell his police buddies? And what action would they take anyway? It's not as if she . . . well, she attacked me but I'm fine. How can they take pre-emptive action for what she might do in future?'

'Let's just forget about it then,' Rishi suggests. 'I heard there's a small lake nearby where we can hire a boat. Let's check it out.'

Nisha's lack of response is her answer. She feels bad for Rishi. She really loves him, and she knows he's truly concerned for her. Is she really thinking too much about yesterday's incident? Should she just forget about it and take things as they come?

That bitch Avni wouldn't have a gun with her the next time I see her, would she? If she did, where would she shoot me? Heart, face . . . oh God, stop it!

There it is again, her mind, playing the perfect host to all those nasty thoughts.

'Okay, look,' says Rishi. 'Maybe I can send my sister to my place to talk to her?'

'Rashmi?' asks Nisha. 'How would that help?'

'Rashmi has met Avni many times and Avni likes her. Well'—he rolls his eyes—'at least she pretends to like her. She wouldn't do her any harm.'

'You sure?'

Rishi nods.

In the evening, they go to the lake after all, and hire a boat for half an hour. It isn't a big lake, as Rishi had anticipated, but a small, roundish, man-made one. There are a few boats moving slowly across the water.

Rishi pays for the boat to a gangly man, who holds out his hand eagerly for the money Rishi takes out. He leads them to the boat, Nisha's anxious eyes darting around. It is going to be dark soon, and she thinks they don't have much time for the boat ride. But she couldn't say no to Rishi who's been pleading with her to walk around outside, do some activities that will keep the ghastly images of the Avni incident out of her mind. She knows he is right—she's had enough of it.

Hell yeah, if Avni messes around again, I will tell Dad and have her arrested. Dad knows the Delhi Commissioner of Police, for God's sake. Why should I be afraid?

She steels herself and decides not to think of that crazy woman anymore. She holds out a hand for Rishi to take, steps into the wooden boat, and plonks herself down on one of the wooden ledges. Rishi, sitting across from her, gives her a big smile.

'You okay?' he asks.

She nods.

The gangly man pushes the boat clear of the mud. 'Half an hour,' he says.

Rishi holds the two oars and slowly rows them over the surface of the water. Five minutes later, they are in the middle of the lake.

'Just know one thing, Nisha,' he says, his eyes full of warmth. 'I love you and will never let anything happen to you.'

Nisha nods again, reaching across to give Rishi's arm a tight squeeze.

10

There they are again. Meena is standing in the middle of nowhere and those . . . people—*can she even call them that?*—are marching towards her, slowly, one step at a time. There are seven or eight of them, she can't be sure. Their faces are obscured by the dust flying around, and she sees just wavering silhouettes of them. All she knows is that they are getting closer.

She tosses on her bed, her face glistening with sweat, as she strains to see them better. There is the same image—some crippled people approaching her. *Who are they? What do they want?*

She doesn't know.

Shifting her focus from the figures, she tries to identify the place she is in. She squeezes her eyes shut and tries to concentrate. All she sees is a blanket of darkness. Slowly, the darkness fades, and she sees the same blurred images.

There is a piercing light emanating from them. She can't see anything else.

Now she tries to focus on listening. But all she can hear are the soft snores of her parents to her right. She guesses it must be past midnight as they always sleep by ten, and she must have been awake—or in this semi-sleep state—for at least two hours since getting into bed.

Even though she is blind from birth, her mother has told her, rather made her *believe*, that she is gifted and special. She has told Meena that people who are blind from birth have a high sensitivity to their surroundings. They can hear more, smell more, feel more, than normal people. So, Meena has always believed she is special.

Whenever her heart breaks at the permanent blanket of darkness surrounding her, her mother reassures her. 'The world is not that great a place to see, Meena. You're not missing anything.'

'But I want to see, Mamma.' And she'd start sobbing.

Moni would feel so much pain and anguish as if someone had pierced open her heart. But what can she do? It's not that they had not tried their best. All their savings had gone to the many eye specialists they'd consulted in the first five years of Meena's birth.

They all had the same answer. 'The blindness is due to the degeneration of the retina. At present, there is no treatment of this condition.'

But Moni and Babu were determined. They travelled across the country and consulted more eye specialists.

They clung on to each other and hope. But sometimes hope can be a bad thing. In their case, it was eventually crushed, and they finally had to accept that their daughter would never see the world.

It broke their heart. Every shred of their body complained at the unfairness of it all. They were good people, worked hard, never harmed a soul, so why had this happened to them? They didn't know and quietly went on with their lives. Everyone does, eventually.

But her mother's words stuck in Meena's head like the tune of a catchy song you've heard over the radio.

'You are special, Meena. You are gifted.'

Perhaps it was this consistent thought, this belief, playing over and over again in her mind, day and night, that gave her some special powers.

She grew aware of her gift a little more than a year ago. She heard a boy screaming in her mind. *'Help! Help!'* She also heard splashes of water. Both sounds juxtaposed together in a consistent babble that rang in her ears all morning. She didn't know what to do about it. She didn't even know if it had any significance or if she needed to act. So, she ignored it.

In the afternoon, her mother told her that the little boy, Manu, staying in the cottage behind theirs, had fallen into the nearby lake. By the grace of God, he was safe.

Meena felt the windows of the world open for her. She could *see* things. Her mind became a strong, powerful magnet that attracted visions out of the ordinary activities around her. She found that when she focused very hard, she could even see her surroundings—wavery, blurred, but *something*. But when she told her mother, she laughed.

'Meena, how is that possible?' Her mother stopped laughing. 'And like I always tell you—the world is a bad place. You don't want to see it.'

Then, once when her mother read out a story to her about some blind children (Meena always wanted to hear stories about blind children to understand their experiences), she heard of the phenomenon known as 'sight-sharing'.

'That's just a fantasy of these children, Meena,' her mother warned her. 'Don't believe it. Writers will write anything just to sell their books.'

But it stuck with Meena—the idea of getting in someone else's mind and seeing the world through their eyes.

Some months earlier, she had used her mother as a guinea pig. She concentrated hard when she was around her, and slowly, the black cloud in front of her eyes cleared and she could see blurry images of a sea of greenery around her. The world wasn't a bad place at all. In fact, it was beautiful. She cried hard that day, leaning against the wall behind their cottage.

Her mother had lied to her. But she had done so for her. So Meena wouldn't be sad. And so, she decided she wouldn't tell her mother that she *could* sort of see the world, that the world was *not* a bad place, so her mother wouldn't feel sad for her.

Drying her tears, she'd stepped into the cottage and put her arms around her mother. 'I love you, Mamma.'

So, what is happening now? All day she has been seeing these visions of strange creatures approaching her and cannot figure out what they mean. In the evening she tries to get in her mother's mind when she is making tea to try and *see* them, but nothing registers on her radar.

So, they're not here yet, she concludes.

She runs a hand across her face, wiping off a fine mist of sweat, and realizes she is thirsty. She gropes under her bed for a few seconds till her fingers touch the copper bottle. She sits up, takes a few sips, and puts back the bottle. She lies down again and tries to relax.

It's nothing, the sane part of her mind tells her. *I'm just imagining these things.*

But she can't get rid of the wave of disquiet that has settled over her, and she does not sleep the entire night.

11

The next morning, the guests assemble at the breakfast table. Coincidentally, they are all out at the same time and earlier than yesterday. They fill their plates with *poori-chole* from the buffet table and sit down to savour their meal. The delicious smell of the food wafts around them—perhaps the reason for their early breakfast.

Nisha seems to be in a much better mood today; she is cheerful and chatting with Rishi who seems intent on keeping her thoroughly entertained. A giggle escapes her at one of his jokes and she puts a hand over her mouth. Roy and Monica, on the other hand, appear to be engaged in an intense discussion. Anand is observing both the couples out of the corner of his eye. In the distance, Moni and Babu are on standby, Meena by their side wearing her oversized dark glasses.

Monica murmurs to Roy. 'Do it now.'

They are sitting across from each other and Nisha is adjacent to Monica.

Roy raises his eyebrows and gestures with his right hand. *What's wrong with you?*

'I want it today.'

Roy shakes his head in disbelief.

Anand, sitting at the head of the table two chairs away from them, notices the stark difference in the two couples. Nisha and Rishi appear to be very much in love. Their eyes lock when they talk, they smile at each other, they hold hands. The second couple, on the other hand, does not appear to be lover-like; they come across as business associates. Monica is always dictating terms, and Roy surrenders meekly.

He has noticed this on several instances. Just yesterday, during evening tea, Roy got a call on his cellphone. Both looked at the screen at the caller's name, and then Roy shrugged, putting the phone back in his pocket.

Anand was smoking just few metres away, his eyes darting towards them.

'Pick it up,' Monica said.

Roy ignored her at first. But perhaps it was something in her eyes, Anand thought, that made Roy reach again for the phone in his pocket. By the time he got it out, the caller had disconnected the call. Roy put the phone back inside.

'Call back,' Monica told him.

'Why?'

'Do it.'

And Roy gave in. He pulled out the phone again. They walked away and spent the next twenty minutes on the phone, speaking in turns.

Now, Anand notices that Monica seems to be repeatedly telling Roy something in whispers and Roy is rebuffing it with a frown. Not for long though, he knows.

'Hey Monica,' he calls out. 'What are you troubling Roy for now?'

Nisha and Rishi are distracted from their conversation and look at him.

Monica isn't pleased. She turns her head in his direction, and says, gritting her teeth, 'Do you mind minding your own business, Mister Bad Writer?'

Anand lets out a laugh. 'Someone is in a bad mood today.'

Monica shows him the middle finger.

'Hey,' Anand continues, 'at least tell me what's it about? I can't hear you guys from here.'

Monica doesn't react verbally but the expression on her face—ripe as a tomato now—says it all.

'Stop troubling her, man,' Rishi suggests. 'You've started with the bickering again.'

'I *loooove* troubling her.'

There is silence for a minute or two before Anand starts again. 'Hey, at least tell me the topic of your discussion. You both look so stressed.'

Roy pushes his chair back with a clatter and gets up. He charges towards Anand.

'Oh, I'm so scared now,' Anand says dramatically. 'Please don't hurt me, tattooed lover boy.'

Roy stops close to him and glares at Anand. 'Stop it!' He points a menacing finger at him. 'I'm warning you!'

Anand snorts. 'Just go back to her. I'm done for today.'

Roy stares at him for a good minute before walking back and settling in his chair. Just as he sits down and takes a small bite of a poori, his right hand flies over his heart, and he winces.

'What is it?' Monica asks, worried.

Roy starts shaking and his face contorts. One hand hits the plate in front of him and it drops to the ground, shattering in pieces. At the sound, Babu and Moni run towards the table. By now, Monica and Rishi are hovering over him, and Nisha is rubbing Roy's back. Anand is still on his chair and closely watching the proceedings.

Roy's whole body is trembling, and he emits a groan before falling from his chair. He is now on the floor, his arms and legs jerking.

'Oh my God!' Monica cries. 'What's happening?'

'Is he—is he having a fit?' Nisha asks Monica.

Monica shrugs, her forehead creasing with wrinkles.

'Does he have a history of fits?' Nisha asks again.

'I-I don't know.'

Saliva and mushed food particles dribble out from Roy's mouth and the trembling continues. Nisha drops to her knees and tries to turn him on his side. She cannot move him.

'Help me!' she shouts. 'We need to keep his airway clear. He shouldn't choke.'

Monica and Rishi bend and help Nisha push Roy. Nisha holds his right arm and Rishi and Monica push his back so that he is lying on his left side.

'Quick,' Nisha says. 'We need to make him lie in the recovery position.'

'What's that?' Rishi asks.

'Just push his right leg up,' she replies. 'We need to put him in that position to keep his airway clear and open. That'll ensure that vomit won't choke him. Monica, please loosen his shirt a bit.' She points towards the top button. 'Open up a few of them.'

Nisha observes him closely, and a few minutes later, Roy stops shaking. His eyes are shut but he breathes normally. Nisha notes that the fit lasted less than two minutes.

She has taken enough medical courses to know that this means the situation is not so bad. However, she knows his condition needs to be monitored, and if the fits return, he might have to visit a hospital.

Roy slowly opens his eyes and grimaces. He wipes the saliva dribbling from his mouth with the back of his hand and looks around. All of them, including Anand, have formed a ring around him.

He tries to push himself up with his left elbow.

'You okay?' Nisha asks.

He nods slowly.

'Do you have a history of seizures?'

He nods again.

'Don't worry,' Nisha assures him. 'You're fine now. Just call me if you don't feel well.'

'Thanks,' Monica tells her. 'Thanks a lot, Nisha.'

12

I don't understand what happened today.

So, get this: I was teasing Miss Pretentious, that self-obsessed, brand-conscious, superficial woman, when her weirdo, tattooed boyfriend charges over to me, threatens me, then wanders back to his seat, and suddenly gets a seizure.

Is that how a seizure occurs? I mean, shouldn't there be a catalyst that triggers such a reaction?

I'm not sure—I can't be sure, but it does *feel* wrong.

The doctor . . . dentist, Nisha, may have done an analysis of it, but from a layman's perspective, there certainly seems to be more to it than meets the eye.

Anyway, chuck that. No point wasting my precious time on them. Let me concentrate on my short story. My mother always tells me not to dwell on people you don't like.

Think about the good things in life, about good people. Makes so much sense. She is a wise woman.

In my story, I think I know what the problem should be. I've been thinking about it for the last two days. There needs to be animosity between our first and second couples. The second couple, clearly more powerful than the first, inflicts some damage on them. Roy is a tall, strong man and Rishi is your average guy. I'll put my money on Roy any day if they were to fight in a ring.

Moving on.

Maybe there is an argument between the two women—that Monica is anyway nasty; any woman would have a fight with her. This is believable. Good. Then the men get in. As is always the case. The men start fighting. Again, believable. They get into a verbal duel first, which then breaks into an all-out fist fight. The women try to stop the fight.

What happens after that?

Okay, here's what could happen—Monica accidentally gets struck by Rishi's elbow smack on her face, and it breaks her nose, or cuts her lip, or . . . *whatever*. Who cares? She bleeds a lot—yeah, I'd love to write about that.

This incenses the second couple who hatch a plan. They decide to hurt Nisha. How?

They kidnap her. Do they hire someone to do it?

This part feels right. I don't know what exactly they do, but I think I'm on the right track. If I can write it up effectively, it would be a good short mystery story. The only thing left to figure out is what they do with Nisha.

Do they make her disappear? That has a nice ring to it. But how?

13

Monica is very worried and angry. How could Roy never share with her that he has a medical condition? They've known each other for over ten years. She knows all his secrets and he knows hers.

She knows he has a fetish for a woman's well-manicured hand. He knows she has a fetish for branded clothes, bags, shoes—anything branded.

So, how did she not know this?

Roy is now safely ensconced in his bed and people have gone back to their own cottages. After thanking everyone profusely for helping bring Roy in—well, except that scum of a writer—and shutting the door, Monica bursts out. 'You get fits? Since when? Is this a regular thing? Why didn't you tell me?'

Roy starts chuckling.

'How is that funny?'

'It's very funny,' he replies and breaks into a guffaw.

Monica doesn't understand. Is that an extension of the fit? Is he getting another one? Nisha had told her it was a common occurrence—a fit can precede another, and that is when it gets dangerous.

Meanwhile, Roy continues laughing, a large belly laugh.

'Are you okay?' Monica asks softly. She approaches him slowly. She is very, very concerned now.

'How could you not notice?' he asks her after he has managed to control his chuckles.

'Not notice what?'

Roy shakes his head. He sits up and puts his hand in the pocket of his pyjamas.

That's when she sees it.

It's a Cartier Tank Solo watch, the 18K pink gold model. Nisha's watch.

'What!' she screams in delight. 'When did you do it?'

He rolls his eyebrows. 'When do you think?'

'Oh my God, oh my God!' She jumps on the bed and gives Roy a tight hug. 'You stole it? For me?'

She holds the watch in her hand, looking at it in wonder.

A thought strikes Roy. 'Hold on—didn't you say it costs more than two lakh rupees?'

'Yes, it does.'

'So, we're going to sell it, right? That's why I stole it.'

Monica gets off the bed and wanders around the room, dreamily caressing the gleaming watch.

Well, he's right. That's exactly what she had thought, wasn't it? That they'd sell the watch. They need money to be able to steal more money. They have to enter the big league, do a bank robbery. Enough of the baby robberies. But they need to hire a few people, get hold of weapons, and you need money for that. The irony is not wasted on her—you need money to make money. How on earth do poor people ever become rich?

She looks at the watch again. It's just so beautiful that a voice in her head keeps calling out, 'Keep it, keep it, keep it.'

'I'd like to keep it.'

Roy shakes his head in disbelief but smiles. 'Alright, put it on.'

Monica puts on the watch. She loves the way it embraces her wrist. It's just made for her. The colour, the style, the brand . . . of course, the brand—it's *Cartier*, come on! She loves it.

'I want to keep it.'

Roy waves his hand. 'Of course,' he replies. 'I knew you'd say that. Keep it.'

'Thank you so much, love.' She plants a kiss on his cheek.

'You're most welcome, sweetheart.'

'This is your best gift *ever*.'

14

A woman steps out of the elevator and looks around. She knows the flat is to her right, but she pauses before walking towards it. At the door, she hesitates again before ringing the bell. She waits for a minute; the door remains shut. She rings the bell again.

Nothing.

She bites her lip, wondering if she's doing the right thing in the circumstances. She is doing it for family, she thinks, and there is nothing wrong in doing anything at all to protect them. Rishi is her baby brother, eight years her junior, stupid but lovable, and she'll do anything for him.

So, when he called her yesterday explaining the situation to her and requesting her to speak to Avni, she'd agreed in a heartbeat. 'Of course, I can do it.'

But what she can't understand is why Avni would go to such extremes. She's known Avni for as long as Rishi has known her. How long is it? Three years, four years?

Alright, she is a little . . . well, batty, if she can use that word. Avni has no friends, no family—heck, she calls them her only family. Why? Where was the rest of her family? Nobody knows. She's never talked about them.

She has no doubt that Avni loves her little brother madly. It's the way she looks at him, talks to him, and almost always flatters him—'Oh Rishi, you are such a kind-hearted man', 'Oh Rishi, you look so good', 'You're such a talented guy.'

But Rashmi has never taken all this seriously; she is sure Avni feels the same about every other guy. Come on, the girl has no one in her life. She is so lonely. What can you expect from such a person? But then lonely people are the most dangerous people, aren't they? They have so much time to brood. Look at the crime statistics anywhere in the world— chances are that the majority of crimes are committed by lonely weirdos.

Rashmi makes a mental note: 'Stay away from lonely people.'

She rings the bell again. 'Where's she today?' she murmurs under her breath. 'I need to sort this out.'

But now she hears footsteps approaching, the doorknob turning, and the creak of the door opening.

'Hello, Avni.'

Avni looks at Rashmi in surprise. 'Hi,' she replies. 'How come you're here?'

Rashmi enters the apartment. 'Haven't seen you in a while, so I thought—'

'You're here for that bitch, aren't you?' Avni snaps. 'Aren't you!' she screams now.

This surprises Rashmi. She has never seen this version of Avni. Hasn't she always been soft-spoken? Love can make you a very different person. But was it even love? Rashmi didn't know, and now, she didn't even know how helpful this little trip to Avni's place would be.

Avni's expression softens. 'I'm sorry, but I don't know why Rishi is saying he loves that bitch. He has always loved me. What happened suddenly?'

Rashmi realizes she must handle this conversation very tactfully. The girl is insane. When did Rishi tell her he loved her?

'Tell me,' Avni starts again, 'what happened to him? Both of us have . . . in fact'—she shakes her head—'all three of us have spent such amazing times together.'

Rashmi does a mental count of the number of times all three of them have been together.

One.

They had gone out just once for a movie. This was six months back when she was going for a film with her brother. In the hallway, Avni had suddenly appeared like a ghost, and begged them to take her along.

'Do you know why he is doing this?' Avni asks, her tone now completely mellow. 'Is he angry at me? Is he taking revenge for something?'

'No, I don't think that—'

'He loves me, I know that. I've always known that.'

'Listen, Avni—'

'Maybe he's just pretending he loves that bitch, so I'll get jealous and love him more. Men do that, I know.'

'You have to listen to—'

'But Rishi is such a nice guy. He's not like other men. Then why is he doing this to me?'

'Alright, enough, Avni. Please. Now you listen to me.' Rashmi comes forward and puts a finger on Avni's lips. 'Rishi has never loved you. You've just been his friend. In fact, you've even forced that friendship on him. But you've got to leave him alone. He really loves Nisha.'

Avni is quiet and seems to be taking it in. Then her body starts shaking and she grinds her teeth. She punches Rashmi smack in the face, so hard they hear the crunch of a bone breaking. Rashmi falls back and screams in agony. Her hand flies to her nose and she feels the sticky blood oozing out. The pain is excruciating.

But Avni isn't done. She moves forward and strikes another blow when Rashmi's guard is down, assessing the damage to her nose. Same place. Same strength.

This one is too much to take for Rashmi. The pain is red-hot, unbearable. In place of her nose, there's a pulpy mess of meat and blood and bones.

Finally, Avni pushes Rashmi to the wall, places her left hand on Rashmi's shoulder for a firm hold, and lands punch after punch in the same place until she has to catch her breath. When she lets her go, Rashmi slides to her knees. She is delirious with pain, and when she looks up, Avni is towering over her, ready to hit again.

Rashmi folds her hands, begging her to stop, and crawls to the door. The white of her shirt is soaked in blood dripping down her nose . . . or whatever is left of it.

At the door as Rashmi manages to struggle to her feet, Avni screams, 'Never tell me again that Rishi doesn't love me! Never tell me again that he loves someone else! Never!'

Rashmi barely manages to nod. Her vision is blurred, and she feels she will faint any moment. Blood continues to spurt out through her right hand covering the mush.

'Say it!' Avni screams again, clutching Rashmi's arm.

Rashmi somehow leans across to press the button to summon the elevator.

'R-r-rishi l-l-loves y-y-you,' she manages to mumble. Through her tears, she sees the elevator is still on the ground floor. The door to the stairs is on her right and she stumbles towards it, trying to free herself from Avni's grip. 'P-p-p-please let m-m-me go.'

Avni finally lets go of her arm. 'If you say again that Rishi loves someone else, I'll kill you, and I'll kill that bitch and I'll kill anyone who comes between Rishi and me. You hear that? *You hear that?*'

Rashmi staggers down the stairs, afire with pain, desperate to escape with her life.

15

The story is clear to me now. I've been writing non-stop for the past six hours. Sometimes, stories write themselves without much effort from the person typing it. This is one such story.

The characters evolve as easy as pie, like they are sitting in front of me telling their story. In particular Roy and Monica. They're open-book characters, a writer's delight, laying out their life in front of me naturally and easily, like rolling out a carpet. Their motivations and intentions are so clear; they hide nothing. I do not need to dig down into their hearts to glean information about their darkest desires. Plain and simple! They want to hurt Nisha because they hurt the queen, Monica. Miss Pretentious. Roy loves Monica and he'll do anything for her.

Nisha and Rishi are not what you would call a writer's delight. They unfold slowly, one layer at a time. But I manage to understand them. Deeply, madly in love. They'll cross the oceans if they have to, to be with each other.

I have reached the end and I'm deciding on the story's conclusion. It's close to a five-thousand-word story and it doesn't escape me that I've created a new record for myself for the word count in a day.

Phew!

It's love, isn't it? Whenever I write about love, the writing gushes out of me. The emotion is so strong that I can't contain it. I have written about each character's perspective on love and then derived his or her actions accordingly. Love drives us all, doesn't it?

Sometimes I think I should forget Maira and move on. Live a normal life again. But is life normal without love? How does it matter if she isn't with me today? I think I'll always love her with all my heart. I would rather be a guy who does crazy things for love than someone who hasn't experienced love in its truest and fullest form, and thus isn't driven by it.

To all the novice lovers out there—I have some advice. Love more deeply. Love more passionately. Because when you love, the world is a better place.

Right then. Let me conclude this story and see how far these characters would go for love.

16

The flashes of those creatures walking towards Meena are a regular feature now. She cannot escape them. She has tried on several occasions to access her mother's or father's mind and see through their eyes. But she sees nothing. Just a column of black wherever she turns, like a blindfolded child trying to look for his friends, his arms splayed out.

She wonders if sight-sharing is a real thing after all, or just some writer's imagination, as her mother said. Did she, on the few occasions when she thought she could discern wavery, blurred images of her surroundings, actually see something or was it her imagination? She knows blind people imagine their surroundings a lot. They try to assign images to the sounds they hear. She does it all the time.

She doesn't know the answer to her questions. All she knows is those creatures are real and they are approaching. She can't be wrong about that. In the kitchen, helping her parents prepare breakfast, she feels disquiet settle over her again. Her heart beats slowly but loudly, like a drumroll.

They are not far. What do they want?

She gives it one more shot. She squeezes her eyes shut and blocks out every image, every thought from her mind. She waits for a minute or two. *They'll come.*

And just like that, they do. There are five of them. She sees them clearly despite the darkness. She's standing in the garden. The moon is full above her, throwing its gleam upon the earth. The trees are lit by it; she sees their branches swaying in the wind. The five creatures are wearing loose, baggy clothes. They have a crooked gait, bending to their left as they march forward slowly. Their faces scare Meena. One of them has a bloodied face with big, bulging eyes. Another one, a skinny fellow, looks at the ground, something sinister in his lack of attention. The other three wear ragged clothes, their eyes staring ahead blankly.

At the far end of the resort, there is an open field. There are no trees here, just wild bushes. A wooden fence marks the boundary of the resort.

Meena feels a cry building up in her throat and she has to clamp her teeth against it. Those creatures are in that open field.

Oh Lord! They are here!

17

Monica has made up her mind. Now she wants Roy to steal Nisha's leather bag. Although Monica tried to decipher the brand name of the bag earlier, she couldn't, as the letters carved on the bag were too tiny. And it's not like Nisha carries the bag every time she walks out of her room; Monica has seen it just once. But she is certain that it would be 'branded enough', which makes it steal-worthy. The girl wears a Cartier; her bag's got to be branded.

That Tia, she thinks, *always uploads her pictures with that MK bag on Insta, now I'll show her.*

But Roy is not happy at all and he shakes his head in disapproval as they step out of the cottage.

'No, baby,' he pleads, 'not again please. They're going to catch us if we keep stealing from them.'

'How?' Monica raises her arms in despair. 'Why're you being such a sissy? You were never like that.'

It's true. When they started stealing together, Roy had nerves of steel. The act never made his pulse race. Monica has always told him that he has such a poker face while shoplifting, as if he owns the store, that no one would even dream that he was a thief. He was marvellous. Monica would simply trail him, her heart battering inside her chest at the thought of getting caught.

But now, look at the way he talks!

Slowly, she learnt the ropes and became as good as him. Soon, she overtook him in the nerves-of-steel-while-stealing department. Stealing came naturally to her. She never felt like a thief; she would just pick whatever she liked, as if it belonged to her. And then she held her nose high, and passers-by took her for another wealthy, snobbish lady. Her sartorial taste was so chic (stolen alright, but chic), who would dare mess with a woman like that?

'You're doing it,' she demands. 'And tonight.'

'Tonight?'

'Tonight.'

The first thing Anand notices when he arrives for breakfast is that horrible device which allows you to click innumerable pictures of yourself, customize the pictures to your taste, and then post it for the world to see through the dumbest medium ever invented: social media.

Miss Pretentious has pulled it out of the pocket of her jeans and is posing for the camera, her red lips pouting. *Click! Click! Click!*

Roy joins in, posing behind her, giving a thumbs up, without much interest. Monica clicks a few buttons and there it goes—some more kilobytes out in the world, which is already brimming to the surface with asinine, senseless data.

'Thanks, Miss Pretentious,' Anand mutters under his breath, 'for making the world a better place.'

With the pictures done, Monica and Roy walk over to the dining space. Babu and Moni have just started placing food on the buffet table. Anand doesn't see Meena with them. He cannot see his favourite couple as well.

It doesn't matter now. He has completed the story and he sits there with the smug satisfaction only a writer who has just finished writing a great story can feel. It's how a non-writer would feel after an orgasm-filled night. Relaxed. Content.

And there they are. Nisha and Rishi.

They look sad. They walk out seemingly with no enthusiasm for the new day, which has dawned bright and shining—a perfect contrast to their morose demeanour. They've just heard about the assault on Rishi's sister by that crazy woman who claims to be his lover.

Monica notices Nisha's empty hands. The bag is in the cottage, waiting for her to grasp it. It belongs to her, not someone who doesn't even bother carrying it. Bags, just like clothes, are very full of life. They need proper care and attention.

What would this dimwit know? Lady born with a silver spoon in her mouth, huh!

Monica is sure everything in Nisha's life would have been presented to her on a platter, like a meal in a fancy restaurant. Has she ever struggled for anything? What would she know about the joy of holding something in your hand that you truly desire and fight for?

Monica assumes Nisha has been brought up in a nice bungalow in an elite neighbourhood in a posh part of Delhi, servants in white gloves bowing and scraping to her. *Your wish is my command, madam!* Whatever she wants will come true. Nice boyfriend. Nice family.

And she feels an overpowering dislike building up within her for Nisha, for her easy, trouble-free life vis-à-vis her own life replete with struggles. She wishes with all her heart that something terrible happens to her.

Meena's arms are shaking now. Her face is sweaty. It's good her parents are outside, so they can't see her. She feels like screaming and telling everybody about what she saw. But she knows no one will believe her. And she doesn't want people to laugh at her. She doesn't want to embarrass her parents in front of the guests. She can already hear the jibes people would throw at her. *The little blind girl has gone crazy!*

But those people or creatures—or whatever—are here, and she doesn't know what to do about it. Panic claws at her throat. Her hands press the kitchen counter so hard her knuckles turn white. She lets out a desperate cry of anguish.

Something's got to be done. But for that she needs to be sure she is right. That those flashes are real. Those creatures are real. And that they are here to hurt someone.

Meena closes her eyes again and hopes to not see them again. But she does.

18

The rest of the day proceeds uneventfully. At night, Nisha is searching for her watch in the cottage. She finally realizes she hasn't seen it since yesterday. She opens the bedside drawers. Nothing. She runs her eyes over the study table by the television. Nope. She checks her bag, the bathroom counter. Nada.

'Have you seen it?' she asks Rishi who is fidgeting nervously in the living room.

'No,' he replies disinterestedly, his face twisted in a scowl. 'I already told you!'

'But I need to find it.'

Rishi wipes the sweat from his face. 'There are more important things than your watch right now. We'll find it. That bitch Avni hurt my sister and I want to get back at her.'

Nisha looks at him in despair; now she's more worried than she was earlier when they landed at this place. How can

Vikrant Khanna

a woman be so wild? She broke Rashmi's nose. She has seen the picture Rishi's mother sent him. How did she manage to do that? There was almost nothing left there . . . just a mush of . . . she spares herself the thought.

Rashmi will need a full-thickness skin grafting to reconstruct her nose. Even if that is successful, she will be deformed for life.

Nisha shivers as the hairs on her arms stand on end. She sees the same fear reflected in Rishi's eyes. She knows purging Avni from their life will not be easy . . . hell, living a normal life won't be easy.

'I'm going out for a walk,' Rishi tells her. 'I need to do some thinking.'

Nisha nods.

At the door, he steps back and walks towards Nisha. He cups her face in his hands and says, 'I love you, Nisha, I really do, and I'm going to keep you safe.' He kisses her on the cheek. 'I'm going to do everything I can to keep you safe. Don't be scared.'

They hug for a minute or two. As he draws back, he says again, 'Don't be scared.' And then he walks out of the door.

He doesn't see her again.

84

PART 2

The Investigation

19

By morning the following day, the Himachal Pradesh police have arrived at Writer's Hill. The Station House Officer is Arun Raghuveer aka Raghu, of Renuka Ji police station in Sirmaur district, about twenty kilometres east of Writer's Hill. He is a tall, heavyset, brooding guy whose khaki uniform fits him perfectly. He is wearing aviators, which are of no use as the day is dark and gloomy, much like the atmosphere of this place today.

A twenty-three-year-old girl has disappeared under mysterious circumstances. Somebody had been ringing his phone since four in the morning and he hadn't picked it up. *Nothing that the sub-inspector on duty cannot handle,* he had thought, and silenced his phone, snoring his way back to sleep.

Now he gets out of the jeep and looks up at the resort. The place looks dead. He hears no sound other than the soft chirping of the birds overhead.

'What's the name of the girl, Prakash?' he asks the sub-inspector, a thin, short wisp of a man.

Prakash opens the file in his hand. He looks at the first information report. 'Nisa—Nisha Dastur, sir.'

'Hmm.' He pauses. 'And who lodged the report?'

Prakash opens the file again. 'Her friend Rishi.'

'Hmm.'

They take the stairs towards the resort. At the top, a man is rushing towards the stairs with a girl in his arms. A woman, crying in short bursts, is hurrying along with him, another man at her heels.

'What happened to her?' Raghu asks.

The first man stops in his tracks. 'Sahib, I'm Babu, the caretaker of this place. This is my daughter Meena. I don't know what has happened to her. She's been unconscious since the early hours of the morning.'

'Sh-she's not waking up,' cries the woman.

Raghu and Prakash exhange glances.

'There was . . . there was . . .' The other man struggles for the right words. 'Something . . . *something* happened last night. Very strange.'

'We'll talk later, sahib,' Babu begs the inspector. 'Please let us go to the hospital first.'

Raghu nods and moves sideways to let them pass. He beckons the other fellow. 'Who are you?'

'I'm Anand, a writer . . . uh—I'm a guest here.'

'I want to speak with you.' He gestures to Prakash. 'You take them to the hospital and let me know the girl's condition.'

'Yes, sir.'

Raghu waits for them to pass and watches the jeep drive away, a plume of dust flying in its wake. He looks back at Anand. 'So, what were you saying?'

'Inspector, something strange happened last night.'

'Strange? Isn't there a girl missing here?'

'Yes, yes.' Anand nods. 'But before that we all heard strange sounds . . . like that of a wild animal crying in pain, or a group of them, I don't know . . . fighting with each other. There was a flash in the sky, like lightning, only much brighter.'

Raghu has stopped paying attention to him. He's had a rough last week. His wife Palak had left him after big fights between them for the better part of a year. She wanted a child and Raghu didn't. 'He never wants any responsibility,' his wife would say to her friends. 'Family means nothing to him.'

So, when she broached the topic one last time the week before, Raghu showed her the door and told her she was free to leave.

She left.

Raghu has been struggling to figure out since last week the reason women make a big deal of everything. So, he didn't want a child. Was it that big a deal? Was he the only one in the world to not want a child?

Family this. Family that. Family is important. Screw her, he thinks with a violent shake of his head. He is better off without her. *I can live my life alone.*

'What the fuck are you saying?' he snaps at Anand. 'You are a writer, you said?'

'Yes, sir.'

'Don't make up things. Just tell me what happened.'

'Inspector, this is exactly what happened.'

Raghu shakes his head in exasperation.

'Where's that . . . um . . . Rishi? He got the FIR done, right?'

'Yes.'

Anand leads the inspector to Rishi's cottage. Raghu sizes him up from behind, noting that Anand is at least four inches taller than him. But he is thin as a straw; his shoulder blades jut out from his over-sized shirt which is rolled up to his elbows. He takes long steps with his back bent slightly forward, and Raghu has to play catch-up with him.

'Hey, what's your name again?'

Anand looks over his shoulder. 'Anand.'

Raghu takes a few quick steps and draws level with him. 'And what do you do apart from writing?'

'I'm a full-time writer.'

Raghu thinks about his next question and shoots, 'You got a family?'

'Of course.' Anand nods, giving the inspector a sidelong glance. 'Everyone has a family. I live with my mother. She's the best mother in the world.'

Well, guess what? Everybody doesn't have a family. Surprise! Surprise! Well, unless you don't throw them out.

They reach Rishi's cottage, and the door is ajar. Anand knocks before entering.

Rishi is sitting on the edge of the bed, his head resting on his palms. He doesn't turn around to look at them. Just sits there.

Raghu can hear his soft sobs. They walk towards him and he clears his throat.

'I'm Inspector Raghu, in charge of this case.' He offers his hand.

Rishi looks at him and Anand before rising. He takes the hand in a loose grip and wipes his eyes with the back of his other hand.

'Please help me, inspector,' Rishi says, his voice shallow. 'I can't find her.'

'How's she related to you?'

'She's the love of my life.'

The inspector nods. He walks around, taking in the room. Everything appears normal, in order. He asks Rishi a few generic questions—about himself, how Nisha and he met, the duration of their stay. Rishi answers in detail.

'And when did you see her last?'

'Around 11.30 p.m. yesterday,' Rishi replies. 'I had gone out for a walk after that.'

'Why did you not take her with you?'

Rishi swallows hard. 'I . . . I . . . she didn't want to come.'

'And did you ask her?'

'I . . . I don't remember.'

The inspector waves his hand. 'Anyway, what happened after that?'

'Something strange happened here last night, inspector,' Rishi replies thoughtfully. 'I don't know how to explain it to you. There was a strange sound. It was like a bunch of people or animals wailing in deep pain. It was so horrific and sad. I think it was some . . . some kind of an invisible power . . . I don't know like . . . like—'

'Like something paranormal,' Anand finishes for him.

'Yes, yes,' Rishi nods in agreement.

The inspector wipes his brow. 'What are you both talking about?'

'No, no, inspector, please believe us,' Anand continues. 'It caused that little girl Meena you just saw to fall unconscious. She was thrown with a powerful force at least a dozen or so metres in the garden.'

'And what were you doing outside at night?'

'I was out for a smoke.'

Raghu is sceptical. One is a writer and the other is heartbroken. Are they both imagining things? *But the same things?*

He knew that couldn't be possible. But how could *this* be possible? Sounds of crying animals, light in the sky, invisible force, paranormal activity? None of that made any sense. Even if it did, how did it relate to—

'Hey,' he asks both of them, 'so how does this explain the disappearance of Nisha?'

No one replies for a minute or two.

'I don't know, inspector,' Rishi replies finally. 'I just know that when I came back to my cottage, Nisha wasn't there. I called out her name. I walked back out to the garden, looked in all the common areas, screamed her name, but couldn't find her. Anand was with me too. Babu and Moni came rushing out later, but we couldn't find Nisha.'

'And then what did you do?'

'I drove down to the police station. The constable or whoever was on duty didn't pay any attention.'

'And how did you get my number?'

'From the Himachal Pradesh Police website. All telephone numbers are listed there.'

That explains the hundred calls at four in the morning, Raghu thinks.

'Okay.' Raghu nods. 'Do you have a picture of Nisha?'

Rishi pulls out his phone from the pocket of his jeans, swipes across the screen a few times, and hands Raghu the phone. Raghu looks at the picture, observing her sharp features.

'Okay, send this picture to my phone,' he says, handing the phone back to Rishi. 'You already have my number. Does anybody else live here?'

'Yes, inspector,' Anand replies. 'There is another couple in the first cottage. Do you want to meet them?'

Raghu mulls it over. 'No.' He shakes his head. 'Not now.'

He walks out of the cottage feeling a strange sense of disquiet. He has to admit this is a pretty unique case.

Vikrant Khanna

Like something paranormal. Anand's words flash in his mind. Normally disappearances result from kidnappings, accidents, and in some cases, murder, but this one, he feels, will not be straightforward.

But he'll get the sub-inspector to work on it. Right now, he has enough going on in his own life.

As he comes down the stairs, his phone rings. It's the Superintendent of Police (SP) of Sirmaur district, his boss.

'Yes, sir.'

'Raghu, a girl has gone missing last night from the hills here.'

'Yes, sir.'

'You have forty-eight hours to find her.'

'But what—'

'I'm getting calls from the big guns. The Deputy Inspector General (DIG) of the southern region has called me up and he wants the girl found ASAP. Do whatever it takes. She is the daughter of MP Dastur, a close friend of our Director General of Police (DGP).'

'Okay, sir, I'll do my—'

'Forty-eight hours.'

94

20

Ten minutes later, Raghu is in Roy and Monica's cottage. He is sitting on a chair, right leg crossed over his left. Roy and Monica sit across from him on the bed.

He isn't liking the case so far—a girl missing from an influential family, the girl's father a good friend of his boss' boss' boss, a supernatural or perhaps bogus incident that doesn't make any sense, and the hunger pangs, God . . . the hunger pangs. He feels his stomach will start eating itself. He hasn't had anything to eat since morning. Or was it since last week?

He hates to admit it, but his wife is an organized woman who used to take care of things at home very efficiently. To top that, she is a great cook, and on bad or extra busy days when he returned home late, she'd always have a special meal ready for him. He misses that food. All he has been eating since she left is eggs, cup noodles and more eggs.

95

But that is not the only reason he misses his wife. She's also a good listener, and his discussions of cases with her invariably yielded results. She'd calm him down and offer the perfect outsider's perspective that an officer in charge of a difficult case needs.

But she left. So be it.

'Okay,' he starts. 'Let me know your names.'

'Sir, my name is Roy, and she is Monica, my girlfriend.'

'How did you meet?'

'We met, uh . . . several years ago at an orph—'

'At a pub,' Monica interjects. 'We met at a pub in Delhi some years back. Our common friend introduced us.'

Roy shoots her a furtive look from the corner of his eye, before stealing a glance at the inspector who doesn't appear suspicious. Still, Roy debates if she did the right thing by lying. A girl is missing two cottages away from their own and this might not be the best approach to take.

'Go on,' Raghu nods. 'Tell me more about yourself and your family.'

'Well,' Monica resumes, confident as a lion, believing every single word she utters, 'my father is a prominent businessman from Delhi. Export-import, you know, that sort. I love Roy and Dad doesn't like it, because . . . well, because he is an orphan, brought up in an orphanage. My dad wants me to be with someone from our class, so I left my home to be with him.'

'And you came'—Raghu swivels his head around, moving his right index finger along with it—'here?'

'Well, yes,' Monica replies. 'We like this place—it's very calm and peaceful.'

'And how long have you been here?'

'Almost a month now.' She takes a deep breath and leans forward. 'Please don't tell anyone we're here,' she whispers. 'My father is very strict and there will be, um . . . some very bad consequences for us if he finds out.'

Raghu doesn't respond. The girl is talking more than necessary. He turns to the guy.

'Roy?'

'Yes, sir.'

'Did you see or hear anything unusual last night?'

'Yes, inspector!' he exclaims. 'Indeed, there were some high-pitched shrieks, painful moans, someone crying. I couldn't understand; the sounds were scary.'

'And what did you see?'

'Actually, we didn't step out of the cottage.'

'Why not?'

Roy looks at Monica. 'She was very scared. She wanted me to be with her and not go out.'

Raghu leans back in the chair and crosses his arms across his chest. His eyes move back and forth from Roy to Monica. 'Hmm . . . somehow I find that hard to believe. So, you hear an odd, loud sound outside, she feels scared, and you don't go out to investigate it?'

Roy nods hesitantly.

'So, you didn't see anything?'

Roy shakes his head.

Raghu considers that for a minute. What would he have done? He would have definitely stepped out to see what was going on. Even if Palak was there, scared, he would have at least peeked out from the window.

'Okay, anyway, do you have any idea what might have happened to Nisha? Where would she be now?'

Roy and Monica shake their heads in unison.

'What about her boyfriend, Rishi? How is he? Do you think he might be involved in this? Anything you can remember—a fight, a discussion between them, anything at all? It might be helpful for the case.'

'Well,' Monica says, 'we didn't know them well, but we did see them arguing on several occasions. You're right—he might be involved in her disappearance.'

Raghu nods thoughtfully and rises. 'Thanks for your time.'

21

'What is wrong with you?' Roy screams at Monica after Raghu steps out of the cottage and he bolts the door shut. 'Why did you lie like that?'

'I couldn't think of anything else. He mustn't find out our identity.' She throws herself on the bed, picks up her phone from the bedside table, and begins flicking through the pictures clicked today.

Roy shakes his head and paces up and down the room. He replays the conversation with the inspector in his mind.

Lie number 1: Monica is from a rich family and her father is a businessman.

Lie number 2: She has run away with him.

Lie number 3: They did not see anything last night.

The last lie was perhaps the biggest one in the circumstances. But what *was* it that he saw? With his own eyes he had seen Meena thrown back at least a dozen metres by and with . . . *what*? And what were those sounds? It was akin to a soundtrack from the scariest horror movie he had seen, but far louder and scarier.

Last night, at Monica's urging, he had gone out to steal Nisha's bag from her cottage. From his window he'd spotted Rishi outside in the garden taking a stroll. Roy had tiptoed to Rishi's cottage, assuming Nisha was out with him and their cottage was empty.

Inside the cottage, which was indeed unoccupied, he'd spent less than a minute when he heard those sounds. He abandoned his hunt for Nisha's bag and rushed outside. Rishi and Anand were standing behind Meena who had her arms outstretched, hands splayed in front of her. Her face was contorted in a grimace and it was as though she were trying to push something hard. But there was nothing there. Her feet were rooted to the ground, but she seemed to be slowly getting pushed backwards.

But it was that horrible sound that unnerved him the most, like a horde of animals emitting a painful, keening noise all at the same time, as if they were being slaughtered. Rishi and Anand looked frightened too, their mouths agape. Suddenly, a huge flash of lightning tore the sky open. It was like a burst of electricity that rippled across the sky. At the same moment, he saw Meena get thrown some distance away. And then the sounds stopped, as suddenly as if someone had turned the radio from maximum volume to mute all at once.

Everything seemed to go back to normal then, as if nothing had happened.

Roy didn't want to be seen and sneaked back to his cottage while Rishi and Anand were helping Meena up. He didn't know what happened after that.

'Someone will know I was in their cottage when Nisha disappeared,' he said softly, almost to himself, but Monica heard him.

'But nobody saw you, right?'

'I don't know,' he says, shaking his head. 'What if the police do fingerprinting or, I don't know, footprinting of their cottage? They'd know I was there.'

'Nobody will know anything, sweetheart,' Monica says calmly. 'We are just thieves. We haven't done anything terrible.'

'Are you sure about that?'

22

The main office of the police station is a tiny, untidy room with files piled up in every corner. There are three sets of rusty desks and chairs in the room. Raghu is sitting at the biggest (and the rustiest) of them, his mind spinning with myriad thoughts. He is amazed that thoughts of his wife have chased away the case—of the missing girl—at hand from his mind.

Sub-inspector Shastri is standing by his side. Raghu turns his head towards him. He considers just for a moment if he should ask this question. He's known Shastri the last five years now, has had several drinks with him . . . so what the hell? 'Do you love your wife, Shastri?'

The question from his boss surprises Shastri. He was expecting an update on the missing girl, the next steps to take . . . anything else but this. But he doesn't even take a moment to consider the query, the response emerging spontaneously. 'Sir, she's my wife, so I have to love her. What option do I have?'

Raghu breaks into a smile, the first in many days. The smile transmutes into guttural laughter a moment later. His colleagues from across the room look up and Raghu waves his hand. After a long, satisfying laugh, he looks up at Shastri and pats his arm gently. 'No compulsion, okay?' he asks again. 'Do you then love your wife?'

'Yes . . . yes, sir, why not?' Here again, Shastri doesn't engage the grey cells of his brain.

Raghu nods, but the smile doesn't leave his face.

'Sir, do you mind if I ask—are you missing Palak madam?'

Raghu thinks about it for a moment but doesn't respond to Shastri's query. 'How's that little girl now, uh . . . that blind girl?'

'Meena. Yes, sir, she's still unconscious, last I checked at the hospital.'

'Okay, keep an eye on them. Let me know when she wakes up. I would like to speak to her.'

Shastri nods.

'Oh and yeah, I have told those people on the hill they cannot leave the place for the next forty-eight hours, or until we have something about Nisha. Let's have a van positioned outside the resort with one of them'—he nods towards the hawaldars—'on guard all the time. One of them is most likely responsible for her disappearance.'

'Yes, sir.'

Raghu gives Shastri a nod of dismissal.

So far, he has nothing on the case. Although he feels strongly that Nisha's companions on the hill might have had something to do with her disappearance, he doesn't have any evidence to support his claim. He has sent three of his best men to search for her in the areas around the resort. They are carrying a copy of Nisha's photo and he has given them clear instructions to show that picture to everyone they see within five kilometres of that resort. Somebody would have seen her; she cannot just disappear like that.

But so far, he has had no update from them. He makes a mental note to call one of them for a report.

His eyes fall on the cigarette pack on his desk. Not bothering to control his impulse, he picks it up and heads out of the office. He is trying to control his smoking but has been failing miserably since his wife left.

Even before he lights his cigarette, a police jeep screeches to a halt outside. He recognizes the car immediately.

'Shit!'

He was expecting him but not so early.

The SP of Sirmaur district of Himachal Pradesh is a tall, burly Sikh, taller and broader than Raghu. He steps out of the jeep with a sense of urgency and the air of a man with a lot on his plate. He walks briskly towards Raghu.

'What's the update on Nisha?' he asks Raghu without preamble.

Raghu decides against the smoke. He ponders on the most tactful answer to the question but can come up only with a single word: 'Nothing.'

The SP frowns and gestures with his hand. 'Why?'

'We're trying.'

'How are you organizing the search?'

'Three of my men are searching within a five-kilometre radius of that hill for now, before we expand the search outward.'

The SP frowns again; the frown is more pronounced than the first one. 'Only three people deployed for a five-kilometre radius to search for a missing daughter of a VIP?' He mutters to himself and shakes his head in disapproval.

Raghu turns around and walks back to his desk. The SP trails behind, speculating on the next course of action. This morning, he'd got a call from his boss, the DIG of the southern region of Himachal Pradesh—a phone call that wasn't a conversation but a monologue of the DIG barking into his ear.

'The missing girl *must* be found in the next forty-eight hours. She *must* be found!' the DIG reiterated. 'I don't care what you do, Bedi, just get me that girl. The DGP of the state is involved. You know what that means. She *must* be found soon.'

Bedi had lost track of the times his boss had used the word 'must'. He had politely replied with a 'Yes, sir.'

Bedi realizes he cannot leave the case just on Raghu's shoulders; he needs to get more people involved. Although he trusts Raghu's instincts and believes in him, this case is far more serious and requires more eyes.

'I'm going to call up all the *chowki*s of our district to send more men for the search,' Bedi tells Raghu. 'There are nine of them. That should give us enough men for the search.'

Raghu nods in agreement. 'That's a good idea, sir. I was going to ask you for additional help but didn't as you would have perhaps thought I am not up to the challenge.'

Bedi places his strong hand on Raghu's shoulder and squeezes it. 'Raghu, ask me whatever you want, I have told you so many times. I trust you.'

He withdraws his hand and glances at Shastri. 'Get some tea, yaar.'

Shastri nods in subservience. 'At once, sir.'

Bedi glances back at Raghu. 'You think approaching the Indo-Tibetan Border Police (ITBP) troopers to help us with the search is a good idea?'

'Isn't it too early for that?'

'I know, but this is not a normal case. We want results ASAP. Those guys are really good at this with all their fancy mountaineering equipment and local knowledge.'

Raghu doesn't see a problem with that; it makes his life easy, and if it helps to find the missing girl, why the hell not? He knows he isn't giving his best to the case and now would not be an opportune time for inter-department politics.

'Let's call them, sir.'

'I'll make a few phone calls.' Bedi starts punching numbers on his cellphone and heads outside. 'I'll be back. Keep the tea hot for me.'

An hour later, there are a dozen ITBP and another dozen police personnel searching the hills around the Writer's Hill resort for Nisha.

23

Post a quick lunch, Shastri is driving Raghu downhill to the New Memorial Hospital. Raghu hasn't spoken to Meena's parents yet. He doesn't expect to get much help from them, but they are nevertheless important witnesses.

He has been thinking about the case all along the scenic drive replete with orchards and views of mountains and dotted with modest dwellings here and there. The road is narrow but not bumpy, and Shastri drives cautiously, the car never veering outside the yellow strip on the edge of the road. An old Pahari song plays on the radio without distracting Raghu. In fact, this is the first time since morning that he has been constructively thinking about the case.

There are a few scenarios that could have played out here, he has decided.

First, Nisha might have walked out of her cottage that night to look for Rishi and slipped down the hill in the darkness and been badly injured or killed. But then why hadn't the rescuers found her body yet? It's been six hours already. If they do not find the body in the next few hours, he would toss away this possibility.

Or she just left the resort. But why? Wouldn't her boyfriend or her father know about it? That doesn't appear likely; the way they are panicking, especially her father, pulling all the political strings to locate his daughter. *No.* He shakes his head.

Perhaps there is foul play involved. But who would do it? Her boyfriend? The others? But what about the body? Again, like the first assumption, he might have to rule out this option if Nisha's body is not found.

Or maybe Nisha had gone out for a trek and . . . and— he scratches his head—lost her way, gotten dehydrated, or unconscious, or whatever. This happens in Himachal Pradesh all the time. Just look up the number of missing persons' report in the database. Not just Indian nationals, Americans and Europeans have gone missing from the hills here in alarming numbers. But how does that fit into this case? Wouldn't Rishi know about her trekking escapade? And why would she start at night? Again, why has her body not yet been found?

He rejects this option as well.

What else could have happened to her?

What else . . .? *What else . . .?*

He scratches his head, clicks his fingers, continues pondering.

Then suddenly, a light goes on in his mind. *The supernatural element—what about that?* Could that be the answer?

He turns to Shastri. 'Do you believe in ghosts?'

Shastri utters a squeak. 'Ghosts? From where did this—why . . . why would you ask, sir?'

Raghu looks out the window. 'Those men at the resort talked about seeing some strange things last night.' And why would they talk of such improbabilities unless they did witness them?

So, they actually witnessed such a thing. *So?*

He recalls the conversation he had with them. He zeroes in on the crucial fragments—sounds of animals wailing, crackling lightning across the sky, Meena getting thrown back some distance.

It doesn't make any sense, and even if it did, how is that related to the disappearance of Nisha?

He cannot answer that, but then, he cannot answer a lot of other questions now. Maybe the blind girl Meena can answer some of them. Maybe she holds the key to this whole mess. But she needs to wake up.

He has barely paid attention to his surroundings and now turns to Shastri again. 'How much more time to the hospital?'

'We have already reached, sir,' replies Shastri, and soon brings the car to a halt in the parking lot.

24

At the resort, Rishi is pacing nervously outside his cottage wondering about the search for Nisha. *Are the police close to finding her?* He stops, shakes his head and looks heavenwards, muttering under his breath. He continues looking up at the sky as if expecting an answer. He starts pacing again.

It is late evening and the sun has just about disappeared behind the hills. The sky looks beautiful—a huge canvas of boldly sketched shades of orange, yellow, some crimson.

Anand is sitting on a chair in the garden overlooking the hills, the ubiquitous cigarette in his hand. From the corner of his eye, he is observing Rishi.

Inside his cottage, Roy has drawn back the curtain from the window and has his eye on both of them. He is wondering the same thing as Rishi: have the police found Nisha yet?

Anand rises, drops the cigarette on the ground, stubs it with his right foot, and heads towards Rishi.

'Hey, you okay, brother?' he asks.

Behind him, Roy has stepped out of his cottage and is walking up to Rishi too.

'I don't know,' replies Rishi, gazing at both of them. 'I don't know, man. The love of my life is missing, and I don't know what to do.'

'Hmm . . . if I were you, I would have joined the police in finding her.' This was Roy offering his advice. Although he feels sorry for the guy, the real reason for this suggestion is to clear the way to steal Nisha's bag from Rishi's cottage. Sending Rishi out to join the search seems like a good start.

Rishi doesn't reply. Frankly, he doesn't care if he's being rude. It has been a nightmarish past few days. It was supposed to have been a simple trip with just the two of them spending quality time together and planning their life forward after the Avni debacle.

'Really,' Roy insists, 'I think you should go for the search. It's better than sitting here doing nothing at least.'

Anand gives Roy a sidelong glance, studying him for a few seconds before Roy turns his attention to him. Roy raises his eyebrows, and Anand drops his gaze. He says, 'Not sure how that would help. There are dozens of policemen deployed for the search, aren't they?'

Roy gives him a cold look.

Rishi makes a sound of irritation. 'So, I should just sit here?'

Roy smiles victoriously. 'Exactly!' He pounces at the opportunity. 'Go up and down the hills even if it's dangerous. Step up. Find her.'

'Would you have done the same thing, Roy?' Rishi asks him. 'How much do you love Monica?'

'Absolutely, buddy.' Roy wants to tell him Monica is everything to him, that he'll scale the highest peak in the world for her, swim across oceans, steal whatever she sets her heart on. *For now, it's your girlfriend's bag, but yeah, you get the drift, don't you, pal?*

Roy pauses to study Rishi's expression. It is blank, stolid, like he feels nothing. Almost lifeless.

He decides to answer the second part of Rishi's question as well. 'I love Monica so madly that I'll do anything for her. We all do crazy things in love, right? Well, I've done some myself.'

'Like what?'

The counter-question from Rishi puzzles him. *Weren't we discussing Nisha's search operation? This guy has gone nuts. Like I stole your girlfriend's watch for her because she loves branded stuff,* he wants to tell him. *And now I'll steal her bag if you listen to me and go find your girlfriend.*

But all he can actually voice is: 'Like anything.'

The conversation piques Anand's curiosity. The male characters of his story are discussing love—his favourite subject. He wishes they'd had this conversation earlier; it would have helped him tremendously in penning down his short story. But you can always edit your story to improve it.

He decides to take a deep dive.

'That's a grand answer, Roy,' he says clearing his throat. 'Would you hurt someone for her?'

'I said anything—so yeah, that qualifies.'

Great, Anand thinks. He had no idea their love is so intense; on the surface it appears so callous, so *filmy*, but now it appears that their romance is deep. They came across as a social media couple, constantly clicking and posting pictures for the world to see, accept them, admire them. It's how most people behave nowadays. Suddenly, he doesn't hate them anymore. He likes people who love so passionately and deeply such that nothing can stop them from pursuing it. *That's how love should be.*

'You guys have been together for how many years?' Anand is keen to know more.

'Forever,' Roy says proudly. 'And I plan to be with her forever.'

'Maybe all of us should love like that.' Rishi rejoins the conversation. 'That makes life so easy. Your priorities remain straight.'

'I know you do, brother,' Anand tells him. 'I know you do.'

'How about you?' Roy asks Anand, a slight challenge in his voice. 'Do you love someone so badly that you'd do anything for her?'

Anand thins his lips and stares at Roy. Their eyes remain locked too long for Roy's comfort. He drops his gaze. When he looks up again, Anand replies, 'Yeah, for my mother.'

Roy smiles inwardly. He didn't expect that answer. *But of course. A weirdo like Anand—who'd love him except dear mamma?*

'I'm sure we all have a special someone we'll do anything for.' Rishi glances at both of them. 'That's what makes life worth living, right? What else is there?' He pauses and then adds, 'Yeah, but another question is, how far would you go? There are psychos out there as well who don't understand this.'

'I say whatever it takes,' replies Anand. 'All is fair in love and war, right?'

'Well, if you bring that up,' says Rishi, 'this conversation becomes moot.'

A silence hangs in the air for a few moments. It isn't awkward, but it isn't comforting either.

'So, will you go looking for her?' Roy breaks the silence to bring up this question once more.

Rishi looks at Roy's expectant eyes.

'I will.'

25

Raghu purposefully marches through the corridor of New Memorial Hospital. Behind him, Shastri struggles to catch up. After checking at the reception, they are heading to the general ward.

An overpowering scent of medicine fill their nostrils; the scent of a disinfectant stands out. The place is crowded. This doesn't come as a surprise to Raghu as it is the only government hospital in the area. Raghu sees patients young and old, along with their families, jostling for space. There are patients in wheelchairs, bandages covering parts of their bodies; a woman wailing on a bench; an elderly woman shouting at a man in a white coat; another much younger woman sprinting along the corridor, her left arm brushing Raghu's right one.

They turn left at the end of the corridor. The general ward is the first room to the right. They step inside.

'This side, sir,' Shastri tells Raghu and guides him to the far end of the room past a row of beds.

They stop by Meena's bed. Her mother is sitting by her side, gazing at her, and Babu stands by the bed. Raghu glances at the girl. Her eyes are shut, and it looks like she hasn't regained consciousness. Just below her left elbow, he spots a strip of fresh bandage.

'How's she now?' Raghu asks no one in particular.

Babu folds his hands. 'Thank you for letting us go in the morning, sahib. The doctor has examined her. She had very low blood pressure in the morning and he has given her an injection to increase it. She also had a minor head injury due to the fall.'

'But what happened? And why the sudden low blood pressure?'

There is silence.

'I mean, she's a little girl,' Raghu went on. 'She shouldn't have low BP suddenly, right?'

'Yes, sir,' Moni says. 'The doctor said the same thing. Maybe due to the head injury. I don't know.'

Raghu walks up to the bed and looks intently at Meena. She has a round, sweet face and long eyelashes. He feels a pang of pity for the girl. How hard it must be to live without sight.

'So, when will she be . . . okay?'

'The doctor told us she should be fine and wake up any minute.'

Raghu wants to fire a flurry of questions at them but figures this is not the best time. *I can ask at least a few*, he thinks.

'Did you see or hear something odd last night?'

Babu and Moni glance at each other.

'We did not,' Babu starts. 'We were in our cottage. But there was a loud noise and we came rushing outside. Rishi sir and Anand sir were helping Meena when we got there. She was already unconscious by that time. Rishi sir said that she was thrown back some distance . . . I don't understand how that happened.'

'Hmm . . .' *That matches the version of those guys.* 'And what kind of noise was that?'

'It was just loud and . . . and . . . *strange*,' replies Moni. 'Never heard that kind of noise. I don't know what it was.'

'Okay, do you know what might have happened to the girl Nisha?'

'What happened?' Babu asks, concerned.

Shastri fills them in. Raghu watches their faces turn from concern to astonishment. They ask a few questions about the how's and what's of the incident.

'That's what we are here for,' replies Raghu. 'Do you know what might have happened?'

Babu and Moni exchange confounded looks again. 'We wouldn't know, sir.'

'What do you think of her companion, Rishi?'

'He appears to be nice, sir.' Babu looks at his feet before resuming, 'In fact, it's that other guest, Anand sir, who is a little weird.'

'Weird, how?' Raghu's interest is piqued. So far he has been thinking of the trip to the hospital as a waste of time. 'Tell me what's on your mind.'

It's Moni who answers the question. 'He is more interested in other people's life than his own. In fact, I've seen him a few times outside the cottages of other guests, peeking in through the window. Maybe he knows what happened to Nisha ma'am.'

Raghu nods. 'What else?'

'I can't understand him,' Moni resumes before stealing a quick glance at her daughter. 'Sometimes he's nice to us, to Meena, and on other occasions, he behaves very weirdly. His cottage is always very dirty, cigarette butts and ash everywhere. I think he is a very different person inside than he is on the outside. I don't know what exactly it is, but he is definitely a little strange, sir.'

'Would he peek inside just Nisha's room or that other couple's as well?'

'I saw him outside both the cottages, sir.'

'And what about Roy and Monica—how are they?'

'They mostly keep to themselves,' replies Babu. 'And they always talk to each other in hushed tones, as if they have some secrets.'

'Thanks, both of you.' He nods towards Meena. 'Please let me know when she wakes up. I would like to speak to her as well.' He turns to Shastri. 'Come on, let's go.'

In the parking lot, as they get into the vehicle, he tells Shastri, 'I want you to get me all the information you can about everybody on that hill, starting with that writer Anand, then Roy and Monica.'

26

Raghu reaches home late in the evening. He lives in a two-bedroom apartment in the bustling city of Nahan, eight kilometres south of the police station.

After the visit to the hospital, he had aimlessly roamed the streets around his house for hours, thinking about Palak, his wife. All the conversations of the past few weeks ran through his head over and over again like some old song playing repeatedly. *When did it go so wrong?*

He didn't know, but he certainly knew that it didn't feel right. Life didn't feel right. Just this morning, he was miffed with Palak, but as he paced, his heart gnawed at him. His chest tightened, and he felt as if someone or something had compressed his lungs, releasing all the oxygen from it. He took a few short, quick breaths.

It wasn't that he didn't want a child at all; he just didn't want one now. That was it. Why couldn't Palak understand this? He shook his head violently as he entered a small eatery to pick up dinner, surprised that dusk had turned so quickly into night. He checked the time—it was a few minutes past eight. *How long did I walk?*

He had smoked two cigarettes while waiting for his food and then trudged home with it, trying to banish all thoughts of his wife from his mind.

Now, dropping the keys of the flat on the small circular dining table, he walks over to the cabinet in the corner, pulls open the glass door, and grabs his favourite bottle of scotch. He normally doesn't drink on weekdays, but this week, particularly today, has been miserable. A couple of drinks are definitely called for.

Pouring himself a big shot, he throws himself on the couch. *Neat today.* He takes a sip and grimaces. A bit too strong for comfort. He switches on the television and leans back, stretching his legs on the small table in front of the couch. He flips the channels and settles on NEWS 24.

Before too long the newsreader is announcing the news he was expecting to see. A photo of Nisha flashes on the screen. The anchor clears her throat. 'We have just received reports of a girl, Nisha Dastur, disappearing from Writer's Hill resort of Sirmaur district in Himachal Pradesh earlier this morning. A team of Himachal Police and Indo-Tibetan Border Police are carrying out search operations. Nisha is the daughter of a prominent businessman and MP, Mr Pramod Dastur of Delhi. Raj, our correspondent from Delhi, is presently with Mr Dastur.'

The screen changes to a lanky man with a microphone in his hands standing outside the Parliament. A tall, stout man stands near him.

'Mr Dastur, do you have any update from the police authorities on the whereabouts of your daughter?'

Mr Dastur coughs. He appears to be in his late fifties but strong for his age. 'Nothing so far.' He shakes his head and frowns. 'I don't know where she is, what has happened to her. But I'm sure the authorities are doing a good job and will find my Nisha.'

'What do you think might have happened? Anything you can think of? At some point, I'm sure the police would consider . . . well, maybe kidnapping. Do you have any enemies, Mr Dastur?'

He shakes his head again vigorously. 'No, I don't think so.' He takes a deep breath and dispels air noisily through his teeth. 'I'm told by the police that if I don't get a call within forty-eight hours, it most likely would not be a case of kidnapping. I'm leaving for Himachal Pradesh right away. I have hired local trekking companies to help in the search. I'm confident we'll find her. She's a lovely child and God is with us.'

Damn! This is going to be messy.

Raghu turns off the television. Dastur is a powerful man who will have the entire police force of Himachal Pradesh scurrying around like rats to find his daughter. They must find Nisha, and soon.

He downs his drink in a quick swallow and is rising to get another when his phone rings. He looks at the screen.

It is Shastri. For a moment he contemplates ignoring it before reaching out to pick up his phone.

'Hello,' he answers groggily.

'Sir, we have some information on Roy and Monica.'

'What is it?'

'They are not who they say they are, sir,' Shastri pauses for a moment. 'They are thieves.'

27

Anand and Rishi are out in the garden when they see the police—Raghu and two others, one of them Shastri—march into the resort again. Racing up the stairs, they storm towards Roy and Monica's cottage.

Anand checks his watch. 9 p.m. He raises his eyebrows at Rishi. 'What's that all about?'

Rishi shrugs, his eyes never leaving the cops. 'Let's find out.'

They trot over to Roy's cottage and find Raghu at the entrance, pounding on the door. His subordinates stand behind him; both have their hands interlinked behind their back.

Raghu keeps knocking.

'What is it, inspector?' Rishi asks. 'Do you know something about Nisha's whereabouts?'

Raghu's fist is still on the door. He stops knocking and looks at Rishi. 'How well do you know these guys?'

'Not much,' Rishi replies blankly. 'I just met them some four days ago. Why?'

Raghu grunts and glances at Anand. 'And you?'

Anand shrugs. 'A week. What's the matter, inspector?'

Raghu pounds on the door again. 'You'll soon find out.'

After what feels like an eternity, the door creaks open. And what Raghu does next surprises not just Anand and Rishi, but his subordinates as well; one of them, in fact, claps his hand over his mouth in shock.

Raghu pushes the door with his left hand and delivers three powerful slaps on Roy's face with his right hand, which is adorned by three heavy rings. Roy's hand flies to his face, which is now a deep, scarlet colour. His cheek throbs painfully, and he instinctively rubs it.

'Where's Nisha?' Raghu demands. He is now inside the cottage and the rest of the company is outside the door, closely watching the proceedings. 'Where is she?'

Monica appears behind Roy, her hair tied in a towel. 'What's happening?'

'Where's Nisha?' Raghu is asking both of them now.

'How do we know?' Monica replies disinterestedly. 'Aren't *you* supposed to find that out?'

Raghu nods his head ever so slowly. He knows that the girl is smart; it would be tough to get an answer from her. He turns on his heels and spots Rishi lurking at the door. He beckons him.

Rishi enters the room cautiously. Raghu asks him. 'Do you suspect these guys?'

Rishi's eyes dart from one to the other before moving up to the tall policeman. 'I wouldn't know, inspector.'

'Hmm . . .' He looks over his shoulder at Shastri. 'They are thieves, right?'

Shastri nods. 'An FIR is lodged against them for possession in the Maidangiri chowki in the eastern district. He'—Shastri points a finger at Roy—'held up a gun at a man walking out of an ATM. That man'—Shastri breaks into a giggle, then pinches his lips in restraint, but the sound comes out like an engine of an old vehicle sputtering to life momentarily before dying down—'was a police officer. This man ran but the officer got an artist to sketch his face, which is still pinned on the board in that station as we speak. They are also prime suspects in a number of other robberies.' Shastri pauses to catch his breath. 'This girl is a liar. She was brought up in the same orphanage as the boy, no rich father, nothing. All lies. They were thrown out of the orphanage due to their stealing habits. I suspect they are here to hide after committing some other crime.'

Rishi's jaw drops. 'Actually, Nisha had lost her watch just a day before she disappeared.'

'Now, is that right?' Raghu says dramatically. He turns to the two thieves, staring grimly at them. 'Where's the watch?'

'What watch?' Monica asks. She looks so innocent that, for a moment, even Roy thinks that she has no clue.

'Search the cottage,' Raghu orders the other two.

The two constables begin opening drawers and cupboards, rummaging through them.

'Hold on!' Monica protests. 'Aren't you supposed to have a search warrant before doing this?'

Raghu sniggers and walks slowly towards her, the heels of his shoes clicking across the marble floor. 'Go—complain to the police!'

Monica frowns but stays silent. There's only so much pretence you can pull off. Her heart is battering in her chest now. One of the constables has opened the top left drawer of the almirah, above the shelf where she has hidden the watch. He'll find it anytime now. She has concealed it between some crumpled clothes, but these bastards are thorough. The constable at the almirah is checking that drawer as if he is looking for a pin, carefully running his fingers inside.

He's going to find it. And we'll have to go the prison, Roy thinks. Monica glances at him. She can see Roy is a nervous wreck. But even she doesn't feel very confident now.

The constable opens the drawer with the watch. It's a matter of seconds now.

Raghu notices thick beads of sweat form on Roy and Monica's foreheads. He's convinced they have stolen the watch. Nisha? He's not sure, but it does seem likely they have something to do with her disappearance.

'Is this the watch?' The constable asks Rishi, holding out the gold-coloured Cartier watch. Rishi walks towards him to take a closer look.

Monica can swear she can hear Roy's heart pounding against his ribcage. But she is equally frightened now. They are dead meat.

'Yes!' Rishi exclaims, taking the watch in his hand. 'Oh my God! Yes!' He casts a reproachful look at the two thieves in front of him. 'You stole Nisha's watch!'

Raghu steps forward and slaps Roy again. 'Where's Nisha? I won't ask again.'

This time Monica doesn't utter a word.

'Where's she?' Raghu screams, loud enough to make the two tremble.

'Okay, okay,' Monica says, holding out both arms in front of her in a plea for mercy. 'We stole the watch, but we had nothing to do with her murder.'

'Murder?' Raghu glances at Shastri. The tension in the room suddenly intensifies. Rishi swallows the huge lump in his throat that has formed upon hearing that word. His senses have heightened.

Raghu takes another step forward. 'How do you know Nisha has been murdered?'

28

Avni is watching the news with the sort of excitement she hasn't felt in a very long time. Sure, she felt it seven years ago when she abandoned her parents and left home, but this is even better.

Nisha has been missing for almost twenty-four hours and the police have no clue what happened to her.

'Is she dead?' she mutters under her breath. She hopes so with all her heart. It is fitting punishment for the woman who came between her and Rishi, the only man she has ever loved.

She remembers the day she had moved into this apartment. It was such a relief. Her home in Kurukshetra had been so claustrophobic. She is from a family of priests; the entire clan would spend all day in temples, offering prayers, singing *bhajan*s, and do nothing fun. She never wanted that kind of life. She feels praying is the weakest of all activities a person can do. If you want something, just go for it; why pray to statues?

When she asked her parents this question, her father's thick hand struck her cheek.

'How can you be so impudent?' her father boomed. 'Fear the Almighty who runs the world!'

Bullshit! *We* run the world. Only the weak pray to God and beg for the fulfilment of their dreams. The strong fight against the world to achieve it.

And she is strong. She is going to fight against the world if she has to, so as to have Rishi. Her love is all-consuming. Love has to be like that, she thinks, an obsession; otherwise it isn't love.

She knew this the first time she set eyes on Rishi, just a day after he had moved here. He had inadvertently locked the door to his apartment with the keys and his phone lying inside. With no other option, he rang the bell to Avni's door. When she appeared, he asked if he could use her phone to make a call. Avni had let him in, offered him a hot cup of tea, and given him company until the locksmith showed up.

In those ten minutes, she had learnt everything about Rishi—he worked in a prominent IT company in Gurgaon, he had an elder sister who adored him, he was born in Allahabad and moved to Delhi two years back—and taken a special liking to him, maybe felt the first stirrings of love.

By the end of the month, she was completely in love with him and believed that her love was reciprocated.

A few years later, when she saw Nisha entering Rishi's apartment (after being turned down herself), something in her mind snapped.

She would have killed Nisha that day if Rishi hadn't saved her.

She turns back to the television and laughs when she sees tears in Nisha's father's eyes while answering a question from the journalist.

'She's gone!' she exclaims gleefully.

29

'How the hell do you know that Nisha has been murdered?' Raghu yells again at Roy and Monica and sees them tremble; they look like children being scolded by their stepmother. He notices that Monica's imperious demeanour has vanished; her shoulders have dropped and her eyes are downcast.

'I . . . we don't know,' Monica answers softly.

'Then why did you say it?'

Tears are rolling down Rishi's eyes now. He can taste the salt in them. Nisha had been warning him all along that she expected this trip to be a disaster. What had she said?

I feel it. Something bad is going to happen on this trip.

He curses himself for not listening to her. But how could she have been murdered? How could *that* be possible?

There is only one name that pops into his mind.

Avni.

'Think about it, inspector,' Monica replies slowly. 'There have been more than a dozen people searching for the girl since morning. It's a small resort. Why is it taking so much time to find her? Maybe someone killed her and threw her body in the valley? Or maybe in that lake nearby? It's just a guess.'

'Please, sir, we might be thieves,' adds Roy, 'but we aren't murderers. That gun I pointed at an inspector outside the ATM wasn't even real. It was a toy gun that I had painted black.'

Shastri utters an uncharacteristic shriek. When Raghu glances at him, he mouths 'sorry'.

But Raghu believes Roy. And feels they can't be murderers. He doesn't know the reason for his strong conviction. Perhaps it's the sincerity in Roy's voice or maybe intuition. They come across as simply petty thieves, not killers or kidnappers.

But that's not what he is pondering just now. He is thinking about what Monica has said. It makes so much sense. Her words make his skin cold.

It's a small resort. Why is it taking so much time to find her? Maybe someone killed her.

That is possible, isn't it? Kill her. Then dump the body in the lake. Maybe he should send divers down there? But something tells him he won't find anything there. *Too easy.* There are smarter ways to get rid of a body.

But who would do it? And what could be the motive for the crime?

He turns to Rishi. *Would he kill here?* He gives a barely perceptible shake of the head. Rishi seems like a man genuinely worried for his girlfriend.

'Any news?' he asks Shastri.

Shastri shakes his head. 'The last update was half an hour back—nothing at all, sir. No sign of her, nobody has seen her.'

Raghu turns his attention to Roy and Monica. He points his right index finger at them. 'I'm going to ask you only one time: is there anything else you are hiding from me? Do you know anything, anything at all, about what might have happened to Nisha?'

'Sir, I . . . I swear to God, I just stole her watch,' Roy replies.

'Actually,' Monica adds, 'we were also planning to steal her bag, but we didn't.'

Roy nods. 'Okay, I'll tell you about that as well. Yesterday, I planned to enter their cottage and get her bag, but just after I entered, I heard that sound or . . . sounds that we told you about earlier. I came out of the cottage and ran to see what was happening. Which is when I saw that little girl being pushed backwards and . . . and that's it. Rishi and Anand saw me then, and I came back to my cottage.'

'So then why did you lie earlier this morning when I asked you if you saw something?'

Roy hangs his head and looks at his feet.

Raghu shakes his head in disbelief and exasperation. He feels like holding their heads and banging them together until they crack. 'Do you guys know anything about Nisha? Anything at all?'

Both shake their head. 'No, inspector,' Monica replies. 'We don't.'

'All fucking lies, then, huh?'

He exhales a puff of air. 'How the fuck do I find her?' he whispers in anguish.

30

The next morning, Raghu picks up the newspaper slid under the door of his apartment and settles on the dining table. He has made himself a cup of tea, or rather, a half-cup—most of the water evaporated as he'd left the pan on the stove far too long. Breakfast is scorched egg bhurji. He pours a river of ketchup over it to offset the horrible burnt taste.

He flicks the paper open, and on the third page he sees what he expected to see. Shaking his head, he begins reading.

MP'S DAUGHTER MISSING FROM THE HILLS OF HIMACHAL PRADESH

Nisha Dastur, twenty-three-year-old daughter of prominent businessman and Member of Parliament, Mr Pramod Dastur, has mysteriously disappeared from Writer's Hill, a resort in Sirmaur district. At the time of the paper going to print, almost twenty-four hours had elapsed and there were no signs of Nisha.

'We are doing our best to locate the girl,' says SP Bedi of Sirmaur district. 'There are more than a dozen personnel, ITBP and our own involved in the search. We have our best men on the job, and we are hopeful of having results very soon.'

Raghu tosses the paper aside. So many rescuers involved, so why haven't they been able to find her? Even if Monica's guess is correct, where's the damn body?

He picks up his phone and dials Shastri.

'Did you find out anything about the rest of the people?'

Shastri has some interesting findings.

'Okay, I'll be there shortly,' Raghu tells him.

An hour later, Raghu is at his desk in office, gratefully sipping his second cup of tea of the morning—this time a full cup. Shastri stands by his side.

'Moni and Babu's story matches their statement, sir,' he says. 'They've been working in that resort for the last fifteen years, since it was set up. Before that they were working for the owner, Sodhi, at his place in Delhi. He asked them to run the place as he liked their work.' Shastri pauses to make sure his boss is listening. When Raghu nods, he continues, 'I spoke to Mr Sodhi as well. The girl was born here on the resort, and she *is* blind from birth.'

'What were you telling me about that writer?'

'Sir, there's something wrong with that guy's story. You remember he mentioned he has a mother?'

'Yes,' Raghu nods. 'Why?'

Shastri smirks. 'Well, sir, he was lying. His mother has been dead for ten years.'

Raghu looks up at Shastri in surprise. 'What?'

'Yes, sir.'

'But—' Raghu stops. Didn't Anand say he lives with his mother? He tries to recall the conversation with him yesterday.

'Everyone has a family. I live with my mother. She's the best mother in the world.'

Another liar?

Raghu runs his hands through his hair, ruffling it. This is getting more and more complicated. Why now? When he isn't at his best. When he wants to go on leave and think about his life, about Palak and the future—about whether this is how he intends to continue living, without her, without all those moments of happiness (okay, they fight sometimes but mostly they've been very happy together). He wants to carefully analyze his life, ruminate about what he really wants and doesn't want (loneliness being number one on the latter list). Not be bogged down by a bunch of liars and that missing daughter of a hi-fi politician.

But it pays his bills, so—

'Now, why is *he* lying to us?' Raghu asks, gritting his teeth.

Shastri offers a shrug.

Raghu rises. 'Let's find out.'

31

Raghu jumps into the jeep with the urgency of a ship captain on high seas in stormy weather, turns on the ignition, and pushes the accelerator pedal down to the maximum. Shastri, sitting by his side, jerks backward as the jeep lunges forward like a wild boar. Glancing sideways at his boss, he is intimidated by the expression on his face. Raghu's visage is like steel. The veins on his forehead are standing out, throbbing with warm blood. His hands are grasping the steering wheel so hard that Shastri wouldn't be surprised if it simply popped out of the shaft.

Anand is dead! Shastri thinks.

They reach the resort in no time, although it felt like eternity to Shastri, as he was on the edge of his seat, his hands looped around the seat belt as he prayed for the journey to end. They weren't on the road, Shastri swore, they were mid-air.

He scurries out of the jeep as soon as Raghu brings it to a halt. Raghu races up the stairs, Shastri half a dozen steps behind his boss, in no hurry to catch up.

Rishi and Anand are sitting on a ledge in the garden. Raghu, without preamble, lunges at Anand, throwing a powerful arm around his neck and yanking him forward. Anand almost trips over but manages to find his feet. Raghu closes his right hand around Anand's neck again, this time squeezing it slowly but firmly.

'Why have you been lying to us?' he screams.

Anand struggles to break free from Raghu's hold, turning his head this way and that. He then uses both his arms to try to pull off Raghu's hand, but Raghu is too strong for him. He tries to twist his neck free again but the effort is futile.

'Now that you have tried,' says Raghu calmly, 'and failed at it, I'll suggest a better option to free yourself. Tell me the truth. Every second you waste in answering, I'll tighten my hold around that weasely neck of yours. Don't complain if your eyes pop out.'

Despite the advice, Anand keeps trying to loosen Raghu's grip but to no avail.

Noticing the scarlet colour of Anand's face, Raghu lets go.

'Where is Nisha? What have you been hiding?' Raghu screams again.

Anand's hands fly to his neck, gently rubbing it. He sputters a series of coughs and takes short, sharp breaths. He takes his time in answering.

Finally, he mumbles hoarsely, 'Why would I know?'

This time Raghu steps forward and slaps him—a quick, stinging slap that leaves the imprint of his fingers on Anand's face.

Anand utters a bellow. He feels a ringing pain in his left ear, the greatest point of impact.

'I don't know.' He tries again. He gently rubs his ear, squeezing his eyes shut in pain. His lungs are still grasping for oxygen, and his breathing is fast and shallow.

'So why did you lie about your mother?'

'I . . . I did?' he replies, looking dazed.

'Yes, motherfucker, you did!' Raghu yells. 'You said you live with your mother but she's been dead for ten years!'

Rishi's jaw drops open. He stares at Anand in confusion. *What?* Hadn't he told him and Roy just yesterday about his mother? That he loves her so much he'd do anything for her?

Anand reflects on the question. Why did he lie about it? He knows the answer. But why his mother? Why not his father?

He doesn't have to think too hard for that answer as well. He has never liked his father—he was too . . . insensitive, never cared for him or his mother. He lived alone in Dubai— or perhaps with a second family, his mother would sometimes speculate.

Anand initially lived with his parents in a government flat in south Delhi. When he was around six years old, his father started to disappear for long periods. Initially, he would be absent for a week or so; slowly that stretched to a month, and eventually, his father moved out of the house and relocated permanently to Dubai.

He would see his father once a year from then on. But he never saw any change in his mother's behaviour towards him. She was still the same sweet, loving mother who loved her son unconditionally. She took a job in Anand's school to run the house. When he asked her about his father, she would mostly answer, 'I'm both your mother and father.'

But as he grew older, sometimes she would cry and tell him about her suspicions of his father having another family in Dubai, a family that he loved more.

'Some people are like that, son,' her mother had once said between her sobs. 'They don't know love, its power, its magic. They keep searching for love all their lives, falling in and out of love, when in fact, love should be steadfast, guiding your life—like a lighthouse at sea directing a ship towards safe waters.'

Anand put his head on his mother's lap, and her soothing hand gently caressed his hair.

'You must not be like that,' she continued. 'Always love passionately and deeply. Find that one special person and dedicate all that you have to her. That'll make your life worth living even if everything around you is falling apart. Believe in the power of love. Never deceive love. Never disrespect love. And always remember that you'll be far happier if you're with a person who loves you than with a person you love.'

Anand never asked about his dad again. He could live without his father. God had given him a good mother and a great doctrine on love. That was enough to live a good life.

But when asked by his friends in school about his father, he would lie that his dad travelled a lot. That was why he couldn't come for parent–teacher meetings like the fathers of other kids. The lie reduced his stress, made him feel good.

His psychiatrist is sure the lies started from there. Anand thought it was the day his mother was on her way to pick him up from school on the last day before the winter vacations when he was fifteen years old. She never made it—a veering truck hit her from behind and she died on the spot.

But for him, she was still alive. At least that's what he told himself, and then the other people in his life. When he reflects on it, he is sure that was the time in his life when he became an inveterate liar.

Initially, he would lie only about his mother being alive, but gradually, he began lying about everything. His job, his hobbies, the girls in his life, everything. There was no reason to lie; they just flowed effortlessly, like waves lapping against the shore.

His psychiatrist has always told him that deep within him, the lies made him more self-assured; that is why he carries on with this habit. He doesn't think so. Initially, yes, perhaps, but then later, it was just so much fun to make people believe all those things.

'Oh, you want a Mercedes so bad? *Really?* Well, I drive one all the time in Dubai. My dad has two Mercs.'

'You like that girl? *That* girl? I dumped her like two weeks back, dude!'

'The Clones' show tickets? The guitarist of the band is my buddy! Sure, I can you get you a VIP pass. Come on, dude, that's nothing for me!'

Yeah, sure, that was fun. And people loved him. For a short time, okay, but they did love him and respect him. If they found out he was lying, no problem at all. There are so many people in the world. Last he checked, there were seven billion people on the planet. You can always find someone else to lie to.

No problem at all.

Raghu snaps his fingers inches from his face. 'Where the hell are you lost?'

Anand brings himself back to the present. 'Okay, okay, I might have lied about my mother, but really, I don't know what happened to the girl.'

'Is that another lie?'

Rishi grabs the collar of Anand's shirt and gives him a shake. 'Please tell us if you know something about Nisha. It's been more than a day and we don't know where she is.'

Anand shrugs. 'I really don't know.'

32

Raghu decides to do a quick search of Anand's cottage. He still doesn't believe the guy. They follow Anand to his cottage, and Raghu cannot help but feel that the guy is nuts. *What else has he been hiding?* He turns to look at Shastri and finds the same incredulity in his eyes that he had seen in Rishi's.

Poor guy! He feels for Rishi and hopes that he can put an end to his torment soon. Anand is definitely involved; his intuition tells him.

When Raghu steps into Anand's cottage, a wave of nausea overwhelms him. The room is filthy; it stinks worse than a garbage truck. Banana peels, leftovers of sandwiches and other food have made the floor their home; flies merrily buzz over it all. Cigarette ash is sprinkled all over the floor, and Raghu has to debate if it is intentional when he spots three ashtrays in the cottage. The mattress is on the floor; socks, crumpled shirts and trousers are strewn over the bed.

Raghu turns to Anand. 'How the fuck do you live here?'

'Sorry, inspector, it's a little dirty.'

'A little?'

Raghu shakes his head and advances further into the room. He stops at the messy desk, which has all sorts of objects scattered over it. There's a laptop and Raghu taps a key. The screen comes to life and Raghu finds an open Microsoft Word document.

He looks over his shoulder at Anand again.

Anand shrugs. 'Just a story I was writing.'

'What's it about?'

Anand feels terror striking his heart. It's *that* short story. About Nisha and the rest of them, where he makes Nisha disappear—

Before he can answer the question, Raghu has started reading it.

Soon, Raghu pulls out the chair and sits on it. He is hooked. It's the name of the character that caught his attention, but then slowly, he has found all the people in Writer's Hill in the story.

It takes Raghu ten minutes to finish reading the tale, and when it's done, he is breathing heavily. He rises and storms towards Anand.

'YOU made Nisha disappear!'

Anand feels a huge lump in his throat and swallows hard. 'N-no, inspector,' he replies, but his words sound like a lie even to himself. He fails to understand how he could be so stupid. *Why didn't I delete the story after all this happened?*

Raghu is staring at him with baleful eyes. He thumps Anand on the chest, and Anand staggers backward. 'Where's she? Tell me now or I'll put you in lock-up and torture you such that you won't be able to write a single word for the rest of your life!'

'Please believe me, inspector,' Anand begs but he knows that Raghu doesn't believe him at all. Nevertheless, he tries to fight his case. 'It's just coincidence that my story came true. I don't have it in me to harm someone.'

'Shastri, do you believe him? He wrote about Nisha disappearing in his story and a day later'—he makes quotation marks with his fingers—'voila, she disappears.'

Shastri looks up, adjusting his khaki cap. 'I don't think so, sir. Too big a coincidence.'

'I don't think so, too.' He flicks his right hand. 'Come, let's go to the police station. You won't answer until I bust your ass.'

'Sir, no . . . no, please—'

But Raghu's strong hands are already clutching Anand's wrist, and he is pulled along against his will. He tries to resist, but when Raghu glances at him over his shoulder, his bloodshot eyes scorching him, Anand yields.

Outside, Rishi watches in despair as Shastri puts handcuffs on Anand.

'He might be a liar, inspector, but he can't have harmed Nisha,' Rishi tells Raghu. 'I mean, he's not a bad person.'

'How many days have you known him?'

'Four–five days.'

Raghu nods. 'Then you have no idea if he's a bad person or not.'

'Believe me, inspector,' Anand tries again from behind. 'I can't hurt anyone. Please speak to my psychiatrist. She'll tell you everything about me.'

Raghu stops in his track and whirls around. 'Your psychiatrist?'

Anand nods.

'Why do you see a psychiatrist?'

'B-b-because I'm not mentally stable, or so they say.'

Raghu gives a shout of frustration. 'Is there anything else we should know about you?'

33

Back inside Anand's cottage, Raghu dials a number on his cellphone. He impatiently listens to the rings, staring at Anand all the while. He is still having a hard time believing him. *But why would Rishi stand up for him?*

'Hello.' Raghu hears a strong voice on the line.

'Hello. Is this Dr Banerjee?'

'Yes. Who's this?'

'I'm Inspector Raghuveer from Renukaji police station in Sirmaur district, Himachal Pradesh. I'm calling you to enquire about your patient, Anand.'

There is silence on the line. Then a clearing of throat.

'I'm not allowed to discuss my patients unless it is—'

'Yes, it is,' Raghu interjects, 'a police case and we have strong reason to believe that your patient is involved. In fact, we're taking him to the police station to file an initial charge sheet against him.'

'Okay. What do you want to know?'

Raghu thinks of a few questions on his feet. 'Start by telling us how long you've known him, what you are treating him for, do you think he is capable of committing a crime, and any other related information you can think of.'

There is another silence on the line—a longer one—and Raghu begins to think he'll get evasive answers.

'I've known him for nine years now,' Dr Banerjee starts. 'Anand came to me in acute depression at the loss of his mother and with absolutely no self-worth. He had lost all hope in life and he showed classic suicidal tendencies, you know—like asking questions about whether suicide relieves you of all your pain. Anyway, my first few years with him were difficult and I had to give him a lot of time. His mother was a good friend of mine, so I didn't mind the extra hours. I managed to get him out of the deep depressive abyss, but I realized he is a very unhappy person. Simple reason for that: he was very lonely. He constantly looked for acceptance and adulation by people, he lied a lot to influence friends. In fact, he still lies for no reason at all. I think it gives him some excitement, but I also think he does it to deceive himself. He'd lie about his father. Why? Maybe to delude himself into believing his father is still with him. Ditto for his mother. Lots of people do it. It makes them calm and emotionally stable. Then he also hankers for a romantic relationship. He doesn't want to be like his father who abandoned his mother for another woman—no, he wants the real thing.

'You asked me if he is capable of committing a crime? I really don't think so. He is a kind man at heart, and I'm sure he'll turn the tides, so to speak, to help someone in need. He behaves a little strangely at times, I'll admit, but it is his loneliness that makes him do stupid things. His father left him. His mother died when he was young. What would that do to a young man? All he wants is a little love that he never got. In fact, we all want love to survive and stay sane, isn't that right, officer?'

Raghu grunts uncomfortably. 'There's a girl that has gone missing from a resort here in Himachal Pradesh. I think he might be involved.'

When Dr Banerjee speaks again, her voice is even firmer. 'I told you, officer, I don't think he can hurt someone. Are you sure about what you say? Do you have evidence?'

Raghu grunts again. 'No . . . no, we're not sure.'

'Then you're wasting your time and mine.' She pauses to draw a sharp breath. 'Is there anything else you'd like to ask me?'

'No, thank you.'

Raghu hears a click, and then the soft drone of the telephone line.

All he wants is a little love that he never got. In fact, we all want love to survive and stay sane, isn't that right, officer?

'She's right,' he mutters under his breath.

'Sir, you said something?' Shastri asks his boss.

Raghu shakes his head. He's confused now, and although he would like to take Anand to the police station, beat him up until he gets some answers to his questions, he feels that the doctor may be right. What evidence does he have to pin Nisha's disappearance on him anyway?

The story? But Anand wouldn't so stupid as to write a story of Nisha's disappearance and then make her disappear the following day, with the story still on his computer.

He looks up at Anand who is fidgeting nervously. He's a messed-up young fellow, perhaps caught at the wrong place at the wrong time.

'Let him go,' Raghu orders, and walks out of the room.

34

Later that day, Anand is sitting alone in the garden. He's still as a post; a less keen eye might mistake him for a statue, like the many others in the resort.

His eyes have welled up and his vision is blurry. After a long time, he is missing his mother. He had kept her alive in a mausoleum tucked somewhere in the dark corner of his heart. He talked to her, laughed with her, shared stories with her. He would tell her that he remembers everything she had told him. About life. About love. But she's gone now. Forever.

'What are you doing here alone?' Rishi calls out from behind him.

Anand wipes his eyes with the back of his right hand, and sniffs loudly. 'Nothing.'

'You lied to me about your mother?' Rishi says accusingly. 'What else have you lied about?' When he draws level with Anand, he notes his teary eyes.

'I'm sorry,' Anand replies. His voice is low and unsteady.

Rishi takes a deep breath. 'I trusted you with everything, man.'

'What's going on, boys?' Roy is walking towards them. 'I heard the police had you handcuffed, dear writer.' He chuckles.

Silence.

Anand squeezes his lips, blocking a sob that is waiting to break out. He wants to get the hell out of this place. Away from everyone. He wants to be alone in his room, switch off all the lights, and tuck himself tightly under the covers. He doesn't want anyone to see him, talk to him; all he wants to hear is the soft tick-tock of the wall clock in his bedroom.

'Are you okay, Anand?' Rishi enquires, placing an arm on his shoulder.

Anand shakes it off. 'Yeah, please leave me alone.'

Rishi glances at Roy and shrugs.

'I thought you were going to join the search,' Roy says. 'Weren't you?'

'We're not allowed to leave this place for a few days. And why do you care so much? So, you can enter my cottage and steal Nisha's bag?' Rishi gives him an angry shove. 'Why did you steal her watch?'

Roy bows his head. 'I'm sorry,' he replies. 'I really am. I did it for Monica. I told you earlier—I'll do anything for her. Wouldn't you do anything for Nisha if she asked you to?'

Rishi doesn't reply at first. He just stands there with a grouchy expression. Then he says, 'Of course, I'll do anything for her, you idiot, but that doesn't mean I'll go out and steal something!'

Suddenly, they hear a cackle erupt from Anand. He rises in some pain, his eyes fixed on the ground. 'The things we do in love,' he says, shaking his head, and slowly walks away to his cottage.

Rishi and Roy's eyes follow him to his door. When Anand firmly shuts the door behind him, they turn to glance at each other.

'You have no idea what I'll do for her,' Rishi tells Roy. 'No idea at all.'

35

A couple of days later, posters of Nisha are ubiquitous at every corner of the district of Sirmaur. Nisha's father has offered a reward of twenty-five lakh rupees to anyone who provides information about Nisha. Her big, beautiful eyes in the picture cry out for help. Thousands of passers-by have gone past it, taken a close look at the picture.

Nobody has seen Nisha.

Nisha's father has also paid for ads in the local newspapers and other media. He has provided four phone numbers and exhorted people to help with any information of Nisha's whereabouts.

Along with a team of more than a dozen professional trekkers, he has covered the hills around Writer's Hill more than a few times. The good sign is that they haven't discovered her body, so she is definitely out there; the bad sign, of course, is that nobody has a clue.

Pramod Dastur is at a tea stall on one of the hills along with his team, when he gets a call from the SP. 'Yes, Bedi. Any news?'

'Nothing about Nisha, but I got a call from Raghu, the officer in charge of the case.' Bedi pauses and takes a deep breath. 'There might be another angle to this story. The guests at the resort had spoken about some'—he hesitates and clears his throat, doubtful as to how his boss' boss' friend would react to what he was going to say next, because he didn't believe it himself—'some supernatural element. They heard something strange that night, and the daughter of the caretakers was hit badly by . . . in their words, a powerful force. Now, I know this sounds ludicrous but—'

'Where is that girl now?' Pramod interjects.

'She was unconscious in the hospital, but she's fine now and heading back to the resort.'

'I'd like to meet her.'

Raghu has been thinking a lot the past few days about what the guys had told him—those strange sounds, blinding lightning, Meena getting thrown back. He had more or less dismissed it as hogwash initially and gone on with the search, sure in his heart that they would find Nisha.

But it's been almost a week now and they have had no luck. Maybe there is an otherworldly element to this. Maybe what the guys had told him was true. And the most likely person to confirm this was Meena who was getting discharged from the hospital today.

At five in the evening that day, Raghu drives towards Writer's Hill. He had spoken to Babu earlier and told him about needing to see Meena for a few minutes.

When Raghu reaches the resort, he calls for Rishi. Babu scurries towards Rishi's cottage.

'He's not here,' remarks Anand who has emerged from his cottage.

'Where's he?'

'Gone out looking for Nisha. He said he'll ask everybody that he meets about Nisha, that surely someone would have seen her.'

'Now, is that a lie?'

Anand shrugs disinterestedly. 'Why would I lie about it?'

'I don't know,' Raghu replies. 'You tell me?'

'No, inspector, I'm not lying.' Anand's tone is firm, steady.

'Ring him up,' Raghu says. 'I want to speak to him. We might be getting close to her.'

He turns to Babu. 'I'd like to talk to Meena now.' He follows Babu to his cottage, the smallest one in the resort. As he enters, Raghu asks him, 'How's your daughter now?'

'She's fine now, sir. The doctor has asked us not to stress her.'

The bedroom is tiny with just enough space for a queen-sized bed. Meena is lying on one side of it, her mother sitting by her side. When Raghu enters the cottage, both of them look up at him.

'Hello,' Raghu says. He walks towards the bed and asks Meena, 'Feeling better now, child?'

Meena nods slowly.

'Can I ask you a few questions quickly please?'

She nods again.

Babu gets a wooden stool from the kitchen and offers it to Raghu. He thanks Babu, pulls it close to the bed, and sits down.

'Now, I want you to think very carefully,' begins Raghu, 'about that night. Did you feel anything odd, hear anything odd? Most importantly, who pushed you, causing you to fall unconscious?'

'Sir, is it the right time to ask her these questions?' asks Moni, concerned. 'She just got released from the hospital.'

Raghu glances at her. 'I understand your concern, but that girl Nisha has been missing from this resort since last week. I have reason to believe that Meena can help me find her. Please. This is really important.'

Babu goes over to Moni and gives her arm a little squeeze. 'Sure, sir, you go ahead. We too want Nisha ma'am to be found.'

'Thank you.' Raghu turns back to Meena. 'Please think carefully.'

Meena nods.

There is a sudden knock on the door, which makes them all jump. Babu walks over and opens the door.

It is Nisha's father accompanied by two burly men. Nisha's father looks even heavier built in the flesh than he does on television, Raghu observes.

He enters the room and Raghu rises to greet him.

'Has she said anything?' Pramod asks without preamble. 'I believe she might be the key to my daughter's disappearance.'

Raghu lets out a laugh. 'That's not what I told Bedi sir. I meant she might know something that we're missing.'

'Oh . . . okay.'

Babu brings another stool and Pramod sits next to Raghu. Raghu glances at Meena. Her face is turned towards him questioningly. Raghu notices that her dark glasses are too big for her small face, almost reaching the tip of her nose. She has an innocent, sweet look, and Raghu feels a pang of pity for her.

'Okay, sweetheart,' he starts again. 'Have you thought about it? Can you please tell us all that happened? That night, a young woman went missing, and her father here is shattered. We have to find her.'

There is silence in the room for a minute or two. Anxious eyes lock into each other wondering if Meena would be any help at all. She is blind, after all—what could she have seen?

Meena starts in a shaky voice. 'I . . . I just remember there were some animals around . . . no, I mean I didn't see them, but I . . . felt them. They were howling and in pain.'

'Where were they?'

'Here, in the resort . . . I don't know—it felt like that, or was it just a sound in my head? I'm not sure.'

Raghu and Pramod exchange looks.

'Actually,' Raghu says, 'what you are saying matches what the others said.' He looks around, speaking to no one in particular, 'But what was it? *Animals?* Where did they come from?'

'Sir, that can't be,' replies Babu. 'We don't have any animals in or near the resort. Maybe they all heard something else.'

'Yes, maybe,' Meena says.

'And who pushed you?' Raghu asks.

'I don't know.' Meena shakes her head. 'I just . . . I felt a strong jolt. Before I knew what happened, I was on the ground.'

Raghu doesn't like what he's hearing; he doesn't like it at all. It's raising more questions than answers. He comes back to that question he asked Anand the first day: how does this explain Nisha's disappearance?

Even if some supernatural phenomenon happened that night and howsoever outlandish it was, whatever happened to Nisha? Where did she go? And where's her damn body? Did those animals or whatever *eat* her?

Raghu's mind is pounded by a barrage of questions, like a volley of gunshots in a battlefield. Unlike a soldier who gets to fire back, Raghu has no way of responding. He is clueless. It's not that he's a cynic who dismisses unexplained phenomena; no, he's a believer and accepts that certain baffling events do occur in life. So, although he wants to agree that there might be something uncanny going on here when nothing else has yielded answers, he cannot connect the dots.

'And you heard nothing after that?' he persists, hoping against hope for that one clue that will sort out the puzzle. 'Do you know where Nisha was at this time?'

Meena shakes her head slowly; she appears dejected at not being able to help. 'I . . . I don't know.'

'Anything else you can remember?' Raghu pushes again. Desperation has crept into his voice. 'Do you have any idea at all where Nisha might be?'

Meena shakes her head again.

'It was a waste of my time.' Pramod gets up and walks out the door.

Raghu glances at Meena one last time before rising, and thanks them for their time.

36

By the time Raghu walks out of the room, his mind churning even more than earlier, Pramod is stepping into a car in the parking lot below. *He's really disappointed*, Raghu thinks.

The past few days, the case has occupied him; he has barely thought about his wife. But now, images of Palak suddenly come rushing to him when he sees Pramod's car zipping away. Maybe it's the abject sorrow on Pramod's face at the disappearance of a loved one that has triggered memories of his wife.

Or maybe he genuinely misses her.

He doesn't know, and he doesn't want to answer the question. But the fact remains that his heart sinks every time he remembers her absence. He hates to admit that he feels a burning desire to see her. He has loved her for five years after all. *How can you forget someone you love so easily? If it was that easy, there wouldn't be any love in the world.*

Then don't forget her, go and get her, a voice calls out from inside his heart. It is the same voice that has been trying to communicate with him for the past two weeks, which he has been busy ignoring. But he now realizes he might have to listen to it. *The heart wants what the heart wants, right?*

Almost convinced, but not a hundred per cent. There is another voice, the antithesis of the first voice (anti-love, pro-war this one—*is that the mind speaking?*), which tells him it won't work out. *You are both different people. Different people want different things. Duh!*

He leaves the two voices to sort it out among themselves and ambles over to Rishi's cottage, rapping on the door before pushing it open.

Rishi is sitting on the bed, bent over, his face covered by his hands. Anand is leaning against a wall, his right leg crossed over his left.

'You're crying?' Raghu asks.

Rishi lifts his head and gets up on his feet in a flash.

'Sorry,' Raghu holds his hands up in apology. 'Didn't mean to startle you.'

'No, no, it's okay.' Rishi nods towards the chair beside the bed. 'Please take a seat.'

'Thanks,' Raghu says and sits down.

Rishi sits on the bed facing him. 'Please tell me you know where Nisha is.'

Raghu glances at Anand before shaking his head as he looks Rishi in the eye. 'Afraid not.' He observes grief settle back on Rishi's face. The poor guy probably thought Raghu had some news for him about Nisha. 'What have you been doing here all this while?'

'After you allowed us to step out of the resort, I just come here to sleep at night and spend the day looking for Nisha, asking every man, woman or child I meet if they have seen Nisha.' His face contorts in sorrow, tears brimming in his eyes. 'But no one has seen her. No one.'

Raghu nods and pats his shoulder. 'All of us have been trying very hard, but . . .' He trails off. 'How long have you known her?'

'A few months now—fell in love with her almost at first sight.'

Raghu smiles. 'That is sweet.' He pauses. 'Listen, I . . . I'm really sorry we haven't been able to find her so far, but I promise we will.'

Rishi nods ever so slowly. 'Thanks.'

Raghu bobs his head towards Anand. 'So, you friends with this guy now?'

Rishi allows a small smile to appear on his face. 'He's a nice guy, inspector. I know he lied and all. I think he's messed up like all of us and lonely, I guess . . . but he's a good guy. He's been a great support.'

'I'm sorry I lied, inspector,' Anand takes over, 'but I wouldn't hurt someone. I'm a man of love, and I would do anything to help someone be with their love. I *love* love, if you know what I mean.'

Raghu hesitates for only a second before confessing, 'I know how it feels when you miss someone, that perpetual heart-sinking feeling, the unsettled mind not being able to focus, the impatience gnawing at you . . . I know how it feels.'

'Inspector, if I may ask, who are you missing?' Anand says.

Raghu waves a hand in a dismissive gesture. 'No one.' He looks around, as if for an escape route, but the words are out before he can stop them. 'It's my wife.'

And then it all pours out of him—his love for his wife, her love for him, the conflict, and the separation. He admits it was his mistake, that he had been very negligent and taken for her granted. He misses her intensely and is desperate to see her again.

'You know, inspector,' says Anand, 'my mother would tell me to always love passionately and deeply. Find that one special person and dedicate all that you have to her. That'll make your life worth living even if everything around you is falling apart. Maybe her words can help you.'

'Your mother is a wise woman,' Raghu says.

'Was,' Anand corrects him. 'My mother was a wise woman.'

'I'm sorry.'

'Then do it, inspector, call her, go see her,' Rishi says after a moment. 'What's stopping you?'

'I'm sorry,' replies Raghu. 'Why am I discussing all this with you guys? I was here to discuss Nisha.'

'Don't worry about it,' Anand replies. 'Maybe you saw your pain reflected in Rishi's eyes and felt like talking about it. It's fine.'

Raghu smiles. He rises slowly. 'Yeah, buddy, you're right. I do feel pain. A lot of it.'

'Then call her, inspector, and tell her that.' Rishi also rises and leads Raghu to the door, Anand waves from his position against the wall. 'Love, family, they're so important. What else is there in life?'

Raghu nods. 'Yeah, you're right. Nothing else.'

37

There is news the next morning. One of the ITBP personnel, Prasad, a tall, wiry man, has discovered the body of a woman about fifteen kilometres away from the resort.

While relieving himself on the side of a mud track leading off the main road, Prasad was casually glancing around when his eyes fell upon what looked like a bundle of clothes about three hundred metres down the slope. He squinted hard and thought he could discern the shape of a woman's body. Zipping up, he slid down the slope towards the mound.

He didn't inform his colleagues just then. The closer he got, the surer he was that he had found Nisha. *My God*, he though, *will I be eligible for that twenty-five lakhs award?* But the thought melted away as soon as it appeared. *No, that's part of my job, they will say.*

Prasad proceeded nonetheless with the energy and enthusiasm of a child presented with a new bicycle. A few minutes later, he was staring at the body of a young woman. There was a big cut on her left temple. When he peered at her face, he thought it matched the photo of Nisha he had pulled out from the pocket of his trousers. He squatted on his haunches to place a finger below the woman's nostrils and felt a slight puff of air on his hand. She was breathing.

He then alerted his colleagues on his walkie-talkie and, half an hour later, an ambulance arrived.

Now, Pramod's car stops at the site and he dashes out of the car. There is a throng of journalists jostling for space, reporters already speaking to cameras. There is a cacophony of voices, but the question that rises above the rest is: 'Has Nisha Dastur finally been found?'

'Where is she?' Pramod asks one of the security personnel.

'We have just transferred her to the ambulance.'

Pramod rushes towards the ambulance. Raghu and Bedi have just arrived and they join him, elated at the thought that Nisha has been found. But when Pramod gets into the ambulance and looks at the woman on the bed with a green blanket draped across her body, he knows immediately.

'That's not Nisha!' he screams.

Back in the police station on his desk, Raghu feels drained. When he heard the news that a woman, alive and breathing, had been found, every cell in his body was convinced that it was Nisha. How could she just disappear into thin air after all? But unfortunately, it was a different case altogether, of violence inflicted on a woman, registered a day ago at another police station.

Believing the case was about to close, Raghu had made plans to go on leave for the entire week, and just relax. Do nothing. And yes, talk to his wife. He had every intention of being with her. Nothing felt right without her.

'Love, family, they're so important. What else is there in life?'

Rishi's words ring loud and clear in his mind, and he cannot agree more. He has felt so empty the past few days—as if someone has plucked out his vital organs. And he hopes his wife feels the same way. *Should I wait for her to call me first?* he wonders. *She left, not me.*

He quickly douses the flames of ego beginning to form, picks up the phone, and dials his wife's number.

38

Some months later, the posters of 'Missing: Nisha Dastur' are peeling off the walls. People walking past no longer pay them any attention. Nobody is talking about Nisha any more. The police, too, had termed the case a mysterious disappearance and closed the file.

For the first three weeks after the disappearance, Raghu forbade the other guests from leaving the resort. He couldn't get rid of the notion that one or more of them were involved in Nisha's disappearance, and sooner rather than later, the truth would surface. But when they started protesting, especially Monica, Raghu realized he had no grounds to keep them captive and had let them go.

They all left with alacrity. Except Rishi who'd joined the police in their hunt. He accompanied them on their trips around the hills. But last month, he'd left as well. Raghu couldn't look him in the eye and say goodbye. All he could say to him was to not lose hope. Rishi shook his head and walked away.

TV channels stopped covering the disappearance as well, and the print media soon followed. There was nothing left to report. The girl was lost and couldn't be found.

Last week, there was an article, 'The mysterious disappearance of Nisha Dastur', in *HP Times*. It spoke of the failure of the government and the police authorities in the search operation for the missing girl. The closing lines of the article rubbed salt into Raghu's wounds. 'She was the daughter of a prominent politician and businessman, and yet they failed abjectly to find her. What would happen if a common man or woman disappears?'

He concluded with an open mind that the media is a business after all, and if they do not sell exciting news, no one would read them. He knows he and all others involved tried their utmost to find Nisha. Not just because she's the daughter of a VIP, but because it's their job.

There is a personal angle for him as well: Raghu had started feeling pangs of pity for Rishi. He didn't want to see him lonely. It was Rishi who had suggested to Raghu that he should take the first step in getting back together with his wife. And it had worked so well. Raghu feels their relationship is now stronger than ever. He owes Rishi big time but is unlikely to be able to pay him back.

Raghu had warned Roy and Monica to be careful, to watch their back. He didn't have anything substantial against them, but he exhorted them to clean up their act.

'I'll be watching,' he told them.

Anand, on the other hand, didn't get a reprimand from Raghu on his last day. He just had some advice for him.

'Find that special someone that you talk about.'

'I will, inspector,' Anand had replied. 'I will.'

'And stop lying!'

As he went on with his life, Raghu became sure that none of them had anything to do with Nisha's disappearance.

He couldn't have been more wrong.

PART 3

The Conclusion

39

One year later . . .

In one of Central Delhi's prominent bookshops, a writer is reading a passage from his book. There are at least fifty people in the room listening in rapt attention.

'Love can make you do crazy things. It can make you run, hide, lie; it can make you take bold decisions you wouldn't imagine you were capable of. I know of a couple who did unimaginable things for love; they fought all odds to be together.'

He stops reading and is rewarded by a big round of applause which dies down when the compère, a pleasant-looking young woman, gestures for silence.

'So, readers, are you ready for the questions? Who wants to go first?'

More than a dozen people raise their hands.

'Alright you first,' says the young woman, nodding to a teenage girl.

'Sir, I read in your blog that you are planning to write a mystery novel. So then did why did you write a romance?'

Anand—for the author is none other than him—breaks into a smile. 'You're right, I was going to write a mystery novel. In fact, I had completed most of it. But then I met a fascinating couple at just that time and realized that love is such a powerful emotion that I *had* to write about it.'

'Thanks for your reply,' the teenage girl says and takes her seat.

'Okay, you next.' The compere points to a man in his mid-twenties.

As he rises, Anand instantly recognizes the familiar face. 'Can you throw some light on the couple you mentioned?'

Anand breaks into a chuckle and people in the audience wonder if they missed the humour in the question.

'Thanks for the question, Mr—'

'Rishi.'

'Well, I met them on a trip. They didn't initially like me, in fact'—he guffaws—'they hated me!'

His remark sparks laughter around the room.

'So anyway,' he continues, 'we grew really close some days later. They were an extraordinary couple who would do anything to be with each other. Their love story inspired me to write this book, and for that, I'll always be grateful to them.'

'Wow! Sounds like an amazing couple,' Rishi replies and sits down.

'Yes, they are.' Anand smiles again.

An hour later, Anand is nearly done with his book signing duties. His readers had crowded around him, asking questions, expressing admiration for his work. Never in his life has he felt so important. So wanted. It makes him feel damn good about himself. His father never wanted him. His mother, unfortunately, hasn't been around for a long time. And he has no friends.

But now, he has Rishi.

And Nisha.

After the book launch, Rishi and Anand saunter to a nearby café. They are meeting after almost a year. Anand notes Rishi's relaxed demeanour—a huge contrast to a year back when they were in Writer's Hill. Rishi was a nervous wreck, struggling with the weight of Nisha's disappearance, but now he is as calm as a summer sea.

'How have you been?' Anand asks with an impish smile. They have got two cappuccinos and settle at a table by the window overlooking the busy Delhi street.

Rishi chuckles, taking a sip of his coffee, savouring it. He places the cup back on the saucer and wipes his lips with a paper napkin. 'What do you think, man? Couldn't be better.'

'I'm very happy for you guys.'

'I know, man, I know.'

Rishi has no doubt this statement is true. He reflects that sometimes first impressions can be very wrong; eventually, when you get to know someone better, you might be in for a pleasant surprise.

That someone was Anand. *Who would have liked Anand after meeting him for the first time?* Rishi asks himself. He was slovenly, laidback and so nosy. He didn't even mind that people knew he was staring at them, no, ogling them; he just carried on doing so shamelessly. Many times Nisha had (before her disappearance) complained to Rishi: '*That man is staring at me again!*' And when Rishi would glance his way, Anand never dropped his stare; those dull eyes continued to be fixed on Nisha with surprising tenacity.

Many a time Rishi had thought of confronting Anand, perhaps punching him in the face and knocking out some of his teeth, but Nisha always held him back.

'We're in trouble anyway,' she would tell him. 'I don't want any more trouble please, Rishi. He's definitely a psycho, much like another one we know—Avni, don't you think?'

And Rishi would heed her words.

Now, Rishi shakes his head as he looks at Anand. They had hated him, but it was he who stood by them and helped.

'What are you grinning at, buddy?' Anand says, noticing the sudden smile on Rishi's face.

Rishi shakes his head. 'When we first met you, we thought you were such an asshole. You were eccentric and nosy, and then a few days later, I find out that you are an inveterate liar. You lied about your mother and . . . okay, forget it.'

Anand narrows his eyes and tilts his head to one side. 'Where did that come from?'

Rishi waves a hand. 'I was just thinking about how, sometimes, we can be so wrong in judging a person.'

Anand nods.

The real reason behind all that eccentric behaviour, Rishi deduces, was simply one problem with his friend: that he was lonely.

Nothing else.

A lonely man can be more dangerous than an outright villain. But in Anand's case, his loneliness drove Anand to be emphatic towards them. When he got to know about their problem, he agreed to help them no matter what the cost. What had he said? Rishi tries to recall.

'I would do anything for true love, anything to help you guys out. There aren't many true love stories out there and we need more love in the world.'

What happened to Nisha was an idea that he came up with.

'Thanks again.' Rishi offers Anand his hand across the table. 'I can never forget what you did for me. For us.'

Anand shakes it gladly.

'And I'm dying to read your book.'

Suddenly, Anand looks nervous. 'But you don't read books.'

'But I want to read my friend's book.'

'N-n-n-o-o . . .' Anand stutters, 'it's . . . it's not that great. You won't like it.'

Rishi is confused. Shouldn't a writer want as many people as possible to read his books? Why was Anand behaving so strangely about his book?

'I'll take it for Nisha.'

40

More than sixteen hours later, Rishi disembarks from Samvat Express and walks down the long platform of the railway station of a small town in southern India.

He checks his watch. *Well on time.* Anand's book is clutched in his right hand; he didn't get the chance to read it. There was a loquacious lady in his compartment who jabbered through the day. She didn't shut her mouth for even a minute, spilling out her entire life story during the journey.

Rishi couldn't care less. Although he nodded every now and then to not appear disrespectful, his mind was far away. He was thinking about Nisha, her disappearance, the year that passed after that. He wondered for only a moment whether they'd done the right thing.

'Of course we did,' a voice in his head replies instantly. 'We're together now.'

An hour later, he rings the bell to his apartment. The door opens and standing in front of him is the woman he loves so madly that, in Roy's words, he'd do anything for her.

And, well, he *did* do crazy things for her.

'Hello, sweetheart,' greets Nisha in her gentle voice that Rishi loves. 'I was expecting you later.'

'The train reached on time. It made up for the delay at the start by moving at a rollicking speed for some stretches.' Rishi enters the apartment and gives Nisha a kiss. 'You okay?'

'Couldn't be better.' Her eyes fall on Rishi's hands. 'Is that Anand's book?'

Rishi nods, pulling his luggage from outside the door. He hands the book to Nisha. 'Here, take it. I bought it for you.'

Nisha holds the book in her hand and feels a sense of wonder that she knows the writer of the book.

The Things We Do for Love reads the title in big block letters—she can't wait to start reading it.

'Let me know what you think of it.'

As Nisha bustles about getting dinner ready, she can't help comparing the apartment with her home in Delhi. The entire apartment might be smaller than her own room in the Central Delhi mansion where she'd spent her entire life. But she doesn't complain. Not at all. Here, she can be with Rishi, and that's all that matters. Had they not taken this step, this wouldn't have been possible. Sure, she misses her father, but she has sent word to him that she is safe and will reach out to him soon. Life without love is no life at all, and she'd rather be dead than live a loveless life.

She smiles at Rishi who is sitting on the couch watching the news.

'Come, sweetheart,' she calls out. 'Dinner's ready.'

Rishi jumps up and strides over eagerly. What a bonus. He didn't know earlier about Nisha being a splendid cook whose sumptuous dishes rival those of chefs in fancy restaurants.

Over dinner, they discuss the book launch and the conversation Rishi had with Anand. Nisha is delighted that his book is doing well, and that he has many fans.

'I'm sure he'll be happy,' Nisha says. 'He deserves it.'

'Yeah.'

'I think life has been unfair to him. But he doesn't complain and goes all out to help strangers.' Nisha thinks of all that he did for them. 'What a gem of a person, no?'

Rishi nods.

'I just hope he finds someone as nice as him.'

'I'm sure he will,' replies Rishi. 'Good things happen to good people.'

Nisha switches on the bedside lamp, dimming the light just enough so she can read. She turns to her side; Rishi is already snoring softly. She pulls the sheet over him and gently kisses him on his cheek.

'Sleep tight, sweetheart.'

She picks up Anand's book from the table and begins to read.

41

The Things We Do for Love
Chapter 23

Nisha and Rishi now realize something has got to be done. They cannot sit idle and wait for Avni to plan her next move. They love each other far too much to leave their fate to destiny. They want to be in charge. Take action. All their conversations I've overheard in the past few days indicate their desperation.

Then, there is a soft knock on the door.

Nisha and Rishi exchange confused glances. Rishi looks at his watch.

'Who could it be at this time?' Rishi wonders.

I am outside their cottage, peeping in through the window. I can't see the person knocking on the door. The lights go off early here in the hills, so I can understand the astonishment on their faces. It is late—10.30 p.m.

Rishi opens the door and I see the blind girl Meena enter. What is she doing here?

'Meena?' Rishi glances over his shoulder at Nisha and raises his eyebrows. Then he turns back to Meena. 'Everything okay? Did you lose your way?'

Meena shakes her head and steps inside. 'They are coming!'

Nisha advances towards Meena and holds her hand, guiding her to the chair beside the bed. Meena sits down but does not release Nisha's hand.

'They are coming!' Meena repeats, terror discernible in her voice this time.

I catch a quick glimpse of Nisha before she heads towards Rishi and my view of her is blocked. There is horror on her face, and I can imagine her heart thudding inside her chest.

Nisha and Rishi slowly walk towards Meena and are back in my line of sight. Rishi bends and asks Meena, 'Who's coming?' His voice is not steady.

Meena shakes her head. 'I . . . I don't know but I know they are here to hurt her.'

Rishi turns to Nisha before looking back at her. 'Who? Nisha?'

'Yes,' Meena nods.

'But what . . . how do you know?'

Meena doesn't reply for a minute. Nisha's chest is heaving, and I can almost hear her wheezing breaths. Her face resembles that of a scared kid watching a horror movie alone at night.

'I just know,' replies Meena in a flat, eerie voice. 'I can see things.'

The tension in the room seems to jump a hundredfold. Rishi rises and slowly turns around. He begins pacing the room, his hands interlinked behind his back. Nisha simply sits motionless on the bed adjacent to Meena. Her eyes stare blankly in the distance. Nobody speaks for a minute or two.

Then Meena starts talking again. 'Somebody wants to hurt you. I can see that . . . yes, I can see that.' Then she murmurs to herself, and even from here, I can see the hair on Nisha's arms stand on end.

'But who is coming?' Rishi hunkers down and sits on his haunches in front of Meena.

'It's those strange people . . . I don't know if I can call them that . . . but I see them all the time. They're coming here, and now they're very close.'

'But who are they?' Rishi tries again, horror stealing into his voice.

'Ghosts,' replies Meena flatly.

42

The Things We Do for Love
Chapter 24

I knock on the door at that moment. I just feel like I can help.
I know Nisha and Rishi, and I have great admiration for their
love story. Somehow, I feel it's my duty to help them.

Rishi opens the door looking apprehensive and is flabbergasted
to see me.

'Can I please come in?' I ask politely. 'I might be able to
help.'

I have never seen a man more confused. Rishi swallows
hard, looks over his shoulder, back at me, back at Nisha again,
before letting his eyes settle on me. He is perspiring heavily despite
the nip in the air; as if on cue, he retrieves his handkerchief from
the pocket of his tracks and wipes his face.

'What are you talking about?' he asks.

'May I come in first?'

Rishi steps aside and I enter the cottage.

'Okay,' I begin, 'first things first. I have a confession to make. You're a lovely couple and sometimes I spy on you. Please accept my sincere apologies.'

Nisha is too exhausted to react, but Rishi's face twists in an exasperated scowl. He looks like a man who is denied a seat to a ride back home after a jungle expedition.

'What are you talking about?' he asks the same question again.

I let a sharp hiss escape my teeth. This is going to be very difficult to explain. 'Okay, sometimes I eavesdrop on you guys and I know there's a girl called Avni who loves you madly and who hurt Nisha. And that you are still scared of her. Now, Meena here tells you that some people'—I roll my eyes—'are here to hurt Nisha, I don't know how she knows that but—'

'I'm not stupid!' Meena snaps. 'I'm blind but not stupid. I know there are evil spirits here who want to hurt Nisha didi. I think . . . I think someone has used bad magic to call these spirits here. I'm not sure but I don't have any other explanation for these visions. They've got to mean something, I know that!'

'Bad magic? You mean black magic?' Rishi asks, bewildered. I can almost hear his heart thudding against his ribcage.

I nod. 'I wouldn't be surprised. It's common in our country, man. People use these powers to hurt others all the time.'

'So, you think Avni has—' Nisha breaks off.

'But would Avni go to that extent?' Rishi's mouth drops open and he doesn't look at anyone, simply stares at the wall in front.

204

I can tell that he is very confused, overwrought. His sweat glands are working overtime—there is a fine mist of sweat over his face again. 'Yes, she . . . she could,' he answers his own question.

Nisha says quietly, 'You told me once she's from a family of religious fanatics, right? So, don't you think she could have learnt—'

Rishi's eyes slide to Nisha. 'Yes . . . yes, you are right.'

'That makes sense,' Meena says, nodding slowly. 'So, what I was thinking may be true.'

'But what do we do now?' Rishi asks, looking at all of us in turn. 'How do we save Nisha from them?'

Normally ideas do not come to me in a flash. I almost never have an epiphany. I am one of those who struggle to procreate and to bind a cohesive plan together.

But not in this case.

I had an idea.

43

The Things We Do for Love
Chapter 25

The idea is simple. Nisha must disappear. No one should know about it. When Avni finds out, she should think she won. That her idea worked. Nisha would be safe then.

'But what about those . . . those spirits?' Rishi asks me. 'They'll still hurt her, no?'

'I can . . . I can try and take care of them,' interjects Meena in a small, wavery voice.

Nisha makes a visible effort to collect herself. 'God! Are you guys hearing yourself? What are we talking about—ghosts, black magic?' She shakes her head and manages a dry laugh, exhaling a puff of air through her nose. 'Am I dreaming? Is this a nightmare?'

Meena clears her throat. 'No, Nisha didi, it's all really happening, it's not a nightmare.' She reaches out for Nisha's comforting hands, which Nisha shook off when Meena starting talking about black magic. Nisha sees Meena's beseeching arms fluffing through the air, moves closer to her, and takes her hands in hers. Satisfied, Meena opens her mouth again. 'Those creatures I see in my visions are real. I've been seeing them for the past few days. And they're here for you. I don't know how that girl Avni managed to spawn them. I don't know how they know that you're here—maybe Avni followed you here. I don't even know how I know it's you they are after—I just saw it in my visions. But what I do know is that if we don't act now, they will hurt you.'

Her fairly extended monologue educes a deadly silence in the room.

'So, what do you suggest we do?' Rishi says slowly, finally breaking the silence.

Meena takes a deep breath. She squeezes Nisha's hands. ' I think she should disappear.'

'How far do you think those . . . whatever . . . creatures are?' I ask Meena.

'Very close,' Meena replies. 'We need to act fast.'

'So, you've got to disappear tonight, Nisha,' I suggest. 'At night, so no one can see you. And we need to pull off a charade that she's actually missing.'

'But what happens then?' Rishi asks.

'And where would I go?' Nisha asks both of us, glancing back and forth.

'Anywhere, but not your home,' I reply. I haven't thought of the plan in detail and am just thinking aloud. 'Maybe settle in a city away from here. Perhaps, later, Rishi can pull off another

dramatic charade, blame Avni for something or the other, and then storm out of that apartment. Hopefully, Avni will leave you guys alone then, content that at least you two aren't together.'

'But what if someone identifies Nisha later? She can't disappear forever,' Rishi points out.

'Hmm.' That's a good question. What do we do in such a case?

I know a very resourceful guy Adi. He is the kind of person you want to keep in touch with, his number safely stored in your phone contacts. He knows everybody in the world. Hacker, scientist, investor, thief, you name it. If he doesn't, one of his friends would, if they don't their friends would—and that way, all sorts of people are accessible to him and those who seek his help.

When I call him to ask how to make someone disappear, he freaks out. After I explain the situation to him, he tells me he does know someone who might be able to help. I take down the number.

'Call him in ten minutes after I explain the situation to him,' Adi says tersely, and hangs up before I can thank him.

After ten anxious minutes I look at Nisha and Rishi. 'You want me to call and find out?'

They are tense, their faces taut with foreboding. They stare into each other's eyes for what seems like forever. When they look back at me, they both give barely perceptible nods.

'I'll take that as a yes,' I say and dial the number.

Our potential saviour declines the call after the first ring. I call again. He declines it again. Confused, I glance at Rishi. A few moments later, I get a call from an untraceable number.

'Hello,' I say.

I listen for a few minutes without saying a word. When I finally hang up, Nisha and Rishi look at me hopefully.

I speak without any melodrama. 'He told me that he can make Nisha disappear forever, but she would have to get a different identity and live in a different city. More importantly, for her safety, she can't establish any contact with the people she knows in her present life.'

Rishi looks aghast. 'What is that supposed to mean? So, she can't even contact me?'

I shake my head. 'No, she can. It's just that she has to live with a different identity. He told me he'll get her a new name, a new identity card, passport, drivers' licence, permanent account number, etcetera. She cannot contact you or anybody using her old credentials. He'll even tweak her appearance a bit—her hair, her lips, I don't know, the shape of her nose, the eyebrows and so on. Basically, Nisha has to die if she has to live.' I roll my eyes. 'Sorry, that didn't come out the way I intended it. All for a price, of course.'

'Does it make sense to you?' Rishi asks Nisha. He looks over his shoulder at Meena who is mumbling something. 'You okay, Meena?'

'They're coming now,' Meena says very softly. 'They're coming. She needs to get out of here now. NOW!'

44

The Things We Do for Love
Chapter 26

Night falls over the gloomy resort, consuming it with its darkness. The moon is full today, lending its grand luminance to the charcoal sky. An owl hoots in the distance. A slight, intimidating breeze blows from the north; the trees rustle with an eerie sound. Other than that, I hear nothing.

We have just said our farewells to Nisha. Meena has asked her to run as fast as she can, down the hill, and not look back. I have told her to ensure no one notices her and take advantage of the darkness. Rishi hugged and kissed her, tears streaming down their cheeks as they exhorted each other to be careful. I felt a bit emotional myself.

Now, I am standing with Rishi in the tiny veranda of their cottage. Meena is a few metres to our right; her hands are spread out like fangs over her ears and her head is moving slowly from side to side. This strange disposition frightens me, and I feel a prickling sensation on the back of my neck running all the way down to my lower back. I'm not sure if she can hear more clearly this way, or if it's just an act.

'What the heck is she doing?' Rishi whispers beside me. His voice is laced with terror.

'I'm wondering the same thing.'

We stare at her for a minute or two before glancing at each other.

'She's going to be fine, right?' Rishi asks me. 'Please tell me Nisha will be fine.'

I continue looking deep in his scared eyes and don't reply right away. The correct answer is I don't know. But I don't want to tell him that. It'll break him, particularly since it'll be a long time before he sees her again.

But isn't this the best we could have done in the circumstances? Our first priority was to get her out of impending danger. Okay, we don't know if there really was *a danger; we're just relying on the visions of a blind twelve-year-old girl. It doesn't seem like the smartest decision but if you'd experienced the conviction and force of little Meena's speech, you wouldn't think our actions were dumb. What she saw was real, I believe her. Surely there's something coming . . . what exactly, we don't know—yet.*

'I think we did the right thing,' I finally answer Rishi's question calmly. 'At least she's out of danger now. And believe in

your love, man. You guys are phenomenal. Nothing will happen to her.'

'Thanks, buddy,' Rishi's gratitude is heartfelt.

I nod, and just as I do that, I hear the most peculiar sound. I don't know how to describe it. If you've ever been in an old, rusty elevator that descends with a loud, rumbling sound and a constant grrrrr, you'll be able to associate, except that the sound is far more screechy and annoying. It pricks our ears, and we both press our hands over them.

Rishi whimpers, 'Oh my God, what on earth is that sound?'

'I don't know,' I whisper back.

Meena slowly starts walking towards the sound, which is coming from our right. Our eyes are fixed on her, even as we keep our ears plugged. But the sound finds its way in. I hear the piercing cry of an animal next, but I see nothing. Nothing but a blanket of darkness—even though the moon is full—beyond Meena who continues walking towards the sound.

'Where's she going?' Rishi asks me.

'I don't know,' I say again. 'I'm as clueless as you are.'

The sound abates slightly and Meena stops moving. We climb down the four steps of the veranda and slowly walk towards Meena. We see nothing, but Meena has her arms spread out in front of her, the fingers splayed out. They move like the fingers of a puppeteer manipulating his marionettes in front of a packed audience. We stop a few metres behind her.

'Meena,' I call out.

No answer.

'Meena,' tries Rishi.

Nothing.

We gaze at each other and both of us are filled with a sense of foreboding. And then we hear her screaming. A hair-raising scream. We stumble a few steps back.

Then I hear the strangest sound I have heard in my life—it sounds like several animals crying in unison. It's so horrific and sad. But I see nothing. I swivel my head around. Nothing. Only darkness. Where the hell is the sound coming from?

Meena continues screaming and her fingers move faster now; her screams coalesce with the painful wails of – of what? – I'm not sure, maybe animals, procreating to form a portentous babel.

And then there is another sinister occurrence, as if the night had not already been the weirdest night of my life. I hear a loud lightning—loudest and widest that I have ever seen—tear open the sky through its various fragmented branches. It easily covers one-third of the concave sky. But the weird part is that lightning normally strikes on a cloudy sky, but this—I look up—is as clear a sky as it gets; there are hardly any clouds. I don't understand, but then there are a lot of other things I don't understand about this night either.

The wails and Meena's screams reach a crescendo. There's a last chilling shriek from her and then she seems airborne, flying backwards and landing a few metres away with a thud.

Then, there is silence.

45

Nisha glances at the bedside clock. It's 3 a.m. She feels chilled to the bone. He heart is pounding in her chest and her breath is coming in quick, shallow puffs.

He wrote our story? OUR story? Everything?

She stares blankly ahead, trying to make sense of this. *Why would he write this? It was his idea. He helped us. He asked me to disappear. So why bring our story out in the open now? Wasn't this supposed to be a secret?*

Terror seizes her when a name pops into her mind. *Avni. What if she has read the book? What if she knows?*

She feels a cry building up in her throat and clamps her teeth against it. But she can't stop the scream, and Rishi, who has been snoring softly, is sitting bolt upright by her side the next second. 'What happened, Sheena?' he asks groggily, his eyes half-shut.

'No point addressing me by my new name!' she snaps. 'It's all over. You might as well call me Nisha and I revert to my old identity.'

'What are you talking about?'

'This book,' she says, holding out Anand's book with one hand and thumping it twice with the other. 'Everything is there. All our secrets revealed. That ass wrote about us. Our story.'

'What?' Rishi is suddenly wide awake; it is as if someone has poured a bucketful of water over him.

Nisha nods.

'But this was supposed to be a secret!'

'Exactly!'

Rishi places his hands over his eyes; he can't believe it.

'He has written everything,' Nisha or Sheena continues. 'About Avni's assault, Meena's visions, my plan to disappear, Meena's fight with those creatures, our charade that I went missing because of them. Everything.'

'But *why*?'

Nisha shrugs.

'It was his idea. Why would he publicize it to the world?'

Nisha doesn't respond. In her mind, she is already contemplating the worst possible outcome. Avni reading the book. Finding out about this whole drama. Finding Nisha. Engaging another set of those creatures. And then the end.

Rishi puts his arms around Nisha. 'Take a few deep breaths and try to calm down, sweetheart. Please don't imagine the worst right away. I know what you're thinking now.'

'So, what do you want me to think, huh?' Her voice cracks. 'I'm fed up of this.'

Rishi takes a deep breath. 'We'll find a way out of this as well, trust me. Let me call Anand tomorrow. Let's get some sleep.'

But they don't sleep the entire night.

In the morning, Rishi dials Anand's phone number. He doesn't take the call, so Rishi tries again. Then again. After more than a dozen calls, he still can't get through. He gives up.

Nisha and Rishi barely talk that morning. An ominous silence hangs in the tiny apartment. Rishi wants to tell Nisha that everything will be alright, only he doesn't believe that himself. Their secret is out in the book, and what are the odds that Avni won't find out? Sooner rather than later, she or a friend or an acquaintance will read the book, and Avni will know what they'd done, and that Nisha is alive and well. That they are together. What will she do then?

Rishi feels his knees buckle as he stands alone on the balcony of the second floor. Nisha is in the bedroom and he doesn't feel like rehashing it all with her and creating more tension.

He dials Anand's number again. This time he picks up.

'Hello, my friend,' Anand's voice is low, regretful.

'What the fuck did you do?' Rishi says sharply. 'Why?'

'I'm so sorry.'

'You wrote about us!' Rishi cannot keep his voice down. 'Why would you do it?'

There is silence on the line.

'Hello?' he says. 'Are you there?'

'Y-yes.'

'Tell me, man. Why did you spill the secret? I remember you telling me on that hill that we shouldn't share this with anybody, that it'll be dangerous for Nisha. And then you go home and write a book about it! I'm going crazy here. Please help me understand. Why would you do such a stupid thing?'

All Rishi hears is the soft rustle of Anand breathing. He waits for a couple of minutes before losing it completely.

'Tell me, you asshole!' he yells. 'Tell me! Why did you put Nisha in danger again after helping her?'

'I'm really sorry,' Anand finally replies and hangs up.

46

You already know I'm a liar. I've lied about a lot of things. First, I lied about my mother. You know about that.

And then my father. Although in his case, it wasn't as much a lie; it was just convenient omission on my part.

See, when my mother died, I was shattered. I spent days locked in my room with the curtains of the windows drawn to evade the outside world. I couldn't separate day from night, and for weeks I didn't have any human interaction. Then, one day, I thought—where's my father when I'm going through this? He hadn't even bothered to check if his son was alright. He was busy with his second family. That infuriated me so much that I decided to go see him in Dubai.

Three months after Mom's death, I gave him a call. That surprised him, as I *never* called him. The conversation was stilted; once I told him his wife was dead, there was nothing more to talk about.

'You want to visit me?' he asked just when I thought of hanging up, and the offer surprised me.

'Yes,' I replied. 'In fact, the other day I was thinking about it.'

Two weeks later, I was on a plane to Dubai with Daddy-sponsored tickets. The resentment I felt for him for leaving my mother and me was still blazing. We could have been a family if he hadn't been so self-centered, and maybe, just maybe, my mother would have been alive.

My father had a plush four-bedroom apartment in a luxurious condominium on the upscale Sheikh Zayed Road. His family wasn't home then and I remember feeling a wave of calm wash over me at that; I wasn't interested on meeting them at all.

Daddy was unusually kind to me. He offered me a cold beer as soon as I walked in. I declined but thanked him. I was awed by the opulence of the apartment—high ceilings with a gigantic, plush chandelier hanging in the centre of the living room; huge glass windows offering breathtaking views of the city from the twenty-eighth floor; a humungous nine-seater leather sofa; a 75-inch ultra slim LED television nestled opposite it. I wanted to take that beer he offered, switch on the television, play one of the million DVDs that were in the cabinet by the side, and dig my buttocks into that sofa for the rest of the evening. But it wasn't my home, so I restrained myself.

I walked up to the glass windows and glanced below. People appeared tiny from up here, like mice. I could spot a huge swimming pool and a children's play area within the complex.

'Are you okay?' Daddy called out behind me.

I turned on my heels and gazed at him, gritting my teeth. 'Does it even matter to you?' I shook my head. 'Did you ever miss Mom or me?'

I could hear his sigh of frustration. He walked towards me. 'Why?'

'What do you mean why?'

'Why did you come here if you hate me?'

'It didn't even matter to you that she died!'

He put a hand on my shoulder. I shook it off. 'Don't touch me!' I yelled and moved away from him.

'I fell in love with someone else,' he said. 'I am sorry about what happened to you, but I'm not sorry for falling in love again.'

I felt something constricting my throat and my lips started to tremble. 'But couldn't you be with her for her, for me, for our happiness?'

He made a scoffing sound. 'Are you listening to yourself? Would *you* be with someone you don't love for somebody else's sake? This is a selfish world we live in. You need to grow up, Anand, and start thinking about yourself.'

'I will,' I replied firmly, looking in his eyes. 'I will if I have to. The world needs more love and for that it needs better people than you. Like Mom.'

'Like your mom, ha ha,' he scoffed again. 'She was a bloody crazy and impractical woman!'

Instinctively, my hands clenched into fists, and I could feel my nails dig into the meat of my palms. I'm not sure what made

221

me do what I did next; I still think about it till this day if my action was warranted, but back then, it just happened. I grabbed him by the collar, shook him a few times, then flung him with all my strength. He staggered backwards and his head made contact with the glass window with a thud. I saw him wince, his knees slackened, and he dropped before me like a man shot.

'Oh God!' I cried and ran to him. I bent and tapped his cheek a few times. 'Daddy! Daddy! Can you hear me?'

Blood was starting to run from the back of his head, and I panicked. I looked around. 'Daddy.' I touched his cheek again. 'Wake up! Please, wake up!'

I lifted his right hand and tried to feel for a pulse on his wrist. Nothing. I put a finger below his nose to feel a breath. Nothing.

Tears were now streaming down my cheeks. 'Oh God! What have I done?' I patted his cheeks a few more times. Still nothing. After a few minutes, as reality sank in, I realized I had to make a choice. Call the police or get away now. I got up, picked up the phone next to the couch, and dialled the Emergency number, exhorting them to send an ambulance ASAP.

Then I sprinted from the apartment and took the next flight home. I don't think he died, as the police never contacted me. But I didn't bother finding out—he was anyway dead to me. I do not discuss this event with anyone. What's the point?

Now that we are at it, let me be honest and tell you that I also lied about Maira—the girl I claimed to be in love with and who left me. I discuss her with everybody, even my psychiatrist. Even she doesn't know that Maira is just a figment of my imagination. Please don't tell her. Honestly, I don't even know anybody by that name. But I wish I did. I just wanted to believe that, like everyone else, I too have a love story. But the fact is that I have never truly been in love. And my heart aches when I say that.

Nothing is more important to me than love. And that is the reason I helped Nisha and Rishi. I truly wanted them to be together. I admire the love that they have for each other.

So why did I write a book about their story and spill their secret to the world, you must wonder? Let me just say that I do not have a straight answer to that. But take a moment to spare a thought for Avni.

Whatever she did, she did for love. No matter how much I admire the love story of Nisha and Rishi, I also feel awe at Avni's passion, that she gave her all to separate them. What great love she harbours for Rishi. You've got to give her that.

I know it was my idea to make Nisha disappear so she could be safe, but when our plan went off perfectly, I found myself thinking a lot about Avni. Did I not fool her? Did I not disrespect her love? My mother always told me that you should never deceive or disrespect love, but I'd done exactly that, and began to be consumed by guilt.

By that time, I had made up my mind that I would write a love story, and I was thinking of inspiration. That is when

I thought of writing Nisha and Rishi's love story as is—it all connected perfectly, falling into place like a jigsaw puzzle. If Avni reads about it, it is her destiny, and she can do whatever she wants to. If she doesn't read the book, I would take it that Nisha and Rishi's love is eternal. But either way, my load of guilt would lighten. I wouldn't be responsible for Avni losing in love.

And that is really important to me.

But now, after speaking to Rishi, I think I made a mistake. They trusted me and I betrayed their trust. It saddens me. Their love shouldn't suffer because of my need to purge my conscience.

I had to do something.

47

Three months later . . .

I am sitting in a café. The girl sitting across me is not classically beautiful, but she is pretty enough and a smooth talker. She mentions that she reads a lot, but she hasn't heard of my book. I am glad. She tells me that she is from a family of priests, 'a boring profession', she adds and wrinkles her nose. I tell her I have no family. She reaches out and squeezes my arm. Her hand is cold. I wince.

'What happened?' she asks me.

'Nothing,' I reply.

'You're a great guy, Anand. I really like you.'

I don't want to say it, but I've got to. For them. It's my fault and their love shouldn't suffer because of me. 'I like you too.'

PRAISE FOR THE BOOK

'A daring attempt to understand Naxalism'—*Hindustan Times*

'With direct access to the top Maoist leadership, the author gives us a graphic account of how the radical Reds entered Bastar in 1980 and set up their elaborate network there'—*Times of India*

'Rahul Pandita has done something few others have the dedication or courage to do: Spend time with Naxalites—somewhere along the Maharashtra–Chhattisgarh border—getting a glimpse into their lives and ways. Heady stuff'—*Forbes India*

HELLO, BASTAR

THE UNTOLD STORY OF INDIA'S MAOIST MOVEMENT

RAHUL PANDITA

PENGUIN BOOKS

An imprint of Penguin Random House

I

GIVE ME RED

To be radical is to grasp things by the root.

—Karl Marx

Inside us there is something that has no name, that something is what we are.

—Jose Saramago

The spasms had been troubling him again. In fact, amoebic dysentery had been his constant companion, a result of a harsh life of more than three decades. And an enlarged prostate too. He was more comfortable with the pain these afflictions caused than the feel of the cold metal of a gun in his hands whenever he had had to hold it. But that was on very rare occasions, deep inside the forest along the Eastern Ghats: memorial meetings for fallen comrades, ceremonial parades or military drills. Presently, though, he was hundreds of miles away from the jungles of central India.

He was in Delhi.

The Molarband Extension colony of south Delhi's Badarpur area was a different kind of jungle. Early in the morning, thousands of men swarmed through the narrow, sewage-ridden roads, locust-like, on their ramshackle bicycles. They worked in factories as fitters or cutters or as daily wage labourers at construction sites or as private security guards. Life was tough. In recent times, it had become more difficult to survive, with the prices of food and daily necessities going through the roof. Many men stayed alone, leaving their families behind in small towns or villages. Fathers waiting for a little money to come by for a cataract operation. Widowed mothers. Unmarried sisters. Impoverished wives hoping to save enough for the education of children. Out of their meagre incomes, the men struggled to send as much money as possible to their families.

For years, the poor workers took solace from an old film song: *Dal roti khao, prabhu ke gunn gao* (Have dal-roti, sing paeans to the Almighty). But now with dal costing almost Rs 100 a kilo, the poor didn't know what to eat and in the cruel city, who to sing paeans to.

The city ran on a very complex arithmetic. It was a city drunk on power, a city from where a handful of people decided the fate of over a billion others, from Kashmir to Kanyakumari, as messages painted on highways by the Border Roads Organisation would remind one. These few people were India's political leaders. Their abode was the Parliament in the heart of New Delhi, a place referred to as 'pigsty' by the man and his comrades.

On Sundays, the city's middle class would come out in hordes, in their small and big cars, enjoy ice cream at India Gate and then watch a movie at one of the multiplexes. This would cost a family of four at least Rs 1500, more than what 74 million households or 37.2 per cent of India's population earned in two months. The city was a paradox. People would come out to rally for the rights of pet animals, and others would brand their underage maidservants with a hot iron. It was a city where the malnutrition rate was 35 per cent,[1] far worse than sub-Sahara. In the same city, surveys[2] revealed that 40 per cent

---

[1]*The Hindu*, 7 May 2010.

[2]A survey conducted by AIIMS.

of schoolkids were overweight. For the Commonwealth Games, the homes of the poor were being dismantled. Leviathan billboards were being put up to eclipse slums so that foreign athletes would only be able to see glitzy shopping malls and departmental stores selling soy milk and broccoli.

There were two things Delhi didn't want: monkeys and poor people. Thousands of beggars were being bundled into municipal vans and there were negotiations with other states to take their beggars back. A few years earlier, the capital city had tried, in a similar manner, sending its monkeys to the wilderness of other states. And now, for the Games, hundreds of thousands of people would be displaced in all. In 2001, the sealing of small-scale factories in residential areas had rendered thousands of workers jobless. It was the ensuing unrest that the comrades wanted to take up as a cause, and motivate young labourers and workers to channel their anger into something 'meaningful'. To be close to such workers and win them over, the man had been living in the Molarband Extension colony.

Over the past few weeks, the man had also been getting treated for his ailments at a city hospital. He was using a voter identity card, bearing the name of Dilip Patel, for all official purposes. His contacts in the city had made these arrangements.

For purposes of communication, he shunned modern devices such as the mobile phone. Most of the communication was done through a human courier. He had one trusted courier who had been with him for about five years.

Oblivious of what his trusted lieutenant had been up to, the man went about doing his work. On 20 September 2009, he arrived at the Bhikaji Cama office complex, next to Delhi's diplomatic enclave.

Unknown to him, a few men sat in a car, waiting for him.

It was a Sunday, and the regular crowd of office executives who otherwise would be out at this hour for a quick smoke or lunch was missing. The handicapped man who sold soft drinks and cigarettes on his special cycle had no customers to attend to—he passed his time reading a Hindi newspaper. The passport office where thousands of ambitious youth would come every day to try their luck at foreign shores was also shut.

Inside the car, a deputy superintendent of the Special Intelligence Branch of the Andhra Pradesh Police was getting restless. It was hot inside the car and, as he wiped the sweat from his brow, he looked at the man sandwiched between him and his colleague. 'Are you sure he will come?' the officer asked him. The man nodded quickly. He looked at his watch and then looked outside. He was the only one who could identify the man they waited for, the man he had served as courier for years.

At about one p.m., the tall, thin-moustached man appeared and stopped at the bus stop next to the complex. A jute bag was slung across his shoulder. The courier now signalled. In a minute or two, the operation was over. The man was bundled inside the car and taken to the Special Cell Branch of the Delhi Police, near Delhi's famous cultural hub, India Habitat Centre.

Two days later, the police made an announcement.

They had arrested Kobad Ghandy, they said, one of the seniormost leaders of the Maoist movement in India. The leader of a large mass of men and women, which had recently been declared India's gravest internal security threat by none other than Prime Minister Manmohan Singh himself. The men and women known more popularly as the Naxalites. Or simply Naxals.

A day later as he was being produced in court, Kobad Ghandy raised slogans as feverishly as he could while struggling to overcome the exhaustion of sustained interrogation. 'Bhagat Singh zindabad' and 'Anuradha Ghandy amar rahe'. The onlookers who were used to seeing ordinary criminals or terrorists being produced in the court were surprised at these slogans. After all, never before had they heard someone in the court premises or even elsewhere shout praises in favour of India's most popular revolutionary.

And, Anuradha Ghandy . . . who was Anuradha Ghandy?

(Note: This scenario is based on inputs from intelligence sources. However, there still is confusion on whether the courier actually led the police to Kobad Ghandy. A day after his disappearance, the courier is believed to have contacted a Maoist sympathiser in Punjab, who used to work with Kobad, and informed him that Kobad had turned incommunicado.)

On 6 April 2010, in the central Indian state of Chhattisgarh, a group of soldiers belonging to the Central Reserve Police Force (CRPF) was returning after an area-domination exercise. In the early hours of that morning, they were ambushed by a collective squad of Maoists who divided themselves into smaller groups and encircled the CRPF men. Some of the soldiers fought back but they were no match for the Maoists. In no time, 75 CRPF men and a local policeman accompanying them lay dead. Within hours, the images of the encounter, first shot by a local television channel, were flashed across national television.

It was perhaps the deadliest attack so far in any insurgency that India had faced ever since she became independent. In two decades of militancy in Kashmir, aided and abetted by a neighbouring country, never had so many soldiers died in a single attack. Kashmir and India's north-east no longer matched the Maoist insurgency in its ferocity and ability to grab headlines.

Till a few years ago, Maoists were off the news radar. Kashmir was what sold well. But now, India's heartland had become the new Kashmir. It was a very complex situation. Within a few years, the Maoist insurgency had moved from strength to strength and was now spread across almost half of India: Chhattisgarh, Jharkhand, Orissa, Maharashtra, West Bengal, Andhra Pradesh, Uttar Pradesh. The Maoist leaders were everywhere. In West Bengal's Lalgarh, one of the seniormost Maoist leaders, Mallojula Koteshwara Rao alias Kishenji had almost turned into a mythical figure. Appearing every now and then on

8

television, his back towards the camera and an AK-56 assault rifle slung upside down on his shoulder, in his demeanour he was more like a retired professor than a dreaded rebel. He spoke in a feeble voice. But Kishenji was anything but ordinary. He had personally supervised an armed rebellion led by tribals against the state of West Bengal for months now, at one point of time turning the entire Lalgarh area in West Midnapore district into a 'liberated zone'—an area where the Maoists ran a virtual government with no state authority in sight. The local police stations were taken over by Red rebels who ruthlessly killed cadres of the ruling CPM government.

Troops had been deployed but still the armed insurgency continued, and scores of people were killed every day. In one such deadly attack, 24 soldiers of the Eastern Frontier Rifles were killed by a group of Maoists led by a woman commander. Across India's heartland, a war was on. Though the home ministry kept on denying it, the fact remained that a massive military operation had been mounted across the Maoist-affected areas, involving about 100,000 troops of the CRPF and other paramilitary forces. But it was proving to be of little help. The Maoists carried on their operations with impunity. In Chhattisgarh, they had carved out a guerilla zone which the local police referred to as 'Pakistan'. In Maharashtra's Gadchiroli, their writ ran large. In some districts in Orissa, the police would not dare venture out in uniform. In Jharkhand, the Maoists collected taxes, meting out severe punishment to those who did not follow their diktat. In the Naxal-dominated areas, there was no sign of state authority. No forest official, no policeman, no district collector ever visited there.

In Chhattisgarh, the guerilla zone of the Maoists was called the Maad division. For outsiders, it was Abujhmaad. This area had remained out of national consciousness for decades now. In fact, it was never in the thoughts of those chosen by the people to take India to newer heights. The name of this area itself signified what it meant to India: *Abujh* in Hindi means something that cannot be figured out. It was only after the Maoist insurgency had started hitting the headlines that people heard about Abujhmaad for the first time.

In the womb of the land now referred to as India's Red Corridor lay hidden mineral resources worth thousands of billions of dollars. And this was also the land where India's poorest of the poor lived. And now, it was where perhaps India's bloodiest battle would be fought.

The government had sent in its forces. But they had not been able to do much. What could they possibly do? Inside the villages how were they supposed to distinguish between a Maoist and a tribal villager? In a number of cases, they didn't bother to do so. So innocent tribals were picked up, brutally tortured, accused of being Maoists and then put in jail. Or just shot dead after being branded as Maoists. Instead of solving the problem it lent further fuel to the insurgency, more manpower to the Maoists.

On national television, the Maoist insurgency was being discussed threadbare. Is it a socio-economic problem or a mere law and order problem? Can it be resolved militarily? Are we ready for the costs? How far are the Maoists from our cities—from seizing power from the State? Is development the only solution to the Maoist problem? Or should military action and development go hand in hand? In television studios, a horde of politicians, retired military, paramilitary and police officers and civil rights activists sweated it out almost daily since every day some incident would occur. A CRPF group ambushed. A police van blown up in an IED blast. A politician killed. A train derailed. Alleged Maoists killed—most of whom later turned out to be innocent tribals. Tribal women raped by Special Police Officers. A Maoist camp dismantled.

Till a few years ago, India's homeland security was in the hands of Shivraj Patil, a Congress loyalist who was known for his devotion to a godman and his penchant for changing his clothes frequently. After intense pressure in the wake of intelligence failure leading to the 2008 Mumbai terror attacks, Patil was now being replaced by another senior politician who had steadily risen through the Congress ranks. From being the Tamil interpreter of the English speeches of Indira Gandhi, the suave lawyer from Tamil Nadu, who was better known for his stints as the country's finance minister was now in charge of the home ministry. And sure enough, Palaniappan Chidambaram made enough news from day one to show that he meant business.

He said that the Naxals were 'simply bandits'. He snubbed those who called for development in this area instead of sending in military forces, branding them Maoist sympathisers. In a Parliament address he called them people 'who write 33-page articles', a reference to writer-activist Arundhati Roy who had spent a few days with the Maoist guerillas and written a long essay in *Outlook* magazine. It would seem that instead of fighting Maoists, the home minister's whole energy and that of his aides was directed at hurling diatribes at members of the civil society. Those who went as a part of fact-finding missions to Naxal areas would be targeted and branded as Maoists. That was not all. The government issued a decree that those found to be aiding the Maoists would be dealt with severely and charged under the anti-terror law UAPA (Unlawful Activities Prevention Act). It was like the cowboy doctrine propagated by the former American President George Bush after the 11 September 2001 attack: Either you are with us or against us.

Many saw it as a repeat of the infamous 1975 Emergency. After all, it was not very long ago that Binayak Sen, a doctor and an activist working in Chhattisgarh had been incarcerated for eighteen months on charges of being a Maoist. Scores of other people had been put behind bars on similar charges. Many others were wary that they would meet the same fate. And subsequently, towards the end of 2010, a local court in Chhattisgarh found Binayak Sen guilty of sedition and sentenced him to life imprisonment. These were indeed dark times. Across the world, personalities like the political activist-philosopher Noam Chomsky and Nobel laureate Amartya Sen had condemned Sen's arrest and subsequent sentencing. But it would not move the government. On the other hand, the tribals suffered terribly, caught as they were, between the Maoists and the State. In many pockets, though, the tribals supported the Maoists. In their areas of influence, the local population acted as the eyes and ears of the Maoists. As a senior police officer who had served in the Naxal-affected Chandauli district of eastern Uttar Pradesh said: 'The line between a Maoist and a tribal has blurred. So, the Adivasi you saw plucking dead tree branches during the day might turn into a gun-toting Naxal in the night.'

The void created by the State had been filled by the Maoists.

II

HISTORY'S HARVEST

To remain ignorant of things that happened before you were born is to remain a child.

—Cicero

Everything repeats itself and everything will be reincarnated, And my dreams will be your dreams.

—Arseny Tarkovsky

Sometimes history acts like a housewife. It whispers in the ears of the present what bearing events of the past could have on the future. It is up to the present to pay heed to it. But those who represented India's present always acted as arrogant husbands. They never listened. They never took note. In the case of the Maoist insurgency, the writing on the wall was clear even before India's present could take shape, even before India could attain what it thought was freedom from its colonial masters. The colonial masters indeed went away but for the poor of India freedom remained elusive.

The handful of men and women who hid in the bushes near a field in a remote village in West Bengal on a hot May morning in 1967 would know it in a few minutes' time. Spread over an area of about 500 sq km, the Naxalbari area of West Bengal was covered by three police stations: Naxalbari, Kharibari and Phansidewa. The Naxalbari area lay along Nepal and East Pakistan (now Bangladesh), and was inhabited mostly by tribals from the Santhal, Oraon, Munda and Rajbansi communities. Most of them were landless peasants, who worked on a contractual basis on the land owned by zamindars. It was not a peaceful coexistence. The landlords provided seed and agricultural tools like ploughs but would take a lion's share of the crop. The tribal peasants after working like oxen in the fields would not even get enough to eat. Disputes over the sharing of crops were very common.

In the mid '60s India was facing a severe food crisis. Millions of people were affected by the shortage of food. Many died of starvation. The government, as usual, refused to accept that people in independent India were dying because of lack of food. When the situation turned grim, the babus in New Delhi called these deaths a result of malnutrition. More than 40 years later, New Delhi is still in denial mode. Whenever starvation deaths are reported from Orissa and even from non-Maoist areas like Rajasthan, the officials go to great lengths to show that the deaths had in fact occurred due to, say, cholera or diarrhoea. What they do not know or will not admit is that these diseases kill because the body of the victim is badly weakened by lack of food. Even as it sends missions to the moon and boasts of being a nuclear power, India has so far failed to ensure that nobody goes hungry. There have been cases where foodgrains were left out in the open to rot while the godowns of the state-run Food Corporation of India were rented out to liquor companies to store alcohol.

So, yes, in the '60s the cultivable land in the country was owned by a small group of people, mainly big landlords. According to a survey[3] of land ownership conducted around that time, it was revealed—and these were termed as conservative estimates—that 40 per cent of the land was owned by only five per cent of rural households. Life was a constant challenge for India's landless poor. On top of it,

---

[3]National Sample Surveys.

famines struck across India, in states like Bihar and Madhya Pradesh.

To tide over the food crisis, the government envisaged and implemented the Green Revolution. While it did increase India's foodgrain output, the Green Revolution also created further disparities in society. It benefited only those farmers who could afford to buy chemical fertilisers and modern agricultural equipment.

It took the government two years to realise this. Speaking at a conference of state chief ministers in New Delhi in 1969, the then Union home minister Y.B. Chavan warned that the Green Revolution may cease to remain green if it were not accompanied by measures for social justice.[4]

In Naxalbari, long before those men and women hid themselves in bushes on that hot May morning, a man had been closely examining these developments. From the early '60s in his hometown in Siliguri, the bespectacled man would lock himself for hours in his room and read of a revolution brought about in neighbouring China by a peasants' army led by Mao Tse-tung. The man was deeply influenced by Mao's ideas and believed that similar conditions existed in India wherein militant peasants and youth could be mobilised to overthrow the government through armed struggle.

Like his hero, Charu Mazumdar also believed that war was nothing but politics with bloodshed. He particularly

---

[4]Sumanta Banerjee in his book, *In the Wake of Naxalbari*, quoting a report that appeared in the *Patriot* newspaper on 29 November 1969.

liked to quote one statement from Mao: 'Revolution is not a dinner party, nor an essay, nor a painting, nor a piece of embroidery; it cannot be advanced softly, gradually, carefully, considerately, respectfully, politely, plainly, and modestly. A revolution is an insurrection, an act of violence by which one class overthrows another.'

By 1965, whatever he read and thought had taken shape and in the villages of north Bengal, young men inspired by Charu Mazumdar's ideology were propagating it and organising the poor and landless peasantry.

Earlier, the Communist Party of India (CPI) had split, and a more radical Communist Party of India (Marxist) had taken shape. But even within the CPI (M), there were comrades who were disillusioned with the party's politics and thought that the party had become revisionist. (The word 'revisionist' is perhaps the most commonly used term of censure within the Communist movement, and when one group accuses another of retreating from a particular revolutionary position, it dubs it as revisionist.) Such comrades got in touch with Charu Mazumdar. He in turn set down conditions for those who wanted to join him and there were four prerequisites. First: Acceptance of Mao Tse-tung as the leader of the world revolution and his thoughts as the highest form of Marxism-Leninism of that era. Two: Belief in the view that a revolutionary situation existed in every corner of India. Three: Area-wise seizure of power as the only path for taking forward the Indian revolution. Four: Guerilla warfare as the only means of advancing the revolution.

Charu Mazumdar had an invincible belief that revolution

could be brought about by the formation of underground organisations that would then wage a war against the State and bring it to its knees. He remained dismissive about 'open' organisations such as trade unions or farmers' associations. Backing him were two other prominent leaders of that area: Kanu Sanyal, who had very strong organisational skills and was very popular among the tea workers in the area, and Jangal Santhal, a popular tribal leader who unsuccessfully contested the 1967 election, coming second only to the winning Congress candidate.

With their backing, three cultivators supported by a few CPI (M) party workers armed with crude weapons lifted the entire stock of paddy from a landlord's granary, without leaving a single grain for him.

In the next few months the Communist cadres forcibly occupied land, seized granaries and burnt land records. Any resistance was brutally put down.

The landlords acted swiftly, getting rid of those who worked on their fields. In some cases the landlords took the help of the police. This would be another constant recurrence in the history of independent India: the police mostly acted and worked for the influential and rich or their political masters.

This is what the men and women who had hidden themselves in the bushes realised. A few days earlier, some peasants had gone to work in the fields. In the evening they did not return. A day later, other men went to the fields and they also failed to return home. So, some men and women hid in the nearby bushes to see what was happening. No sooner had another lot of men begun to till

21

the fields than a police party appeared and took the men away. When confronted the police said that the landlord didn't want them to work in his fields and had asked the police to arrest them. This aroused a great anger in the peasants and it was then that they organised themselves into underground squads like Charu Mazumdar's followers had wanted.

Soon, a bloody war was to follow that would make Naxalbari the foundation stone of the Maoist movement in India and also give it a name: the Naxal movement. On 23 May 1967, Inspector Sonam Wangdi led a police party to arrest the leaders behind the agitation. In a confrontation with angry tribals, some arrows were shot at Wangdi, leading to his instant death.

Two days later, a bigger police contingent arrived. Men and women armed with whatever they could lay their hands on came out to confront the police. In the ensuing confrontation, the police fired at the tribals killing nine, including six women and two children.

A full-fledged war was now on.

China was quick to respond to the happenings in Naxalbari. An editorial in *People's Daily*, the mouthpiece of the Central Committee of the Communist Party of China, termed the happenings in Naxalbari 'a peal of spring thunder'. It further added: 'Revolutionary peasants in the Darjeeling area have risen in rebellion. Under the leadership of a revolutionary group of the Indian Communist Party, a Red area of rural revolutionary armed struggle has been established in India. This is a development of tremendous significance for the Indian people's revolutionary struggle.'

But back home, Charu Mazumdar's actions irked the CPM leadership. During party meetings he was termed as mentally sick and even accused of being a police agent. Some said he was working at the behest of New Delhi to destabilise the Communist-led United Front government in West Bengal. Others branded him an American agent. But undeterred by this criticism, the Naxalbari group of Communists went about doing their job, according to the principles laid down by Mao. In mid 1968, Kanu Sanyal, Jangal Santhal and another comrade Sourin Bose went to China along with two others to receive military and political training from the Communist Party of China.

In 1969, on Lenin's birth anniversary, Charu Mazumdar announced the formation of a new Communist party—the CPI (Marxist-Leninist) or the CPI (ML).

Meanwhile, the Congress government led by Indira Gandhi decided to send in the army and tackle the problem militarily. A combined operation called Operation Steeplechase was launched jointly by military, paramilitary and state police forces in West Bengal, Bihar and Orissa.

In Kolkata, Lt General J.F.R. Jacob of the Indian Army's Eastern Command received two very important visitors in his office in October 1969. One was the army chief General Sam Manekshaw and the other was the home secretary Govind Narain. Jacob was told of the Centre's plan to send in the army to break the Naxals. More than 40 years later, Jacob would recall[5] how he had asked for more troops, some of which he got along with a brigade

---

[5]Interview to NDTV, 10 June 2010.

of para commandos. When he asked his boss to give him something in writing, Manekshaw declined, saying, 'Nothing in writing,' while secretary Narain added that there should be no publicity and no records.

In 72 days, the Naxalbari upsurge was over. Most of the guerilla leaders were arrested while Charu Mazumdar continued to evade arrest.

The China factor played a big role in the failure of the Naxalbari struggle. The Naxal leaders had come up with a slogan: 'China's Chairman [Mao] is our Chairman.' The Chinese prime minister Chou En-lai later spoke of this as 'a folly' to guerilla emissary Sourin Bose who had gone to China to seek help once again. While criticising Charu Mazumdar's policy of class annihilation, Chou En-lai also pointed out that China's leader could never motivate the people of India in the same way as a leader from their own soil: they needed to have their own Mao. That was why, he said, the revolution had failed to move Indians in the way it ought to have done.

Charu Mazumdar realised that the movement had failed in Naxalbari. Now they sought a new area from where the revolution could be brought about and the power struggle could go on. For this purpose the Naxalbari revolutionaries chose Midnapore. At that time the largest district in India, Midnapore lay next to the industrial and railway hub of Kharagpur, and was known for its revolutionary activities during British rule. It was there that the young revolutionary Khudiram Bose was born in 1889, and later became the youngest revolutionary to face the gallows at the age of 19 for a failed assassination attempt on a British magistrate.

In Midnapore, the guerillas were led by a Dalit leader, Santosh Rana, who had a Master's degree from Kolkata University and was actively involved in deep Red politics. He was helped by another student leader Asim Chatterjee popularly known as Kaka, who had a huge following in Kolkata colleges, and like most of the Naxalbari leaders had been expelled from the CPI (M).

Under the guidance of Santosh Rana, who only worked upon strategies laid down by Charu Mazumdar, a large number of squad actions were planned and executed. The first one against a landlord Khagen Senapati was led by Santosh Rana himself on 21 September 1969. The most spectacular action took place on 1 October 1969 at a village where thousands of armed tribals attacked a landlord's house. He made good his escape but his house was ransacked.

But even this could not be sustained for long. The losses among the guerilla cadre were too many, far more than those sustained by the class they were seeking to annihilate. This led to frustration among the leadership. In a letter to Charu Mazumdar, published in the CPI (ML)'s Bengali mouthpiece *Deshabrati*, Asim Chatterjee expresses it clearly. It so happened that a few comrades were returning after a squad action. On their way, they were killed by militant goons hired by a powerful landlord. 'The comrades gave their lives. It is unbearable asking comrades to lay down their lives like this. I want to know where we are making mistakes.' Later another prominent leader, Satyanarayana was to say in an interview given to the *Hindustan Standard* on 20 May 1974, 'We now hold that annihilation of individual enemies is nothing but individual or squad terrorism and has nothing [in] common with Marxism-Leninism. It turns the masses into silent spectators and robs the revolution of mass support.'

The Naxalbari movement might have failed but it inspired a whole generation of youth and served as an initiation to radical politics. In fact, the late '60s were heady days for the youth all across the world. In China a cultural revolution was in the offing. America was receiving a beating in Vietnam. On the streets of Kolkata, angry, restless youth were hurling crude bombs at police vans. Students from affluent families, studying in prestigious institutions were bidding goodbye to lucrative careers and going to the forests of Bihar and elsewhere to participate in the revolution. For such youth in India, Naxalbari became the shining light.

Apart from Naxalbari, the leaders of the current Maoist movement were inspired by the sacrifices of their predecessors, first in Telangana and then in Srikakulam in Andhra Pradesh. In fact, the movement in Telangana took shape even before India became free.

In the Telangana region of the then princely state of Hyderabad, popular sentiment was against the Nizam, the ruler of the state. Like most of the feudal lords of British India, the Nizam ruled with an iron fist, oppressing the people he ruled. The administrative structure was feudal.

The ruler and the ruling class were Muslims, the population was Hindu. Forced labour was common and the people suffered severe oppression.

Since the Nizam had banned Communist parties, the Communist leaders got together under the banner of the Andhra Mahasabha in 1946. The Nizam tried to suppress it but was met with stiff resistance by peasants, who rose against the Nizam under the guidance of the Communist rebels. Within a year of the insurrection, the three districts of Nalgonda, Warangal and Khammam came under the control of the insurgents. A peasants' guerilla army was raised which comprised 5,000 members. The feudal landlords were driven away and their land seized.

Feudalism is one big factor that contributed to the rise of Naxalism since the beginning. In his jail diary, Naxal ideologue and poet Varavara Rao describes the plight of women working as labourers in the fields of a feudal landlord, Visunuru Deshmukh. Once the women begged him to let them off for a while to enable them to breast-feed their children who lay outside the fields. He is believed to have ordered them to fill a few earthen pots with their milk. Then he snatched away the pots and threw that milk over his fields.

By mid 1948, about one-sixth of the Telangana region had come under the control of Communist guerillas. In 1948, the Indian state sent its army to tackle the Nizam and overthrow him. Hyderabad was made a part of the Indian dominion.

With the the entry of the Indian Army in Telangana in September 1948, the Communist rebels were faced with several questions. Should the armed struggle be continued as a war of liberation against the troops? Who would then be the allies in such a struggle? Till now the middle-level peasants and the small capitalists had been supporting the anti-Nizam struggle; but now would they support the Indian government hoping for a better future in the Indian Union? This created a division among the Communists. While one section favoured the withdrawal of the armed struggle, the other wanted it to continue against the Indian Army. In 1951, the Communist rebels withdrew the struggle, leaving the poor sections of the rural population in the lurch. This division led to the military weakness of the rebels.

There could be no further extension of the narrow liberated zones and the guerillas had to retreat to the forests on the Godavari river, Karimnagar and the Nalgonda forests. The landless in the Godavari forest area mainly from the Koya tribal community joined the guerillas, and had to pay a heavy price later when the army adopted a plan devised by Harold Briggs, the British director of operations against Communists in what was then Malaya in the '50s. The army burnt down the tribal hamlets and herded the people into internment camps. The same plan would be adopted later in Mizoram and more recently in Chhattisgarh in mid 2000 where 40,000 tribals were forced to leave their villages and stay in security camps.

The formal split of the CPI came in 1964 when those who advocated the continuation of the struggle formed a separate party called the CPI (Marxist). People like Charu Mazumdar joined it and were later dissatisfied with its policies, as already discussed above.

28

The year trouble broke out in Srikakulam was the same as that of Naxalbari. On 31 October 1967, at a place called Levidi in the Parvatipuram agency area of the Srikakulam district, situated on the north-eastern tip of Andhra Pradesh, two peasants were shot dead by the goons of a landlord. Spread over 300 square miles, the area is inhabited by the Savaras, who live on the hill slopes and are popularly known as Girijans—hill people. As is the case with most of the tribal communities, the life of the Girijans too revolved around the jungle. They would eat whatever grew in the forest and also grow some crops through the method of shifting cultivation. But over the years, the Girijans had been trapped by moneylenders and were now absolutely in their grip. It so happened that the newly-implemented national forest law had made it difficult for the tribal communities to sustain themselves through forest produce. The forest officials made life hell for them by not allowing them to even cut a branch from a tree. Since British times any transfer of land in tribal areas could happen between tribals only. But in independent India, the rich landlords and moneylenders, who had influence among the political class, had managed to fleece the poor tribals and usurp large tracts of their land.

In the '50s a few Communist teachers began working among the Savaras and the Jatapu tribals. Prominent among them was Vempatapu Satyanarayana, a charismatic leader. To get a foothold among the tribal community, he had married two tribal women—one each from the Savara and Jatapu tribes. Along with Adibatla Kailasam (the duo was popularly known as Satyam-Kailasam) the two formed the

Girijan Sangam. On 31 October 1967, a group of Girijans was going to attend a conference called by Satyam-Kailasam to discuss their strategy in the wake of large-scale arrests of the tribals by the police. On their way, they were confronted by landlords at Levidi village. Two Girijans, Koranna and Manganna were killed in gunfire.

That is when events took a different turn in Srikakulam. Satyam and Kailasam decided to organise tribals into squads and undertake selected action against 'class enemies'. Armed with bows, arrows and spears and other traditional weapons, the squads attacked moneylenders and landlords, occupied their land forcibly and harvested it themselves. When the police arrived, they took the side of the landlords, further alienating the tribals. In fact, the role of the police follows a more or less similar pattern even decades later: in the 1984 Sikh pogrom, in communal riots in Uttar Pradesh, Gujarat and elsewhere.

But despite this, in Srikakulam, the guerillas managed to work out a better deal for the tribals. The landlords were coerced into increasing the wages of workers, and sharecroppers would now get a two-third share of the crop.

In 1968, all those accused of being involved in the murder of Koranna and Manganna were acquitted. This further strengthened the belief of the tribals that they should not expect anything from the State and that an armed struggle was the only way to make things work. Before this judgement, the guerilla leadership was not fully ready for armed struggle. A Srikakulam veteran later recalled how many police constables had initially offered them weapons like rifles to fight. But they wouldn't take them. So much so that when a guerilla seized a weapon from an American tourist who was exploring the area, he was reprimanded by the leadership.

But the killings of the two tribals and the support to the landlords by the police and subsequent acquittal of the accused changed all this. Also, around that time, Charu Mazumdar paid a secret visit to Srikakulam. He came visiting after an emissary was sent to him to seek his advice. Mazumdar's arrival in Srikakulam in March 1969 gave a fresh lease of life to the Srikakulam movement. He exhorted the revolutionaries to make Srikakulam the Yenan of India. He told them to pursue the policy of 'khatam' or annihilation to the fullest.

Describing a meeting with the Srikakulam comrades which took place at a secret location in the hills, Mazumdar writes about his experience[6]: '. . . These comrades are no idle daydreamers. So, they are not thinking of winning victory the easy way. They realise that attacks are sure to come and that they may even have to suffer serious set-backs. They are quite aware of that danger and are preparing to face such eventualities.

'They are convinced that to carry on revolutionary struggle, they must have a revolutionary Party. That is why they have put the task of building such a Party before everything else. At the same time they also realise that a task of such a revolutionary Party will be to imbue the Party members and the people with the spirit of sacrifice. Chairman Mao teaches us: "Wherever there is struggle

---

[6]*Liberation*, Vol. II, No. 5 (March 1969).

there is sacrifice, and death is a common occurrence." So, in order to win victory in the revolution, the revolutionary cadres must be able to make sacrifices. They must sacrifice their property and belongings, sacrifice comforts, sacrifice old habits and aspirations after fame, rid themselves of the fear of death and give up ideas of seeking the easy path. Only in this way shall we be able to train and prepare the revolutionaries to conduct a hard, difficult and protracted struggle. Only in this way can we inspire the people to make great sacrifices, who then, with tremendous blows, will smash all the power and might of imperialism, revisionism and the Indian reactionaries and thus win victory for the revolution.'

After Mazumdar's visit, the Srikakulam revolution turned bloodier. Unlike Naxalbari, it was in Srikakulam that the rebel guerillas could manage to create liberated zones known as Red territory. Under the leadership of Satyam and Kailasam, the Girijans organised themselves into armed squads and undertook a number of class annihilation actions. Many bright students studying medicine and engineering in various universities of Andhra Pradesh joined the rebel movement. According to estimates, the guerillas had managed to 'liberate' more than 300 villages. Those who were killed were mostly landlords and money-lenders. Some of them were killed brutally, and in some cases the guerillas painted the walls of the house with the blood of the victim or wrote revolutionary slogans with it. Also, a number of policemen were killed in squad action.

In certain cases, the landlords or policemen found guilty of minor offences—which could be anything from harassing

villagers or initial refusal to pay heed to the guerillas—
were let off with a warning or after they paid a fine to the
party. But when the police finally launched a major
offensive against the Red rebels, they showed no such
distinction. Most of the rebels who were caught were shot
in cold blood. Panchadi Krishnamurthy, a young rebel
leader, about 20 years old, was caught with a few other
rebels by the police on 27 May 1969, taken to a forest area
and shot dead. This trend continues even now. In various
cases, the police have arrested top leaders of the CPI
(Maoist) in urban areas, taken them to a jungle, and killed
them. Those thus allegedly eliminated like this include
Maoist leaders like Cherukuri Rajkumar alias Azad, Patel
Sudhakar Reddy, Sande Rajamouli and many others. Later,
a statement would be issued that these leaders were killed
in encounters with the police.

The death blow to the Srikakulam movement was finally
dealt on 10 July 1970 when the police killed both Satyam
and Kailasam in an encounter. In the Andhra state assembly,
some leaders hailed it as Diwali, the slaying of demons by
Rama. Afterwards, the movement just faded away. But
while the Naxalbari movement had shown what arming
peasants could achieve, the events in Srikakulam paved the
way for what could be achieved through guerilla warfare.

Two years later, Charu Mazumdar would be caught
after one of his associates gave in to police torture and
revealed his commander's secret hideout. Mazumdar had
been evading the police for some time. But now, he was
arrested from a house in Entally, Kolkata. He died twelve
days after his arrest. The harsh underground life had taken

a toll and he had developed severe health problems. While in jail he did not receive proper medical treatment, leading to his death on 28 July 1972. With him a major chapter of the Red rebellion came to an end.

But in Andhra Pradesh, a few rebels who had experienced the efficacy of guerilla warfare would keep the spark alive. In India's heartland today, it is this spark that has turned into a major fire.

III

THE RETURN OF SPRING THUNDER

I began revolution with eighty-two men. If I had to do it again, I would do it with ten or fifteen and absolute faith. It does not matter how small you are if you have faith and a plan of action.

—Fidel Castro

It is beyond the power of any man to make a revolution. Neither can it be brought about on any appointed date. It is brought about by special environments, social and economic. The function of an organised party is to utilise any such opportunity offered by these circumstances.

—Bhagat Singh

In Andhra Pradesh's Warangal district, a schoolteacher weighed the losses incurred during the Srikakulam movement. Kondapalli Seetharamaiah had been a participant in the Telangana movement but after the split in the CPI, he had left the party. Then after Charu Mazumdar formed the CPI (ML), Seetharamaiah joined it along with another associate, K.G. Satyamurthy—a man known for his prowess in poetry.

In 1969 itself, while a rebellion was occurring in many parts of the country, Seetharamaiah had quietly sent a one-man squad from Kakati Medical College, a student called Chainsu Ram Reddy, to the Mullugu forests in Warangal. Mao had very clearly laid out the importance of establishing a base area or a 'rear' for the guerillas without which, he said, the revolution could not succeed. As early as 1938 Mao had written: 'History knows many peasant wars of the "roving rebel" type, but none of them ever succeeded. In the present age of advanced communications and technology, it would be all the more groundless to imagine that one can win victory by fighting in the manner of roving rebels.'

From the Telangana experience, Seetharamaiah had learnt that it was not possible to fight without first acquiring a safe base where the guerillas could be trained, and which could also serve as a sanctuary for the rebels. So, Chainsu

Ram Reddy was sent to the Mullugu forests. Reddy was asked to stay with the people in the area and gradually make them politically aware. But in the absence of any support system, he could not sustain himself for long and had to return without achieving much.

Seetharamaiah understood why he couldn't. He was beginning to understand the importance of forming mass 'overground' organisations. But this was something Charu Mazumdar had been strongly against. In the 1970 Congress of the CPI (ML), Charu Mazumdar had made it clear that there was to be no 'overground' party at all. But now, Seetharamaiah was clear that this was necessary. 'One of Seetharamaiah's qualities was that he would first listen to you and then offer his counter-remarks and talk you out of it,' says Varavara Rao. The first violation of Charu Mazumdar's line was the formation of the Revolutionary Writers Association in Andhra Pradesh. Then in 1972, the Jana Natya Mandali was formed. In *Pillapu* magazine, Charu Mazumdar sent a message for Seetharamaiah. 'You are starting a writers' association. Through this magazine, I am sending you a message: this is the period of sacrifice.'

The message clearly meant that Mazumdar had reconciled with KS's policy of forming 'front' organisations. Around this time, many students from Hyderabad's Osmania University and Warangal's Regional Engineering College were attracted to radical politics. From 1974-75, 14 students from the Osmania University took a vow not to have a family and dedicate their whole life to the cause of the people's revolution. Forty other people went underground during the same time from places like Guntur,

Tirupati and Vizag. During this time, KS also saw to it that other 'overground' organisations were formed. The Radical Students Union (RSU) was formed on 12 October 1974 and the first State Conference was held in February 1975 in Hyderabad to strategise on how students' movements could be linked to the idea of revolution. Thousands of students attended the conference. The biggest contingents were from Telangana. Indira Gandhi was then prime minister. Due to her political bungling, the Emergency was imposed in the country in 1975. The 'overground' organisations like the RSU now had to face the full brunt of the repressive machinery. Hundreds of students were picked up and subjected to inhuman torture and then put in jails. Four young students, Janardhan, Murali, Anand and Sudhakar were taken to the jungle and shot dead by the police. Yet, RSU continued its activities in colleges and universities across Andhra Pradesh.

It was after the Emergency was lifted that yet another organisation, Radical Youth League (RYL), was formed in 1978. Together with Jana Natya Mandali and RSU, the members of RYL began what was called the 'Go to the village campaign'. Brilliant strategist that Seetharamaiah was, he devised this method to enable the rebel students to integrate with the peasants. It was an effective method to push the party's agenda among the peasantry.

During the summer holidays, students would form groups and each group would then cover a few villages. The students were so dedicated that in some cases they would be out for days in remote areas. Some comrades would later recall how they wouldn't get anything to eat for days, and a few of them even fainted with exhaustion. During such village campaigns, the student leaders would make the people politically aware and also gather information about the land-based relationships in the rural society. They would also look out for potential activists among the villagers. These names would then be handed over to a Central Organiser. The Central Organiser (CO) was an important man responsible for a particular area. In the guerilla set-up, a squad those days consisted of a CO and his two bodyguards, all of them armed.

The first village campaign began in the summer of 1978. It went on for a month after which the Radical Youth League held its first conference. It was this campaign that sowed the seed of rebellion once again in Andhra Pradesh after a lull of a few years. This culminated in the historic Jagtial peasant movement in Karimnagar district in September 1978. But two years before that, a small group of men waited outside a landlord's mansion in a village in the neighbouring Adilabad district. They were on a mission.

Situated on the southern edge of the Adilabad district, Tappalpur appeared to be a quiet village. But a group of about a dozen men, who lay low outside a mansion on the evening of 25 September 1976, knew that it was not quite so. The village was ruled by the 65-year-old landlord G.V. Pithambar Rao, one-time MLA, who now devoted all his time to managing the affairs of his lands. The Velama caste to which Rao belonged was known for its aversion to engaging in any form of productive work. In fact, there is a saying about the Velamas that even if burning coals land on their thighs, they would expect their bonded labourers to remove them instead of saving themselves.

Around that time, 14 per cent of Adilabad's population was tribal, with Gonds constituting three-quarters of it. The district was also home to the Sringareni collieries, the biggest in south India. But only about six to seven per cent of their employees were tribals. Big industrial houses had business interests here in products such as coal and bamboo. There was a lot of unrest among the landless poor, who were at one time landowners but had lost their land to money-lenders, who had come from Maharashtra and other parts of Andhra Pradesh. In many cases, the poor tribals had cleared large tracts of forest land for agriculture, after paying bribes to the revenue and forest officials. Later, the same forest department officials began evacuating the tribals from the forest area, denying them even the little sustenance that came through cultivation.

It was in such circumstances, Naxalites allege, that rich landlords like Pithambar Rao made life even more difficult for the poor. Rao had been on the hit list of the Naxalites for some time—according to a rebel who was a part of the hit team—because of his alleged cruel ways of dealing with the poor peasants of Tappalpur. The Naxalites accuse him of being drunk on money and political power, and of committing a number of atrocities including the raping of womenfolk. The Naxalites even go to the extent of saying that in those days no family would agree to a marriage alliance for their daughter from anyone in Tappalpur because of Rao's reputation.

Apart from this, the Naxalites had another major axe to grind with Pithambar Rao. In 1972, two peasants, Bhumaiah and Kishta Goud were arrested for murdering a landlord in Adilabad, and were later sentenced to death. Civil rights groups had tried their best to save them from the gallows (even Sartre had demanded their release) but in the middle of the Emergency, on 1 December 1975, the two were hanged in the Mushirabad jail—becoming the first to be hanged in free India (after Mahatma Gandhi's assassin Nathuram Godse). The Maoists believe that Pithambar Rao had played a key role in the arrest of Kishta Goud. That evening a group of them gathered by the walls of his mansion, waiting for the darkness. Later, another rebel group was to join them and then they would attack. The men were armed with axes, knives and a crude bomb. One of the men who waited outside that evening was a bespectacled man, a science graduate, working as a teacher in the neighbouring Karimnagar district. He had recently been made a Central Organiser of the party. Accompanying him was another young comrade known for his physical strength and knowledge of guerilla warfare.

But things went a little haywire. The group that was supposed to join them didn't turn up. As they waited, one of Rao's workers happened to spot them. Another senior Maoist leader who was a part of that group remembers how the young comrade frog-jumped at the worker and prevented him from raising an alarm. But by then the other workers had seen them as well. In haste, the men exploded the bomb they were carrying at the entrance and fled from there.

Though the bomb did not kill anyone on the spot, Pithambar Rao died a few days later. Of a heart attack.

But the group was not yet done. It returned a few months later, this time well prepared. The group had acquired a muzzle-loading gun as well. On the evening of 7 November, the group, disguised as shepherds, pretended to be drunk and initiated a fake brawl among themselves. As the onlookers gathered, one of them shouted: 'Let us go to the Zamindar!'

At the main gate of Rao's mansion they spotted Rao's two sons. Both of them were killed at once along with a police constable. Besides them, a couple of workers and the son of the village head were also killed. The group then left and went to a nearby village where one of Rao's clerks known for his inhuman attitude towards the poor lived. He was found at his house and his throat was slit. The group then raided the house of another landlord and burnt down all the land deal agreements he had with the villagers. Then they went looking for another of Rao's workers who had also played a role in Kishta Goud's arrest. He was fired at but he managed to flee. Later, he surrendered in front of the party leaders and apologised.

This incident is known in the history of the Maoist movement as the Tappalpur raid and it led to the exodus of scores of landlords from Adilabad, Karimnagar and other neighbouring districts. The poor had risen and the Maoists were now leading them.

The young comrade who frog-jumped at Rao's worker

that September night in Tappalpur was Nalla Adi Reddy, more popularly known as Comrade Shyam. He was later killed on 2 December 1999 in Bangalore with two other senior Maoist leaders, Santosh Reddy alias Mahesh and Seelam Naresh alias Murali. Their local guide in Bangalore who had offered them shelter had connived with the police to drug them, after which they were killed. The bespectacled comrade who accompanied the group in Tappalpur was also a Velama, Mupalla Laxman Rao, the man we know now as Ganapathi—the supreme commander of the CPI (Maoist).

The situation in the neighbouring Karimnagar district was no different. There was rampant exploitation of the landless poor and in the feudal set-up formed by the landlords, they suffered a lot. But after the student rebels under the 'Go to the Village' campaign began visiting these areas, they brought with them political awareness. People who were not even allowed to wear slippers in front of the landlords were getting organised under the Maoist leadership.

The first shock to the feudal landlords was administered by a Dalit labourer, Lakshmi Rajam. In Andhra, around the time of Dussehra, it was a ritual that a play called *Dakamma* be performed in the area where the landlords lived. In the village the segregation was complete. Wealthy Velama landlords stayed in the village while the Dalits stayed around the periphery so that they would have no contact with the landlords most of the time. Buoyed by the stories of revolution, Rajam organised this play in the Dalit area in 1977. It was around this time that the Dalits and other landless people began to assert themselves and took over tracts of government land either illegally occupied by the landlords or just left unexploited. The first Dalit to occupy such land was a man called Poshetty. Both Lakshmi Rajam and Poshetty were killed by the angry landlords.

But by then it was too late. By June 1978, the heat had become unbearable for the landlords. The student rebels had sowed a seed of rebellion among the peasants. The Maoist leadership decided to concentrate on the wage issues of agricultural labourers, the abolition of free labour which the landlords forced the Dalits to do, and taking possession of land. Agricultural labourers called various strikes.

There was a sea of landless poor who now wanted a share of the land. All these people, interestingly, made applications addressed to one Mukku Subba Reddy, the secretary of the CPI (ML) saying that they had occupied such and such an area of land and that a patta be issued to them. A senior Maoist rebel, who is now a Central Committee member of the CPI (Maoist) recalls[7] how one of the comrades in-charge, Sai Prabhakar got two full gunny bags of such applications.

On 7 September 1978, over one lakh agricultural

---

[7]Interview to the author in Dandakaranya.

45

labourers and other poor people from 150 villages took out a march to Jagtial town. Hidden in their houses, the landlords watched this development. By the next day a number of them were so shaken by this spectacle that they fled to the cities. The same day, the district collector of the area issued a letter which said that land reforms in Karimnagar should be implemented on a war footing.

Due to the Jagtial march, a rare phenomenon took place, perhaps the only one of its kind till now in the history of India. The poor working class decided to socially boycott those landlords who would not surrender the land they illegally occupied. So for such landlords, washermen, barbers, cattle feeders and domestic servants refused to lend their services. This was the social boycott of the poor in reverse. The same boycott was later extended to the policemen who camped in the area to aid the rich landlords. The boycott was a huge success. Excepting six landlords, everyone else fell in line.

Some of the landlords later retaliated with the help of the police. Village after village was raided by a joint force of police and goons of the landlords. Mass beating and torture took place. In Jagtial taluka alone, 4,000 villagers are said to have been implicated in false cases. Some of them were jailed and many brutally tortured. By end October 1978, Jagtial was declared a disturbed area.

But the men who led and supervised the Jagtial march were a contented lot. The shackles had been broken. That evening in Jagtial, as the poor masses took to the streets, two men would look into each other's eyes and then hug each other. One of them was Ganapathi and the other his friend who would later become his trusted lieutenant: Mallojula Koteshwara Rao alias Kishenji.

By 1979, the party had a substantial number of both 'overground' and underground cadres. The latter carried out a number of operations, mainly killing landlords in the North Telangana area. Also, by this time the members of RSU and RYL had begun working among thousands of coal miners in the area. In a very short time they were able to radicalise the miners who were frustrated by hardships. The management was forced to accept some of the miners' demands.

But KS, as Seetharamaiah had come to be known, was still not happy with the shape the movement was taking. In 1979, KS declared that the Maoist movement had not yet taken the shape of armed struggle. He said that all this while the party had only been carrying out isolated squad actions which could not be termed as 'armed struggle'. Many party members were disheartened and took it as a signal to end all such actions. Some quipped sarcastically that KS wanted Kondapalli toys (wooden toys made in that area) to fight war.

The same year, KS made a historical amendment in Charu Mazumdar's policy of class annihilation. He was speaking on the death of Chinnalu, a former mess worker of the Kakati Medical College. Inspired by the students to whom he served food, Chinnalu had left his job and joined the RYL, rising to become a very popular leader in Warangal district. He was murdered by CPM goons and a breakaway faction of the Maoists who thought KS had broken away from the line of armed struggle. Varavara Rao remembers[8] that speech very well: 'He (KS) said that we will avenge Chinnalu's death but that does not mean that we will kill those who killed him. He said unlike Charu Mazumdar's line we will not go looking for the class enemy, annihilate him, and then organise. We will organise and if the class enemy comes in our way, then we will annihilate him. He gave the example of a farmer. A farmer, he said, while working to prepare a field for harvest removes the thorny bushes, ploughs the land. If a harmless snake comes his way, he will just throw it away. And if it is a poisonous snake, then he will kill it.'

It was a statement that seemed like a contradiction of what the CPI (Maoist) is doing currently by, say, attacking a group of CRPF personnel. 'If they [the CRPF] are in Chhattisgarh, that means they are there for obstructing our work. Otherwise what work do they have in the jungle?' counters a senior Maoist leader.

In a recent interview with me in November 2010, Maoist supreme commander Ganapathi addressed this issue. He said: 'Only when the government forces come to attack us carrying guns do we attack them in self-defence. Our repeated appeal to the lower-level personnel in the police and paramilitary forces is—please do not betray your own class, don't serve the exploiting class, don't

---

[8]Interview to the author.

attack the people and revolutionaries on your own, consciously, in a revengeful manner, join hands with the masses and turn your guns against the real enemies and not on your brothers and sisters. What you are doing is not service to the people but service to the exploiting classes. So stop serving the exploiting classes like slaves. Don't just think of your livelihood, please think about people, think about the country.'

Ganapathi's remarks apart, it is a fact that in many Maoist-affected areas, the security forces are a demoralised lot. But still, operations are on against Maoists in the entire Red zone. The state forces hit Maoists wherever they can, and the Maoists hit back whenever they get a chance. It is a bloody war out there.

IV

HELLO, BASTAR

A strong base of operations must always be preserved and continuously strengthened during the course of the war. Within this territory, the indoctrination of local residents should take place.

—Che Guevara

Whether true or false, what is said about men often has as much influence on their lives, and particularly on their destinies, as what they do.

—Victor Hugo

You could say the idea of Dandakaranya as a rear base for Maoist rebels germinated over a dinner table.

Every summer, or whenever their jobs permitted, Kondapalli Seetharamaiah's daughter and his son-in-law—both were doctors at Delhi's All India Institute of Medical Sciences—would visit Bastar in Madhya Pradesh (it is now in Chhattisgarh) and adjoining areas and treat poor tribals for free. The couple had been witness to the wretched lives the tribals were forced to live. The government just didn't care. For New Delhi, this area didn't exist.

One evening, the couple paid a visit to KS. Over curd and rice, perhaps, they got talking to KS about their experiences in Bastar. Shortly afterwards, a document was circulated among the revolutionaries, which talked about combining four districts of Andhra Pradesh—Karimnagar, Adilabad, Warangal and Khammam into a guerilla zone. The districts are connected to each other through dense forest area. The document said that in order to take the movement towards a guerilla zone, the cadre would have to focus on building the party deep amongst the masses. It also stressed on the formation of village-level party cells that could be built with part-timers. And, of course, mass organisations needed to be built as well. The cadre organised itself into similar formations of Central Organiser plus two bodyguards, all of them armed. Each CO group was to be allocated a fixed number of villages, about 15 to 20.

This is where KS's dinner-time conversation with his daughter and son-in-law came into the picture. The document said that once the party initiated work among the masses, the state forces would be on the alert. In order to escape what it called 'state repression', the document said that it would become necessary to build up 'a rear' in the forests. It was obvious that KS had begun to think of setting up a rear base. It was KS who then proposed that the rear base should be set up on the other side of the Godavari river—that is in the Dandakaranya forests, of which Bastar formed the largest portion. Given this reality, the document pointed out that it was necessary to immediately make proper arrangements for such an eventuality.

On 22 April 1980, Lenin's birth anniversary, Seetharamaiah announced the formation of the CPI–ML (People's War), a new party that would carry forward the line of armed struggle. It was more popularly called the People's War Group (PWG). It was formed after the Andhra State Committee of the CPI-ML came together with the Tamil Nadu unit.

Meanwhile, the thirst for land among landless peasants and tribals was at its peak in Andhra Pradesh. It was Indira Gandhi, say veteran Maoist ideologues, who first created this thirst among the landless in the state. Just before the 1978 assembly elections in Andhra Pradesh, Indira Gandhi arrived late one night in Jagtial in Karim Nagar to address an election rally. People had been waiting for her since late afternoon. It was almost midnight when she finally arrived and went straight on to address the people who had gathered there. Referring to her famous 20-point socio-economic development programme, she blamed her political detractors for her inability to distribute land. As a parting shot, she said: 'If this (distribution of land) does not happen, a bloody revolution will take place.'

The Congress won the elections, but as it happens with most promises, the party did nothing towards alleviating the lot of the poor. Meanwhile, the Maoists had been doing their work, forcibly occupying land in hundreds of villages and distributing it among the poor.

In North Telangana, the Maoist cadre began work among the women and children working in tendu leaf collection. In the entire Dandakaranya forest area, comprising Bastar, the Gadchiroli region in Maharashtra, and in North Telangana, the condition of the tribals was pathetic. They were exploited badly by contractors, forest officials and other government servants. Those who collected bamboo sticks (for paper production) and tendu leaf (used in making beedi) were paid a pittance for their hard labour. For a bundle of 100 tendu leaves an Adivasi would be paid five paise. Similarly, one rupee would be paid for 120 sticks of bamboo. The Adivasi had no say in matters of rate. It was fixed by the contractor in consultation with the village headman.

More often than not, the poor Adivasi worked on an empty stomach. An Adivasi would usually leave a handful of rice or jowar with a little water in an earthen pitcher and then drink that gruel the next morning. The jungle where he worked was infested with snakes, bears, leopards and other wild animals. The sexual exploitation of Adivasi women was rampant. In Gadchiroli's Alapalli village, for example, one tehsildar would just walk into a girl's school, select a girl at his will, drag her into an empty classroom and rape her. In Gadchiroli itself, a forest officer collected one lakh rupees in just three months from impoverished tribals in return for letting them into the forest on which they depended for daily sustenance. The ignorant Adivasis would be fleeced by businessmen who visited from nearby towns. In exchange for a kilo of salt, the Adivasi would be made to part with a kilo of dry fruits or eight kilos of jowar.

The forest officers would not allow Adivasis to clear a portion of jungle and practise agriculture there. Citing archaic forest laws, they would not even allow them to collect firewood or other forest produce, or even thin sticks of bamboo for making brooms. At various places, just before the harvest, forest officials would arrive on tractors and threaten to destroy the crop, and the Adivasi's only recourse would be to pay a bribe or part with a major share of the produce. In their own turn, the government agencies would destroy thousands of acres of land for procuring precious wood like the sagwan or by leasing forest land to mining companies. Thousands of villagers were rendered homeless to make national parks for animals. For the State, the Adivasis counted for less than animals.

In Central-West Bastar, spread over 4,000 sq km, lies the area of Abujhmaad. The combined population of the 236 villages in this region was not more than 12,000.

About 76 varieties of forest produce are found here. The mahua flowers and the tamarind collected throughout Dandakaranya is of premium quality. The Adivasis use mahua for making alcohol and as a food item as well. The businessmen to whom they would sell it used it for extracting oil, making soap and for other purposes. For a kilo of tamarind an Adivasi was paid less than a rupee. The same was sold in the international markets for 400 rupees. Hundreds of thousands of Adivasis continued to live in the Dark Ages.

From these jungles, the then Madhya Pradesh government alone earned a revenue of 250 crore rupees annually. A number of businessmen and traders had bribed their way into buying large tracts of government land and turned it into agricultural farms. There, they employed the landless tribals as labourers, paying them a pittance for their labour. Often an Adivasi caught in the forest area collecting firewood or forest produce would be threatened with dire consequences and then coerced into sending his womenfolk or his cattle to the forest officials. The other set of people who held the Adivasis to ransom were the vadde—the local witch doctors. For Adivasis who had never seen a doctor, the vadde was a personification of God himself. In connivance with businessmen, and because he was feared by the whole village, the vadde often turned into an exploiter himself, usurping land and other resources.

It is under these circumstances that the Maoist guerillas entered the forest area. It was in June 1980 that seven squads of five to seven members each entered the forests. Four squads entered the jungles of North Telangana—one each in Adilabad, Khammam, Karimnagar and Warangal. Two of them entered Bastar and one went to Gadchiroli.

The Gadchiroli squad was led by a young Dalit, 23-year-old Peddi Shankar. Peddi Shankar's father worked in the Sringareni coal mines where the Naxals had made inroads among the miners. After high school, Shankar had worked as a bus conductor. Throughout this area, the Radical Students Union and the Radical Youth League had been trying to garner support among the youth. It was then that Peddi Shankar came in contact with the Maoist activists, and in a short time, he turned into a staunch radical.

One incident in his village, Belampalli, made Peddi Shankar very popular among the people there, particularly those from his own community. Two rowdies, Kundel Shankar and Dastagiri, who were active in the area had spread fear among the villagers. They would openly tease the women, but nobody dared to speak against them. Peddi Shankar and his comrades had warned them repeatedly to refrain from such acts. Finally, one day, Shankar and his close associate Gajalla Ganga Ram (who later died in 1981 when a hand-grenade went off in his hands) waylaid the two in a marketplace and in full public view, hacked both of them to death with an axe.

Later, in 1978, Peddi Shankar also led a major strike of coal miners who were demanding better air supply (called galli supply in mining parlance). But it was the Rajeshwari rape case the same year that catapulted him to legendary fame in this area.

Rajeshwari, a coal-mine worker's wife was raped by a

mine officer, and later died in hospital. It was Shankar who initiated a massive agitation against the rape incident and is believed to have led a violent protest against the accused officer, in which his house was damaged. To quell the protestors, the police opened fire, killing two persons. Afterwards, a case of dacoity and arson and attempt to seize arms from the police station was filed against Peddi Shankar. It was then that he went underground.

By 1980, he had turned into a full-fledged Naxal guerilla. The same year, he was the leader of the squad that crossed the Godavari river and entered Maharashtra. They began work in three villages of Chandrapur district, on the border of Andhra Pradesh: Moinbinpetta, Bhourah and Paidgun. Shankar and his squad members began to talk to the local people, mostly Gond Adivasis, who lived in about 700 huts and had been exploited by the contractors and moneylenders.

On 2 November 1980, Shankar and his friends had stopped for food at a house in Moinbinpetta. It was around this time that Pota, a landlord's henchman, came to know of it and revealed their location to the police. At about 3 p.m., as Shankar and four other squad members were leaving, they were waylaid on the banks of the Pranhita, a tributary of the Godavari. The police party is said to have fired at them from behind. Shankar was shot in the back in full view of a number of villagers who were around. He fell, rose again, ran for a few metres but fell in a jowar field and died. His four friends managed to escape. In a short time, Shankar had become very popular in this area. His body was picked up by the villagers and kept in a school. Three days later, the police took his body. The constable who shot Shankar, Chandrika Deep Rai, was awarded 500 rupees while the other members of the police group were given 100 rupees each.[9]

With his death, Peddi Shankar became the first martyr of the People's War Group. Only a few months earlier, he had received a Mao badge from the party for his work. And now he was dead. The villagers later reclaimed his body from the police and cremated it themselves. It was an emotional farewell to their hero. His father came to know of it only ten days later, and went to see the spot where he was cremated. The police hoped that Shankar's death would put an end to Naxal activities in the region. But his death only served to make the Naxals more popular. Very soon, other squads would enter these areas.

Initially, when the squads entered, the Adivasis would run away from them, thinking of them as dacoits. The Naxal guerillas had a hard time even getting food since the people in the villages that they entered would vanish into the jungles upon spotting them. At certain places, the Naxals would then forcibly catch hold of someone and tell him about themselves, their party and their agenda.

But one incident in 1981 was to turn the Naxal movement into a major struggle in these parts. It happened in Inderavalli in Adilabad district on the Andhra Pradesh-Maharashtra border.

Situated on the western side of Andhra Pradesh, and bordering Maharashtra, Adilabad was the most backward

---

[9]As mentioned in a CPDR fact-finding report.

district of the state. Fourteen per cent of the district's population in the '80s was tribal, of which Gond tribals constituted 70 per cent. According to a People's Union for Democratic Rights (PUDR) report, the district had the lowest literacy rate, medical facilities, electrification and transport facilities in the state.

Since 1978, the tribals, under the guidance of the rebels had begun to organise themselves into Girijan Rytu Coolie Sangams (tribal peasant labour associations) and had begun their struggles against forest officials and moneylenders. The tribals began to demand better wages for tendu leaf collection, control over the forest land and better wages for tribal labourers employed by government contractors. Buoyed by the increasing support of the tribals, the activists announced a rally in Inderavalli village of Utnoor taluka on 20 April 1981. The rally was announced days in advance and posters were put up all the way till Hyderabad, the state capital.

The police sensed danger and a large number of police deployments took place in the area days before the rally. Section 144 was also imposed. But the poor Adivasis who had been informed about the rally in advance had no means of knowing what Section 144 meant. On the stipulated day, they came out in hordes, some of them hoping to buy essential items from the haat. The local Congress workers who had their ear to the ground, had already alerted the senior party leadership in Hyderabad about these developments.

The police clamped down on the tribals. Leading a brutal attack against the Adivasis, the police fired upon them. Officially, 13 Adivasis died, but according to eyewitnesses, more than 50 were left dead and at least 100 injured. Those who tried to rescue the injured were also not spared. Later, the government said in its defence that the tribals were armed. But the fact-finding team that visited Inderavalli right after the incident testified that the tribals were carrying no more than sticks and lathis which they habitually carried. The police did not return even a single body. Instead, they cremated all the bodies, in violation of the Gond custom of burying their dead.

Many say that the Inderavalli incident did to the state's authority in this whole region what Jallianwala Bagh did to the British.

There were a few speakers who were supposed to be addressing the tribals that day. One of them was Kobad Ghandy. Soon, he would be at the forefront of the Maoist movement as one of its ideologues.

The five men had been walking for days. They were exhausted, and the thought came to them that they might die without anyone even knowing. The jungles of Bastar were unending. It was summer time and in the harsh sun, the five men walked slowly, drinking water wherever they could find it. But food had been scarce and they had not been able to eat for two days now. One of them was losing his patience.

The men had entered from Andhra Pradesh, and they

knew that this was the life they had to lead now. Not for days, weeks or months, but for years. Or till a police bullet snuffed out their lives. They were one of the squads sent to establish a base in Bastar. But right now, they were worried about the gnawing hunger in their stomachs. Without food, they would not survive for long—this they knew very well. Even after hours of walking, they would rarely encounter a single human being. In some villages that fell on their way, the Adivasis would be so scared at the sight of them that they would run away and disappear into the jungle. In any case, the Adivasis had barely enough food even for themselves. One of the five remembers watching an Adivasi bring a handful of red ants and making a chutney out of it. The young man who was growing restless could not restrain himself any longer. 'If I don't find anything to eat in the next village, I am returning home,' he told his comrades. His four friends were too tired to try to convince him to stay back.

In the next village, the men found a chicken. They pounced on it, wrung its neck and devoured it after roasting it over a crude fire made of sticks. And they stayed back. The man who had threatened to return became one of the leading lights of the Naxal movement in this area. His name, however, is not known. In the complex history of the Naxal movement, some identities remain shrouded in mystery.

To begin with, the Naxals concentrated upon fighting the authority of the contractors and forest officials. Struggles also broke out against the management of the paper mill and contractors exploiting the forest produce. Massive struggles were waged to increase the rates for tendu leaf and bamboo collection. Within the first year, the Adivasis stopped paying taxes to the forest department. Large tracts of forest land were occupied forcibly for cultivation. Also, large portions of land occupied by traders and moneylenders were redistributed among the landless. Within a few years, thousands of acres of land were occupied through the might of the gun. The Adivasis, buoyed by the Naxalite presence, had begun to assert themselves. They would come out in hordes to press for their demands and, when required, forcibly occupy land.

The Adivasis had now tasted the power of the gun. In Gadchiroli, a woman comrade, Samakkha, took to task a forest officer who had grabbed a vehicle to confiscate forest produce from Adivasis. In front of a huge crowd of people he had dominated for years, the forest officer's collar was grabbed by a single woman, and he was forced to apologise. This left a big impression on the psyche of the Adivasi populace. The tehsildar in Alapalli who was exploiting schoolgirls was caught by the Naxal guerillas, beaten up and then tied to a tree. Then the women of that area were asked to assemble and instructed to spit at his face. One by one, the women approached him and spat on him. Some of them cried.

In many villages in Bastar, even the use of the plough was unknown to the Adivasis. The earth was considered as mother and using the plough, in the minds of the Adivasis, was akin to cutting through her chest. In fact in the entire Dandakaranya region, only two per cent of the land was irrigated. To the Adivasis, even basic agricultural techniques such as weeding or usage of natural fertilisers like cow dung were alien concepts. The exploitation of women was rampant. In the forest, the Adivasis would store forest produce in isolated hamlets called Ghotul. These hamlets were used by forest guards to sexually exploit tribal girls. If the girls protested, they were threatened and in many cases evicted from work. In one such case, when the husband of the woman protested, he was killed by the forest guards and contractors. During a public meeting, this was brought to the notice of the Maoist guerillas. Immediately, the culprits were apprehended and publicly thrashed.

Because of such acts, many young Adivasis were attracted to the Maoist cause. In Gadchiroli district's Aheri taluka was a young girl who grew up witnessing the exploitation of her people by the forest officers. Every year, they would come and take rice and jowar from her father. She would also hear stories of her friends being caught and sexually exploited by them. 'I would ask my father not to bow to their demands but he would catch hold of me and ask me to keep quiet,' she recalls. This was in the early '80s and a Maoist squad had come to their village and set up camp by the river. 'We were not allowed to even venture towards that side since our elders thought the Maoists were dacoits and would kidnap us,' she says. But one day the rebels caught hold of a boy called Raju and explained to him their aim and agenda. The word spread.

A few weeks later, the girl who was then 15 went to the riverside where she met a senior Maoist leader she calls Shankar anna (big brother). By 1986, the girl had become a full-timer. Her first military action commenced seven years later when her squad attacked a police post.

Today, the girl is a woman and one of the senior Maoist guerillas, who goes by the name of Tarakka. She is a ferocious fighter, and in several press reports,[10] she has been described as 'a woman known not just for her commitment to the "Naxalite cause" but also for her beauty'. Her name figures prominently in the October 2009 attack on police personnel in Gadchiroli's Laheri area in which 17 policemen lost their lives. 'But I was not there,' she told me when I met her inside a Maoist camp, somewhere on the Maharashtra-Chhattisgarh border.

Within a few years of entering the Dandakaranya forests, the Naxals held sway over the whole region. Many landlords, contractors, and tradesmen who tried to fight back with the help of the police were annihilated and their properties distributed among the peasants.

The biggest challenge the Maoists faced in this area was that of language. In some areas close to Andhra Pradesh, Telugu was spoken, but once they went deeper, they found that the people spoke only Gondi. The problem with Gondi was that it had no script. The Maoists worked on it gradually. Today, every Maoist guerilla in this region can speak and understand Gondi no matter which part of the country he belongs to. The Maoists have been working on a script for the language and, in the schools run by them, they have tried to introduce textbooks in the language.

Gradually, the Maoists organised the tribals. Many protest

---

[10]Vivek Deshpande, *Indian Express*, 12 October 2009.

rallies and strikes were held under the supervision of the Maoists in support for demands like better wages and better rates for forest produce.

In North Telangana the movement extended to all the talukas of Karimnagar and Adilabad district, except one taluka in each. In Warangal district the focus developed from an urban to a rural movement. In the Dandakaranya forests, the movement spread to Gadchiroli, Chandrapur and Bhandara districts; Bastar, Rajnandgaon and Balaghat of the then Madhya Pradesh and to Koraput in Orissa. In 1985 alone, in two talukas of Gadchiroli district, the Maoists liberated 20,000 acres of land from the government or landlords' control and distributed it among Adivasis.

The area had begun to turn into a guerilla zone.

V

GUNPOWDER IN
BHOJPUR

*Let me fill my nostrils with it, with the aroma of
gunpowder, the soil of Bhojpur is fragrant.*

—Nagarjun*

The most dangerous thing is to be filled with dead peace.

—Avtar Singh Pash *

*Revolutionary poets.

Washing clothes like his father, grandfather and great-grandfather did not interest Ram Pravesh Baitha. He wanted to do a little better in life. But he knew his limitations as well. There was no point dreaming about bigger things. Smaller, manageable dreams would do for him, or so he thought. A pucca house, a proper kitchen for his mother, a scooter for himself. For this, Baitha had realised much earlier in his life, he would have to somehow complete his education. And he did. In Bihar's Madhuban district, however, that a washerman's son would flaunt his graduation didn't go well with the upper-caste pride. So, Baitha was summoned and beaten up badly for possessing a Bachelor's degree. He swallowed that insult. His whole focus was on his dream of a better life. He shifted to another university and completed his Master's as well. And now, his dream was not far from being realised.

Baitha applied for various jobs like most of his friends did. But while his friends secured jobs, Baitha did not find employment. And he realised soon enough why. Apparently he had got a job and had even been sent an appointment letter. But the upper-caste staff at his village post office did not want him to get that job. They tore the appointment letter and threw it away. Baitha joined the Naxal fold. He rose to become the commander of the north Bihar cadre and was later arrested in May 2008.

Caste is one major reason why Naxalism flourished in Bihar. And crushing poverty. The Bihar of the '60s was even more steeped in hunger and caste division than it is today. Most of the land holders were upper caste. The landless labourers and marginal farmers lived a miserable life. The upper-caste zamindars owned gangs of henchmen who would help them to maintain their political clout and also keep the poor suppressed. The poor had no voice. Sexual exploitation of their womenfolk was the norm. It was against this backdrop that the seeds of rebellion were sown in Bihar.

In Bhojpur in central Bihar trouble began when a young educated man, Jagdish Mahto confronted the goons of a landlord who were trying to rig votes during the 1967 assembly elections. He was severely beaten up. Taking a cue from the Naxalbari, Mahto forged a relationship with Naxalite leaders in West Bengal. In his endeavour he was joined by a former dacoit, Rameshwar Ahir, convicted of killing a constable. They were later killed in 1972 and 1975 respectively.

In north Bihar's Muzaffarpur district, the Musahiri block saw major disputes between zamindars and peasants over crop sharing. In April 1968, some peasants forcibly harvested the crop of arhar (a pulse crop) belonging to a landlord, Bijlee Singh. Bijlee Singh is believed to have led his gang of goons sitting astride an elephant. But the peasants fought them back and ultimately Bijlee Singh and his men had to retreat. By 1969, Naxalites from West Bengal had arrived here to spread the movement.

In West Bengal's Jangal Mahal area, two men, Kanai

Chatterjee and Amulya Sen, started an organisation called Dakshin Desh (Dakshin because India is in the south of the Himalayas while China is in the north, hence referred to as the Uttar Desh). The group formed many squads and carried out several actions against landlords.

It is this organisation that was rechristened into the Maoist Communist Centre (MCC).

In early '70s, a Naxalite rebel called Kalyan Roy formed a group called MMG (Man, Money, Gun) that was active around Singhbhum and the neighbouring belt of then undivided Bihar. The group had set up a base in a forest near the steel city of Jamshedpur. In May 1970, a group of Naxalites from this group was arrested from their base including a British woman, Mary Tyler.

Mary Tyler worked as a teacher and a translator, and she had met Amalendu Sen, an Indian engineering trainee working in West Germany while returning to north London from there. The two fell in love and later married in April 1970 in Kolkata where Sen's family lived. Amalendu was a member of the MMG group and both he and his bride left soon after for Singhbhum district, on the Bengal-Bihar border. The police arrested them on charges of raiding a police station. Mary Tyler spent five years in jail, mostly in the Hazaribagh prison. She describes her experiences in jail in her memoir, *My Years in an Indian Prison*.[11] Writing about the condition of the male Naxalite prisoners in the jail, she writes:

'The men are in dreadful conditions. Their yard is as

---

[11]Victor Gollancz Ltd, London, 1977.

dreary and desolate, as ugly a place as one could imagine—
a cemented yard, a water tap and a row of dark little cells,
in which they are locked, five or six to a cell, in fetters,
twenty-four hours a day. Even in the daytime it is dark.
Only if they squat in front of the barred door can they see
to read. At night they do not even have a light inside their
cells. And, to cap it all, one complete madman is locked up
with them.'

She further writes about how some mentally unbalanced
patients and children who had been abandoned or were
lost were made to stay in the prison. She writes about
an 11-year-old girl Satya who was separated from her
father at a railway station in Bihar and was sent to jail for
'safe keeping' . . . 'Unfortunately that was the end of it.
Nobody bothered to trace her family or do anything about
sending her home. When one of the Christian wardresses
offered to look after her, the Assistant Jailers and the Clerk
of the Court warned Satya against it: Christians ate beef
and she would lose caste. Instead, she was left to grow up
in jail.'

She describes the unrest in the country due to shortage
of food. In January 1974, protests against food shortage
turned violent in Gujarat leading to the death of 40 people,
Tyler says. She writes about how a warder, who had just
returned from Dhanbad (in then undivided Bihar) told
her about police wearing gas masks to tackle people who
were in a state of revolt due to food shortages.

'On Republic Day, 26 January, the President V.V. Giri,
appealed to the nation for discipline. I wondered what
they were to discipline—their hunger pangs, may be?

Their crying children? Their wrath against a government that offered them speeches instead of food?' she asks.

Defending the actions of her Naxalite husband and others, she writes:

'Amalendu's crime, Kalpana's crime, is the crime of all those who cannot remain unmoved and inactive in an India where a child crawls in the dust with a begging bowl; where a poor girl can be sold as a rich man's plaything; where an old woman must half-starve herself in order to buy social acceptance from the powers-that-be in her village; where countless people die of sheer neglect; where many are hungry while food is hoarded for profit; where usurers and tricksters extort the fruits of labour from those who do the work; where the honest suffer whilst the villainous prosper; where justice is the exception and injustice the rule; and where the total physical and mental energy of millions of people is spent on the struggle for mere survival.'

In Bihar and later in Jharkhand (carved out of Bihar), it was the MCC that kept the Naxal movement alive along with another Naxal faction called the CPI-ML (Party Unity) or simply Party Unity. But as compared to the PWG, the MCC was considered to be a less disciplined party. In caste-ridden Bihar, the MCC organised massacres of upper-caste men to counter massacres done by upper-caste militant organisations like the Ranvir Sena (formed in 1994 by the upper-caste Bhumihar community). It would also brutally punish 'class enemies' by ordering that they be shortened by six inches—which meant beheading. According to testimonies from Jharkhand, a squad of

MCC would assemble on the outskirts of an upper-caste village. And then in the dead of night, the village would be attacked. Although the MCC maintained that it killed only men, in a few actions women and children would also become victims. On the other hand, the Ranvir Sena would without exception, kill children and women during their attacks. In an interview[12] in 1999, Ranvir Sena chief Brahmeshwar Singh said that his party would kill every Dalit irrespective of age or gender because they provided shelter to MCC squads. Upon being asked why the Ranvir Sena would not spare children and women, he said that Hanuman set the whole of Lanka afire, killing all demons including those in wombs.

But brutal killings apart, the Naxalite groups in Bihar (and Jharkhand) did change a few things. It gave the landless and lower castes a sense of empowerment. It gave them a face, a voice. It was not a done thing now to sexually exploit women of Dalits. Under the patronage of the MCC, a Dalit landless family would just put a red flag on a piece of land belonging to the government or an absentee landlord and then work on it. Though the Naxalite groups boycotted elections, it was difficult for the goons of an upper-caste political candidate to prevent the lower castes from casting their vote. As scholar Bela Bhatia writes in one of her essays[13] on the Naxalite movement in Central Bihar: '. . . their (labourers') perception of poverty

---

[12]*The Times of India*, 13 June 1999.

[13]'The Naxalite Movement in Central Bihar', *Economic & Political Weekly*, 9 April 2005.

as a matter of "fate" (naseeb) has changed; now they often see it as a matter of injustice.'

It is this sense of injustice that turned Ram Pravesh Baitha into a Naxalite. In April 2010, a young Naxal commander, Sandesh Kushwaha took revenge for the killing of his father by killing 57-year-old Badan Mahto and his son in Bihar's Rohtas district. It is believed that in a property dispute, Mahto had been instrumental in killing Kushwaha's father. After his father's death, a young Kushwaha approached a local Naxal commander who asked him to join them and avenge his father's killing. He did that, and at the age of 18, led a squad of about a hundred Maoists to attack Mahto's house and kill him along with his son. Before leaving, they blew up the house with dynamite.

It was not a Bollywood film. It was the everyday reality of Bihar. As an MCC slogan said: *Apni satta, apna kanoon.* Our power, our law.

VI

ANDHRA TO ABUJHMAAD

I remain a song dedicated to the revolution; this thirst will end only with my life.

—Cherabandaraju,
revolutionary poet

An identity would seem to be arrived at by the way in which the person faces and uses his experience.

—James Baldwin

In the mid '80s, the People's War Group decided to take direct action against the police. The place chosen for this once again happened to be Jagtial in Andhra Pradesh's Karimnagar district. In the July of 1985, a policeman was killed by a Maoist squad. In these areas, the police would collude with right-wing student activists like the ones from the BJP's Akhil Bhartiya Vidyarthi Parishad (ABVP), identify students and activists who were sympathetic to the Maoist cause, and eliminate them. But side by side, the Maoist recruitment was on as well, through joint campaigns by the Radical Students Union, Radical Youth League and Jana Natya Mandali. Cultural parties would travel all over, urging youth that 'real men' cared about 'revolution'. Hundreds of youth left their studies, and joined the Maoist movement.

In institute after institute across Andhra Pradesh, particularly in Telangana, former students who became senior leaders in the Maoist movement, would inspire other students to follow in their path. (The Stanford sociologist Doug McAdam calls this a 'strong-tie' phenomenon, essentially meaning that those who join a movement like the Maoist movement have close ties with those already inside. For example, friends.) Maoist ideologues like the legendary balladeer Gaddar would travel from one village to another, talking about hunger, deprivation, marginalisation, caste bias, and sing songs on 'martyrs' like Peddi Shankar. The Maoist campaign was so successful that it would prompt a chief minister to declare: *Aata, maata, paata bandh* (ban on cultural performances, speeches and songs). It was ironical that a man who rode on an anti-Congress wave in the state to form a party and then win elections after calling Naxalites 'Desh Bhaktalu' (patriots) in 1982 would now clamp down even on cultural performances. Nandamuri Taraka Rama Rao, or NTR in short, was a very popular actor of Telugu cinema and had founded the Telugu Desam Party (TDP) in 1982 to counter the Congress government in the state.

Travelling thousands of kilometres across the state in a van driven by his son, NTR campaigned against the Congress. It was also the year when Kondapalli Seetharamaiah was arrested by the police from the Begumpet railway station in Hyderabad. A year later in 1983, NTR rode to power after an impressive victory in the state elections. During this time, the PWG tried to consolidate its position further, entrenching itself deeper in its areas of influence in the state. But soon enough, it was clear that police action against Naxalites would continue in the same fashion.

In KS's absence, his close friend and deputy K.G. Satyamurthy took over the reigns of the People's War Group. But he was a poet and lacked leadership skills. The cadres were confused and didn't know from whom to seek guidance. A veteran Maoist leader remembers that time. 'We would ask him (Satyamurthy) what to do, and instead of displaying some sense of vision, he would break into long sessions of poetry,' he says.[14]

Finally, it was decided that KS had to be freed from prison. On 4 January 1984, KS made good his escape from the Osmania Hospital in Hyderabad after killing a duty constable. The same year, NTR had gone to America, and in his absence, with the aid of the governor, the Congress managed to topple his government on Independence Day. This time KS supported him and wrote about his 'unconstitutional exit' in the party's mouthpiece *Kranti*. This made the young blood in the party very angry. The Warangal secretary of the Maoists, Pulanjaya alias Sagar is believed to have been so furious about what KS wrote that he asked his men to burn the entire bundle of the magazine.

NTR came back to power only after a month. After the People's War Group began targeting state symbols like the police, the NTR government went full-swing against them. A special task force was created to tackle the Naxalites. In some of the worst-affected areas, a number of armed outposts came up. A number of youth were picked up on suspicion and put into jail or killed in staged encounters. In 1987, six IAS officers were kidnapped by the PWG, and a demand for the release of some of their comrades was put forward. A journalist who interviewed KS at the time was told that if need be the PWG would even kidnap Rajiv Gandhi (who was then prime minister). The government bowed this time, but afterwards, NTR toughened his stance once again against the Naxalites.

---

[14]Interview to the author.

By the late '80s, KS had completely lost his grip over the party's affairs. He had aged and had begun to sound incoherent. Later, he was diagnosed with Parkinson's disease. The party brought him to their base in Bastar. Because of what he meant to the party, he was kept in good humour, and the senior leaders, as a mark of respect for him, would sometimes seek his advice. Ganapathi now took over the reigns of the party. Afterwards, he passed a directive about KS: 'We should take his advice when we hardly need it.'

Unfortunately, the Maoists have been used by political parties to further their own interest. In recent times, it has happened in Bihar, in Jharkhand, and in West Bengal as well. In Andhra Pradesh also, political parties would use them for electoral benefits and once they assumed power, the same party, now in charge of the government, would crush them.

In December 1989, the Congress returned to power in the state. Dr M. Chenna Reddy rose to power after doing what NTR did in 1982-83: calling Naxalites patriotic. After he assumed charge, the ban on the PWG was lifted in December 1989. A number of jailed Naxalites were set free. A massive rally called by the Naxalite group in Warangal district was attended by over one million of people.

This was the time when a splinter group of Sri Lanka's Liberation Tigers of Tamil Eelam (LTTE) established contact with the PWG. Some of the cadres were trained by the LTTE rebels in guerilla warfare. And the Naxalites began to develop their expertise in an area they use effectively against the police and politicians till date: explosives. From here, the whole dynamics of the war between the state and the Naxalites changed. The Naxal guerillas could now attack the state machinery from a safe distance inflicting heavy casualties, while minimising the losses on their side.

In 1992, KS was arrested by the police from his ancestral village Jonnapadu in Andhra's Krishna district. The party he had founded had ousted him. He was released a few years later due to his failing health. He died in his granddaughter's house on 12 April 2002, at the age of 87.

A handful of people attended his funeral.

In the '90s, the relationship between the Maoists and the Andhra Pradesh government followed more or less the same pattern: just before elections, a particular political party would warm up to the Maoists and then after coming to power, lift the ban on the PWG. After Chenna Reddy came N. Janardhan Reddy, followed once again by NTR. In 1995, NTR was replaced by his ambitious son-in-law Chandrababu Naidu who staged a coup within the party to become the chief minister. In July 1996, Naidu reimposed the ban on PWG making it into the Maoist hit list. In 1998, the Maoists made a bid on his life by placing the deadly claymore mines in a bullock cart on his route in Karimnagar where Naidu was supposed to address an election rally. The explosive was detected by a police advance party before Naidu passed through. Five years later, in October 2003, however, Naidu came much closer to death when the Maoists targeted his convoy enroute to Tirupati. The impact of the blast triggered off by Maoists using a camera flashbulb was so powerful that Naidu's car was hurled into the air. Naidu was seriously injured and suffered a fracture in his collar bone. His escape could only be attributed to some divine miracle that he acknowledged himself after gaining consciousness later. 'If you look at the blast site, it is difficult to believe that I survived. I am alive today due to the good wishes of the people and due to the blessings of Lord Venkateswara,' he said.[15] The mastermind of the attack on Naidu, senior Maoist leader Sande Rajamouli was later killed by the police in 2007 in an alleged fake encounter. He was a Central Committee Member of the CPI (Maoist) and also a member of its military commission. He carried a reward of 15 lakh rupees on his head. He was married to another senior Maoist guerilla Padmakka who was killed in an encounter in 2002.

But apart from the political dilly-dallying, at least one serious effort had been made in 1989 to annihilate the Maoists. It was senior police officer K.S. Vyas who founded the Greyhound force, an elite police force trained in jungle warfare to conduct surgical operations against the Maoists. Their training pattern was to be similar to NSG commandos and these few thousand men would get 60 per cent more salary than normal pay. Four years later, in

---

[15]*Frontline*, 11-24 October 2003.

A Maoist guerilla sets out to clean a small area before making preparations for lunch. In the Maoist set-up, men and women share equal burden for kitchen work.

A squad of Maoist rebels during a training session somewhere in Chhattisgarh. Women account for forty percent of the Maoist strength.

(Photos: Rahul Pandita)

A Maoist guerilla carries a ration of eggs from one camp to another, somewhere in Dandakaranya.

A Maoist camp somewhere on the Maharashtra-Chhattisgarh border. A camp like this is built in minutes and dismantled in minutes. Depending on the presence of senior leaders, a camp is fortified accordingly.

Rebels sleep at the camp after spending a whole night on sentry duty.

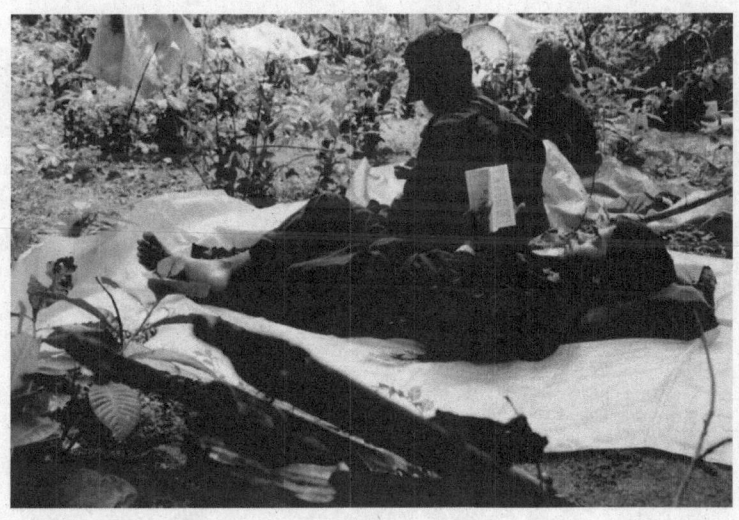

Apart from military training, there is a lot of emphasis on education. Here, a Maoist recruit reads party literature before a class on world affairs.

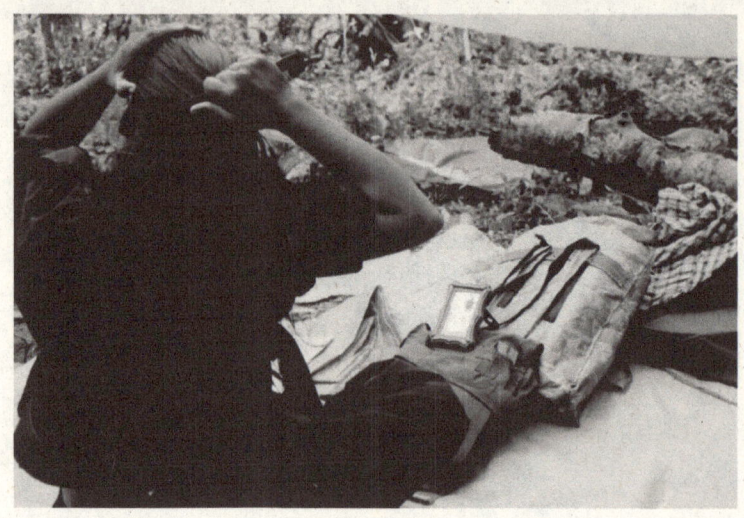

A young guerilla combs her hair inside a camp. In their spare time, girls like to listen to music or do sundry things like combing hair or washing clothes.

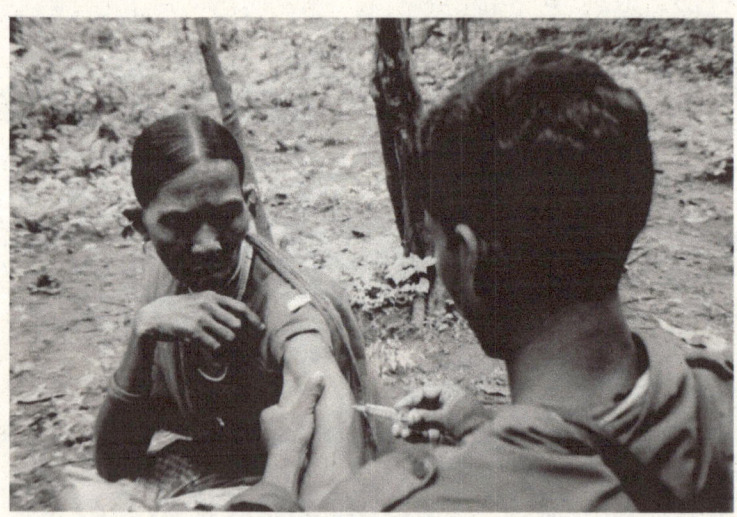

A Maoist guerilla from a medical unit injects anti-malaria vaccine into an Adivasi woman in Gadchiroli, Maharashtra.

Maoist commander Tarakka outside a military camp, somewhere on the Maharashtra-Chhattisgarh border.

14-year-old Suresh is a part of the Maoists' cultural unit, Chetna Natya Manch. After this picture was taken, the group broke into a song about how New Delhi was unleashing a wave of terror and brutality upon poor Adivasis.

The author with two Maoist guerillas in mid 2010. The guerilla on his right is the bodyguard of a senior Maoist leader.

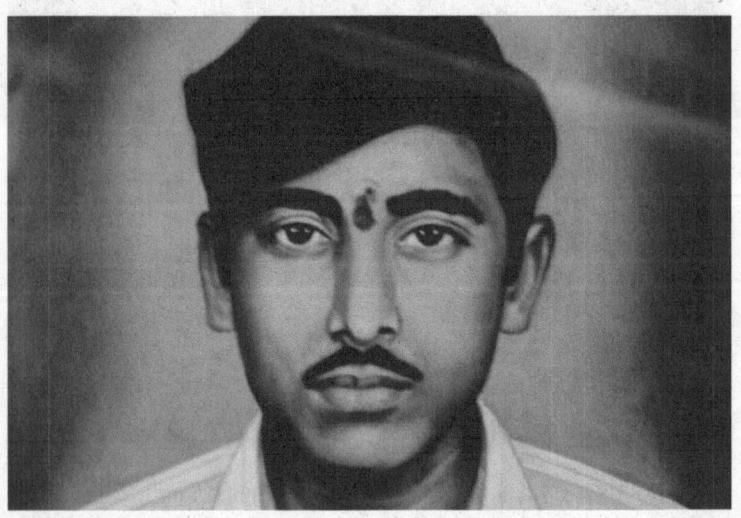

An artistic impression of the first 'martyr' of the People's War Group, Peddi Shankar.

A memorial built by the Maoists for their fallen comrades in a remote village in Gadchiroli, Maharashtra.

One of the victims of an alleged fake encounter by Salwa Judum in Chhattisgarh in January 2009. (Photo provided by the CPI (Maoist))

PLGA fighters at the 2007 Maoist Congress held in the jungles of Bihar (Photo provided by the CPI (Maoist))

Anuradha Ghandy in the PLGA uniform at the 2007 Congress after being inducted into the Central Committee of the CPI (Maoist)

Anuradha Ghandy in a photo taken by her brother on her wedding (Photo courtesy: Ritesh Uttamchandani)

1993, the Maoists managed to kill Vyas in Hyderabad while he was on his morning jog. In a strange twist, the main accused in the Vyas murder case, Maoist hit man Nayeemuddin later turned into a renegade, helping the police eliminate several Maoist leaders as well as some of their sympathisers. He was arrested in 2000 for the murder of a civil liberties activist and later acquitted in 2003 for lack of evidence. In 2007 he made good his escape from a court hearing in the Vyas murder case. He is now somewhere in Hyderabad with his hit squad, allegedly enjoying full police protection.

While the Greyhounds were quite successful in their operations against Maoists, the fact remains that there were a number of human rights violations as well, including fake encounters and custodial deaths. According to the Andhra Pradesh Civil Liberties Committee (APCLC), there have been 1,800 encounter deaths in the state between 1997 and 2007. The police tried to build anti-Maoist militias not only in Andhra Pradesh but in other states as well. In the '90s, a group called Kranthi Sena was forged together in Andhra with the active support of the police. In Maharashtra another such group called Shanti Sena was formed that succeeded in killing a number of senior Maoist guerillas. In Jharkhand, the anti-Maoist group called NASUS (Nagrik Suraksha Samiti) enjoyed the patronage of the police and several politicians. In at least two incidents, the group managed to entrap and poison to death several Maoist guerillas. In retaliation, the Maoists killed politician and Member of Parliament Sunil Mahto near Jamshedpur on 4 March 2007 and NASUS leader

Dhanai Kisku on 5 January 2010. In Chhattisgarh, the anti-Maoist militia took the shape of Salwa Judum.

In 1994, from inside the jail, several arrested Maoist leaders launched an indefinite hunger strike to press the government that they be treated as political prisoners and that the conditions within the jail be improved. After a long struggle, the government finally accepted most of the demands. As a result, in Andhra jails at least, the Maoists enjoy a number of facilities including meeting with visitors outside barracks.

In 1998, the PWG merged with a smaller Maoist group, CPI-ML (Party Unity), active mostly in Bihar. On 2 December 2000, the Maoists announced the formation of the People's Liberation Guerilla Army (PLGA) on the first death anniversary of three senior party leaders Nalla Adi Reddy (Shyam), Santosh Reddy (Mahesh) and Seelam Naresh (Murali). This is the frontal force of the Maoists which carries out attacks against the police personnel and others.

In May 2004, Congress swept to power in Andhra, defeating Chandrababu Naidu's TDP. It was during Naidu's regime that the Maoists were almost eliminated from the state. After taking over from Naidu, the Congress chief minister Y.S. Rajasekhara Reddy kept the pressure on over the Maoists but also initiated peace talks with them. On 8 June 2004, the state home minister K. Jana Reddy invited the Maoists for talks. Eight days later, the government announced a three-month ceasefire. On 11 October 2004, 11 Maoist leaders came overground to hold talks with the Andhra government. The group was led by senior Maoist leader Akkiraju Haragopal known more by his party name Ramakrishna. All of them wore battle fatigues. When Ramakrishna was advised to wear something 'civilian' he replied that he carried nothing else to wear. The Maoist leaders were put up as state guests at a government guest house. A large crowd had come to witness the spectacle. Maoist sources say that on the first day itself, many senior bureaucrats and police officers secretly came to meet Ramakrishna for redressal of various personal problems in the Maoist area of influence.

On 14 October, Ramakrishna announced that the People's War Group had merged with MCC on 21 September to form the CPI (Maoist). Initially, the talks held a lot of promise, said civil servant S.R. Sankaran, who acted as the chief mediator (he passed away on 7 October 2010). But it was clear very soon that the talks would not be successful. Both the Maoists and the government refused to budge even an inch from their positions. The Maoists refused to accede to the government's condition of laying down arms before their demands would be considered. The Maoists said they didn't want anything for themselves and that they only wanted the government to solve the people's problems. On the last day of the talks, land reforms were discussed. The Maoists said that the government was not following its own laws on land redistribution. The government said that it would soon constitute a committee to look into the issue of land reforms. But in two month's time it was all over. Hostilities broke out again. The Maoists attacked a police party on 15 December 2004 in Visakhapatnam. The state retaliated by killing several rebels in January.

While the Maoists used the ceasefire period to breathe easy and regroup, the police used this opportunity to film leaders and their bodyguards and human couriers. Later, many of these were lured by the police to give away the location of several Maoist leaders who were then eliminated.

From then till recently, the Maoists had been on the backfoot in Andhra. It was dubbed as a major success story by the government, and other Maoist-affected states sought to replicate the Andhra model. The Maoists had suffered serious setbacks in Andhra but they had not been wiped out completely. Senior police officers maintained that the Maoists were trying to regroup along the Andhra-Orissa border. 'In Warangal, Khammam and Andhra-Orissa border, they still have a support base and are very much active there,' said Andhra's police chief, Aravinda Rao.

In an interview[16] to the author at the end of 2009, Maoist supremo Ganapathi termed the situation in Andhra as a 'temporary setback' for the Maoist movement and made it clear that the revival of movement in Andhra was very important for them. 'The objective conditions in which our revolution began in Andhra Pradesh have not undergone any basic change. This very fact continues to serve as the basis for the growth and intensification of our movement. Moreover, we now have a more consolidated mass base, a relatively better-trained people's guerilla army and an all-India party with deep roots among the basic classes who comprise the backbone of our revolution.

---

[16]'We shall certainly defeat the government', *Open Magazine*, 17 October 2009.

This is the reason why the reactionary rulers are unable to suppress our revolutionary war, which is now raging in several states in the country.

'We had taken appropriate lessons from the setback suffered by our party in Andhra Pradesh and, based on these lessons, drew up tactics in other states. Hence we are able to fight back the cruel all-round offensive of the enemy effectively, inflict significant losses on the enemy, preserve our subjective forces, consolidate our party, develop a people's liberation guerilla army, establish embryonic forms of new democratic people's governments in some pockets, and take the people's war to a higher stage. Hence we have an advantageous situation, overall, for reviving the movement in Andhra Pradesh,' he told me.

What Ganapathi said about objective conditions is not far from the truth. In Andhra Pradesh, over 20,000 farmers committed suicide between 1998 and 2008. Most of them were tenant farmers (those who take land owned by the landlords on lease). The total number of tenant farmers in Andhra is believed to be as high as 50 lakh. In 2009, there were 2,414 farmer suicides in Andhra. In December 2010, over 50 farmers committed suicide in the state's Krishna district alone.

Veteran police officer and former Director-General of the Border Security Force E.N. Rammohan, who was also appointed by the home ministry to probe the 6 April Dantewada Maoist ambush says that the primary reason why Maoism has flourished in states like Andhra Pradesh and Chhattisgarh is because of land ownership patterns and absence of rights among marginalised communities like the Adivasis. He remembers a time in the late '80s when he was posted in Hyderabad with the CBI, and went to meet the revenue minister along with his friend, the intelligence chief of the state. 'I told him openly that until the government does not implement land ceiling (limiting individual ownership of land) it would be impossible to defeat the Naxals. He said it was impossible and cited a friend's example who owned over a thousand acres of land. He said that friend would not even part with an inch of his land,' says Rammohan.[17]

Of course, that does not deter politicians from taking advantage of the situation for electoral gains. TDP leader Chandrababu Naidu during whose tenure compensation to farmers who committed suicide was withdrawn (by arguing that most of such cases were not related to agriculture) launched a hunger strike to highlight the plight of farmers. When he was the chief minister, the Congress party had bitterly opposed his decision to withdraw such compensation. And now when the Congress party is in power itself in the state, it is singing the same tune as Naidu's. In September 2010, the leading market research organisation IMRB conducted a survey for *The Times of India*[18] in the five districts of the Telangana region—Adilabad, Nizamabad, Karimnagar, Warangal and Khammam. The results were shocking. About two-thirds said that the overwhelming feeling of neglect of the areas

---

[17]Interview to *Tehelka*'s Shoma Chowdhury, 12 June 2010.

[18]*The Times of India*, 28 September 2010.

by the government was 'the root cause of disaffection'. In Warangal, this figure was as high as 81 per cent. Almost 60 per cent said that the Maoists were good for the area. Fifty per cent also felt that the Maoists had forced the government to focus on development work in affected areas.

By the end of 2010, the alarm bells had started ringing in Andhra Pradesh. Intelligence reports suggested that the Maoists were planning to cash in on the unrest generated by the Telangana agitation and the anti-Polavaram dam sentiments (the Polavaram dam project, officially called the Indira Sagar project, is supposed to be built at the Polavaram village of West Godavari district and it will displace about two lakh people, mostly tribals). In December 2010, during the tenth anniversary celebrations of the formation of PLGA, the Maoists finally struck after a gap of four years, killing two men, one of them a TDP leader. There were reports that a large group of Maoists had infiltrated from Chhattisgarh to stage a comeback in the state. Reports also pointed out that they were on a major recruitment drive in their erstwhile bastion. One of the senior Maoist leaders Ramakrishna (who led the talks with the Andhra government in 2004) was believed to be directing operations in the area. This led to a massive troop deployment in the area but owing to fear, night bus service in these areas was suspended.

In the same week, Maoist spokesperson in Dandakaranya Gudsa Usendi[19] said that apart from the PLGA two other

---

[19]In a party press release.

wings had been trained in warfare and would be deployed soon to launch attacks against security forces.

After the formation of the People's War Group, the Maoists adopted the fundamental programme of 'New Democratic Revolution'. It proposed to form the Janathana Sarkar or the People's Government in their areas of influence in Dandakaranya. This party programme is followed now by the CPI (Maoist) as well, in more or less the same avatar. The ultimate aim of the Indian revolution, the programme says, is to seize power. To the masses, the party document, however, guarantees the following fundamental rights:

- To express (speech, write, publication)
- To meet
- To form organisations
- To conduct strikes and demonstrations
- To live according to one's wish
- To have primary education
- To have primary medical treatment
- To gain minimum employment

In return for these fundamental rights, the people are required to fulfill the following duties:

- To protect the country
- To respect the constitution and law
- To protect the government properties

- To provide military services
- To pay taxes

The PWG document provides an assurance that the State (the Maoist state) shall not discriminate towards anyone in terms of tribe, caste, religion, nationality, gender, language, region, education, post and status. It shall deal with all as equals. It shall give equal opportunities to all. Citizens will have the right to believe or disbelieve religion and the state shall oppose all kinds of religious fundamentalism.

The document says that the party will confiscate the lands of landlords and religious organisations and distribute them to the poor, landless peasants and agricultural labourers on the basis of 'land to the tiller'. It shall strive for the development of agriculture.

The document further goes on to say that the party will confiscate all the industries, banks and other organisations of the 'imperialist and comprador bureaucratic bourgeois classes' and that it will dissolve the 'unequal financial agreements that the exploiting government made with the imperialists'.

The document envisages implementing an eight-hour working day for all the workers. It says that the contract work system will be dissolved and child labour abolished. It promises to provide equal wages for women and men and also provide social security and protective working conditions to all the workers.

The document also declares that women will be liberated from household drudgery to make them part of social production, political, military, government administration and other such activities. Prostitution, the document says,

95

will be banned, and rehabilitation would be provided to women. To implement this to some degree, it has taken a lot of effort on the part of women Maoist leaders to change the patriarchal set-up which also afflicts the tribals who form a majority of the Maoist cadre. Senior Maoist leader Narmada remembers[20] how it took time to drill into the minds of male guerillas that women were not only meant for cooking for the squad or performing other domestic chores. Now, the guerillas in a squad do everything irrespective of their gender. That means that while a man may prepare tea, a woman may venture in the forest to cut firewood or perform sentry duty. Initially, when the Maoists entered Dandakaranya, the women guerillas would wear saris and other traditional outfits. Narmada says it was the wife of senior Maoist leader Malla Raja Reddy, Comrade Nirmala, who insisted on wearing 'pant-shirt' like male members of the squad. There was a major debate in the CPI (Maoist) in the mid '80s whether there should be a separate organisation for women. Ultimately the senior women cadre prevailed and the Krantikari Adivasi Mahila Sangathan (Revolutionary Adivasi Women's Organisation) was formed. Today, it has about one lakh women as its members.

On the issue of marriage, the PWG document says that this should be allowed on the basis of 'mutual love and agreement'. The minimum age for marriage would be 20 years. Child marriages are banned and widow remarriages encouraged. Women also have a right to abortion.

---

[20]Interview to the author.

There have been occasional reports on the alleged sexual exploitation of the women cadre among the Maoist ranks. In 2010, a woman commander who said she had surrendered to the West Bengal police accused several high-ranking Maoist leaders of sexually exploiting her. In response to a question on her allegations, Ganapathi claimed that the woman commander had been kept in illegal custody by the police for almost a year and later asked to make such accusations against the Maoist leadership. But he also added that he doesn't deny that 'there are no shades of patriarchy in the party or that the men and women comrades haven't become its victims.' He emphasised that the Maoist leadership was 'fighting against the manifestations of patriarchy by increasing the political consciousness of our comrades and people, by taking up anti-patriarchal rectification campaigns and more than anything, increasing the consciousness, self-confidence and individuality of the women comrades and implementing pro-women policies firmly. It is a part of our practice to take disciplinary actions which include severe warning to expulsion from the party according to the severity of the mistake, on comrades who commit mistakes, however high they may be placed in the party.'

Such allegations notwithstanding, the women cadre is involved in the Maoist struggle at par with its male counterparts. About 40 per cent of the Maoist cadre comprises of women. They take part in attacks on security forces and other operations as much as male rebels. In fact, some of the most daring attacks on security forces—like the one on the camp of Eastern Frontier Rifles in Silda in

West Bengal on 15 February 2010, that resulted in the death of 24 policemen—are believed to have been led by women commanders. Three women Maoists, disguised as dancers, had conducted a reconnaissance of the Silda camp on the morning of the attack. One of them, Sambari Hansda alias Seema was arrested by security forces on 17 December 2010, from the Lakhinpur forest in West Midnapore district.

Maoist documents say that Village Janathana Sarkars may be formed in an area of 500-3,000 population. The Party Constitution reveals that the ultimate aim or maximum programme of the party is the establishment of communist society. This, the document says, will be carried out and completed through armed agrarian revolutionary war. That is the protracted people's war will be carried out by encircling the cities from the countryside and thereby finally capturing them. Hence the countryside and the protracted people's war has remained as the centre of gravity of the party's work from the very beginning.

The military aspect of the Maoist doctrine says that the revolution goes through three phases: strategic defence, strategic equilibrium and strategic offence. A weak force can defeat a bigger and more sophisticated force only through guerilla warfare depending on extensive involvement of the masses. So, guerilla warfare is the method adopted to protect 'people's forces' and 'people's organisations.' As these forces develop into an established army, a 'people's liberation army', it evolves into mobile warfare where, besides self defence, the Maoists wipe out enemy forces. At present the Maoist movement in India is at the stage of strategic defence where in some areas they have been able to shift from guerilla warfare to mobile warfare.

In the 2007 Unity Congress, held in Bheembandh area of Bihar, the party gave a call for getting into the mobile warfare phase. However, Ganapathi believes that in most of the areas, the strategic defence phase will last for some more time. 'It is difficult to predict how long it will take to pass this stage and go to the stage of strategic equilibrium or strategic stalemate. It depends on the transformation of our guerilla zones into base areas, creation of more guerilla zones and Red resistance areas across the country, the development of our PLGA,' he said.

Who can be a member of the CPI (Maoist)? The Maoist document says that any resident of India who has reached 16 years of age, who belongs to the worker, peasant or toiling masses or the petty-bourgeoisie, accepts Marxism-Leninism-Maoism as his/her guiding ideology, accepts the party programme and constitution, actively participates in party activities under any of the party units and observes the unit's discipline, prepares to face the dangers encountered in the course and agrees to pay regularly membership fees and levies that are decided by the party unit, may become a party member. (The membership fee is Rs 10 per annum). Every applicant must be recommended by two party members. It also says that proven renegades, enemy agents, careerists, individuals of bad character, degenerates and such alien class-elements will not be admitted into the party.

In July 1994, the party gave a call for the setting up of new organs of power—the Gram Rajya Committees (GRCs). Led by a party member, the GRCs were envisaged as a rudimentary form of people's government. It is through these GRCs that the Maoists are trying to establish their authority in the villages. A base area, apart from certain military aspects, must have a self-sufficient economy. From the Chinese experience the Maoists have realised that the State seeks to crush a base area not only militarily but also by putting up economic blockades. So, the Maoists have undertaken a lot of development work in their areas of influence. In the south Bastar division, the party mobilised villagers to build a number of tanks to store water. This was done by electing a tank construction committee in every village involved. For example in Basaguda village, people of nine villages formed a tank construction committee and built a dam. Overall, people from 30 villages participated in this project. In Konta area, after a landlord was killed, a big tank on the land he owned was occupied by the local Maoist platoon. As the number of households in that village was only 25, it was decided to mobilise villagers from neighbouring villages as well. A total of 355 people from 12 villages were involved in the work. In some cases, the police would return and damage such projects. In Poosanar village, the police is believed to have damaged a tank constructed by the villagers and used it to ambush Maoist rebels.

The Adivasis' one culinary obsession is fish. The Maoists have introduced fish culture on a large scale. Maoist ideologues say some of it is sold and marketed in Delhi and Kolkata. A large variety of vegetables was also introduced including tomato, brinjal, onion, chilli among others. In 1997-98 alone, about 20,000 saplings of fruit trees were distributed among people in about 100 villages. In 1996-98, about 100 oxen were distributed to a few families in south Bastar. Most of them were confiscated from rich landlords. A number of rice mills were also constructed.

In the field of education, the Maoists have done a tremendous job. All new recruits who join the Maoist fold, are made literate within a year. In hundreds of mobile and permanent schools run in their base areas, the Maoists educate children through BBC documentaries on science. Other modern educational aids are used as well. Apart from the regular curriculum, classes on political education and general knowledge are also conducted. Currently, the Maoists are working hard to create a curriculum in Gondi language. As mentioned earlier, Gondi has no script. But that has not deterred Maoists from introducing textbooks in Gondi language for primary classes in a few subjects including mathematics and social sciences. These books also contain lessons on hygiene and the ills of superstition. At various places, government teachers are encouraged to take classes regularly. In certain cases in Chhattisgarh and Jharkhand, even the teacher's salary and his/her accommodation is being taken care of by the CPI (Maoist). Adult education classes are also run in their villages of influence at times when the villagers are mostly free from their agricultural work.

In the field of health as well, the Maoists often fill in large gaps left by the state. Their mobile medical units cover large distances to offer primary health care to tribals. Most of the guerilla squads have one person trained at a central medical camp. In every village the Maoists choose a few youth to be given basic medical training. It involves identifying common diseases, their symptoms, and then providing medicines for these. Various training camps are held regularly on preventive measures against diseases such as diarrhoea or malaria. The grass-root doctors in the medical squads can administer vaccines, identify a number of diseases through symptoms, and treat injuries that are not severe. Some can even conduct simple blood tests to arrive at a diagnosis. This is a significant advantage in such areas. For instance, on the Maharashtra-Chhattisgarh border, a hospital run by social activist Prakash Amte and his family attracts tribal patients from a radius of 200 km. A number of patients suffering from snake or bear bites or malaria or cholera are often brought on a string cot from afar to be treated at Amte's hospital. In Chhattisgarh's Dantewada district, which has a population of 70 lakh, there are only 12 doctors with an MBBS degree. Out of them, nine are either posted at the district hospital or are into administrative jobs.[21]

But despite all these efforts, the life of the Adivasis is still far from better. As a tribal Maoist rebel, Comrade Kosa told the writer Satnam[22] in the year 2001 in a guerilla

---

[21]Aman Sethi, 'Death stalks disease-hit Dantewada', *The Hindu*, 10 October 2010.

[22]Quoted from Satnam's *Jangalnama* published by Penguin Books India, 2010.

camp in Bastar: 'Would you like to know what we eat here? Fish, rice, wild fruits, etc., appear sumptuous, and from a distance, one might imagine jungle life to be ideal, where there is no dearth of food. But, if you go out of this camp and look around in the villages, you won't find many elderly men or women—our people rarely reach the age of 50, as far as I know. Death begins chasing us right from birth and seizes us as we approach 50 years of age.'

In the early part of this decade, efforts to establish complete guerilla bases were sharpened by the constitution of Revolutionary People's Committees (RPCs). The base is an area where the police or other organs of the state cannot enter at all. It serves as the basic organ of the liberated zone. In Dandakaranya, the most prominent liberated base is Abujhmaad that the Maoists call the Central Guerilla Base.

The Party's Organisational Structure

In February 2007, the CPI (Maoist) held its ninth Party Congress called the Unity Congress (the highest body of the Maoists is the Party Congress). It was held in high secrecy in the jungles of Bihar's Bheembandh area. The Congress was held in a huge area with a number of facilities available for those who attended it. Almost every senior Maoist leader, including its top brass attended the Congress. The area had a parade ground and a huge hall where strategies were discussed and debates held. It had a computer room with a team of operators and translators. Generators were put up that ran for 15 hours a day to enable computers, photocopiers and other electronic appliances to function. The Congress was set up next to a stream from where water was taken, boiled and then used for drinking purposes. An open kitchen ensured two meals and multiple rounds of tea for the 'delegates'. Various groups had been formed that were in charge of security, cultural performances, kitchen, health, media and even electric supply. The security was handled by senior Maoist leader and head of the eastern military command, Misir Besra alias Comrade Sunirmal (he was later arrested in September 2007 in Jharkhand and subsequently rescued by his men from a court in Bihar in June 2009). Many important strategies were discussed and announced during the Congress. It was agreed that till the establishment of Base Areas it is destruction (of enemy power) that will be the primary task and construction that will be secondary, and that in the process of establishment of Base Areas and their consolidation, the relation between destruction and construction gradually undergoes a change. The question of the nature and extent of the changes that have taken place in developed rural areas like Punjab was discussed and also whether in a country like India the election question was one of strategic significance or just another tactical question (it was decided finally that it is of strategic significance). Then a resolution was passed that called for the arming of the People's Liberation Guerilla Army with better weaponry and the arming of militia. It called for intensifying the war in the nine guerilla zones and four Red Resistance Areas and also spreading the war to new areas. Finally, it gave call for the immediate development of Dandakaranya and B-J (Bihar-Jharkhand) into Base Areas.[23]

In the period between two Congresses, the Maoists consider the Central Committee (CC) as their highest body. The Central Committee elects a general secretary of the party who acts as a sort of supreme commander. It also elects a Politbureau (PB). Between one Central Committee meeting and the next, the Politbureau is authorised to take political, organisational and military decisions that need to be later ratified in the subsequent central committee meeting. The general secretary also acts as the in charge of the Politbureau. The PB and CC are on the same level but the PB has special duties and responsibilities which it will fulfill on behalf of the CC in between two CC meetings. In the current PB, there are 14 members half of whom are either in jail or have been eliminated recently. In the Central Committee, there are about 40 members. The CC also forms the Central Military Commission and then there are state military commissions as well.

In the political structure of the party, below the Central Committee there is a Central Regional Bureau that is handled by a PB member. Below this comes various State Committees or Special Zone Committees or Special Area Committees. For instance, Andhra has a State Committee, Dandakaranya has a Special Zone Committee and there is a Special Area Committee in Bihar-Jharkhand. Below this

---

[23]As reported in *People's March*, April 2007.

comes the Regional Committee. Dandakaranya has three Regional Committees. After that comes the District Committee—two or three under a Regional Committee. After that there is an Area Committee, followed by a Village Party Committee. The most basic organ of the party is a party cell, comprising of about five people.

The People's Liberation Guerilla Army comprises of three main sections. The main force consists of armed battalions and companies of Maoist guerillas. A battalion has 250 guerillas while a company consists of about 90 soldiers. The secondary force is made of platoons and local guerilla squads. There are about 30 soldiers in a platoon whereas a squad has about eight to ten guerillas. In the last comes the base force that comprises of civil militia, members of the Gram Rakshak Dal and mass militia also known as Bhumkal Militia. The base force is mainly used to cut the supply lines. In a typical ambush in which, say, a hundred Maoists may take part, more than half will belong to the base force. After the initial assault by the main or secondary force, the base force will snatch weapons or prevent enforcement to come to the aid of ambushed security men. Of the base force, the Bhumkal Militia is mostly used to deal with Salwa Judum, the civil militia supported by the police to counter the Maoists, and they usually carry only traditional weapons. The strength of the hardcore fighting force of the PLGA is estimated to be around 10,000.

The supreme military organ of the CPI (Maoist) is its Central Military Commission (CMC). Various State Military Commissions report to the CMC, followed by various Regional Commands. A number of Regional Commands come under District or Division Commands. The basic military organ is the Village Command. Dandakaranya, for example, has ten divisions.

The Party Congress is held to take care of the following tasks:

- It undertakes the political and organisational review of the party since the preceding Congress.
- It adopts and amends the party programme, party constitution and the strategy and tactics and financial policy and formulates other policy matters.
- Appraises the domestic and international situation and lays down the tasks.
- Decides the number of Central Committee members and elects the Central Committee and alternate CC members. For example in the last Congress, Anuradha Ghandy was elected as a Central Committee member and till her death she was the only woman in the CC (apart from CC member Shiela Didi who is under arrest in Chaibasa jail in Jharkhand).

Funding

The Maoists say that most of their money comes from the taxes or levies they collect from various government agencies or businessmen who work in their area of influence. So, if a government contractor is working on a project in, say, Latehar district of Jharkhand, he has to pay a percentage of his expenditure to the local Maoist leadership. Some believe that in various areas, the Maoists even take a cut from the money available for development schemes like the National Rural Employment Guarantee Scheme (NREGS). It is a different matter that while the Maoists may be content with a ten percent cut, the government official may take even twenty. Of late, the Maoists have also been accused of having a nexus with corporates such as mining companies. A recent report[24] by the Asian Centre for Human Rights cites intelligence reports that at least three Jharkhand-based corporate houses have paid 2.5 million rupees each to the Maoists in 2007-08. It also cites a newspaper report of October 2010 quoting Jharkhand's secretary for rural development, M.K. Satpathy saying that the Maoists had blocked 21 road construction projects sanctioned by the government when the contractors refused to pay them levy. It quotes what it calls the 'secret service reports' of the Government of India according to which the iron ore, mines and crusher units of Jharkhand contribute Rs 500 crore to the Maoists. The Maoists, however, vehemently deny allegations of their nexus with the corporates. 'They (the government) are even alleging that we are collecting 5,000 crores of rupees annually . . . In fact, our party mainly collects donations from the people and funds from the traders in our guerilla zones. We have a clear people's financial policy. And our party also collects rational levy from contractors who take up various works in our areas. A considerable part of these funds is spent for welfare of the people through our

---

[24]India Human Rights Report, July-September 2010.

people's power organs. As for mining organisations, our people are fighting their best not to allow them into our strong areas. Our party is leading these struggles, it is supporting them. So the issue of collecting funds from them does not arise,' said Ganapathi. There have also been unconfirmed reports of Maoists encouraging poppy cultivation, particularly in Bihar, to raise money.

Weapons

Most of the grass-root Maoist cadres carry rudimentary weapons such as muzzle-loading rifles or country-made revolvers apart from traditional weapons such as bows and arrows. Over the years, however, the PLGA has acquired a huge cache of weapons, mostly through raiding police armouries or snatching them from policemen killed in encounters. In a series of daring raids on a police training school, district armoury and three police stations in Orissa's Nayagarh district on 15 February 2008, Maoist guerillas looted more than a thousand sophisticated arms including Kalashnikov rifles and light machine guns. The raids lasted for about five hours. Later, some of the outdated rifles were found abandoned in the forests since the Maoists could not carry them. In February 2004, in the state's Koraput district, the erstwhile PWG cadre had seized more than 500 rifles. The Maoists have also developed expertise in preparing deadly IEDs—Improvised Explosive Devices. The experts among the Maoist guerillas can trigger them with the help of rudimentary things like syringes, camera flashbulbs or even V-shaped twigs scattered in the forest. Reports[25] suggest that they have also developed expertise to clone modern rifles like the AK-47 in factories run by them in their areas of influence.

Over the past few years, the Maoists have developed working relations with various north-east insurgent groups like the Assam-based ULFA or the Nagaland-based NSCN-IM or the Manipur-based Revolutionary People's Front (RPF). In fact, in a joint statement released on 22 October 2008, the Maoists and the RPF declared 'full moral and political support to each other in the liberation struggles to overthrow the common enemy, the Indian reactionary and oppressive regime, respectively.' Police sources say that the Maoists also buy arms that are smuggled mostly through Bangladesh and Myanmar. There have been reports[26] of senior Maoist leaders including Kishenji meeting ULFA leaders, and the Maoists setting up bases for their overground workers in Dibrugarh and Tinsukia districts of Assam. There have also been reports of the NSCN-IM cadre travelling to a Maoist base in Chhattisgarh and offering to provide them with superior training. Security agencies fear that the Maoists may also be looking at some kind of working relationship with the Islamic Jihadis. Ganapathi denies this. 'By propagating the lie that our party has links with groups linked to Pakistan's ISI, the reactionary rulers of our country want to prove that we too are terrorists and gain legitimacy for their brutal terror campaign against Maoists and the people in

[25]Vishwa Mohan, *The Times of India*, 18 January 2010.

[26]R. Dutta Choudhury, *The Assam Tribune*, 13 February 2010.

the areas of armed agrarian struggle,' he said. However he believes that 'it is only Maoist leadership that can provide correct anti-imperialist orientation and achieve class unity among Muslims as well as people of other religious persuasions. The influence of Muslim fundamentalist ideology and leadership will diminish as communist revolutionaries and other democratic-secular forces increase their ideological influence over the Muslim masses. As communist revolutionaries, we always strive to reduce the influence of the obscurantist reactionary ideology and outlook of the mullahs and maulvis on the Muslim masses, while uniting with all those fighting against the common enemy of the world people—that is, imperialism, particularly American imperialism.'

Prominent Leaders and Ideologues of the Maoist Movement

- Mupalla Laxman Rao alias Ganapathi is the supreme commander of the CPI (Maoist). He is from the Beerpur village of Andhra's Karimnagar district. Around 60, he is a science graduate and holds a B.Ed degree as well. A former teacher, he is presently married to a Maoist commander. A photo of his surfaced for the first time when a few videos of the 2007 Maoist Congress were recovered from the laptop of an arrested Maoist rebel. He wears spectacles and changes his location frequently.

- Mallojula Koteshwara Rao alias Kishenji is the man behind the Lalgarh rebellion. He is aged about 60 and hails from Naachpalli village of Karimnagar district. He joined the Maoist movement at a very young age, when as a college student he was drawn to the Telangana movement. He was believed to have been seriously wounded in an encounter in Lalgarh in 2010. But Maoist sources say he is safe but lying low to evade arrest. He is married to a Maoist commander.

- Prashant Bose alias Kishan alias Nirbhay da was the chief of MCC before the party merged with the PWG to form the CPI (Maoist). He is aged nearly 72. Not much is known about him.

- Kobad Ghandy, arrested in Delhi in September 2009. (*See* 'The Rebel' p. 135)

- Sushil Roy, aged 72 is the senior-most Maoist leader in jail, arrested in May 2005 from Kolkata. He is the nephew of the legendary revolutionary of Bengal, Dinesh Gupta.

- Venugopal Rao alias Sonu is Kishenji's younger brother and is one of the first few Maoist cadres to have entered Bastar.

- Amitabha Bagchi, arrested in Jharkhand on 24 August 2009. The Maoists had named him along with Sushil Roy and Kobad Ghandy to talk with the government on behalf of the CPI (Maoist).

- Bansidhar Singh alias Chintan da arrested from Kanpur in February 2010 (*See* 'The Urban Agenda' p. 153.)

- Sabyasachi Panda, aged about 42, believed to be the mastermind behind the Nayagarh raid of 2007 and the attack on Greyhound commandos in Balimela reservoir, resulting in the death of 38 of them. Both his father and brother are politicians. The most wanted Maoist leader in Orissa, he has many admirers including politicians. Orissa's deputy leader of the Opposition, Narsingha Mishra said of him, 'His voice is the voice of 57 per cent people in Orissa who have only Rs 12 to spend per day. It's this injustice against poor, which made him a Naxal. I admire his ideas but disapprove of his violence.' His wife Subhashree Panda alias Mili was arrested in January 2010.

- Narla Ravi Sharma, arrested from Patna in October 2009, along with his wife Anuradha, also a Maoist leader. He has a doctorate in agricultural science and was active in Jharkhand.

- Akkiraju Haragopal alias Ramakrishna is a former teacher who led the talks with the Andhra Pradesh government in 2004. His wife Padmakka, who worked as a teacher was arrested in November 2010. Ramakrishna is believed to be active on the Andhra-Orissa border.

- Malla Raja Reddy, arrested from Kerala in December 2007. He was later released on bail owing to ill-health. He escaped and is believed to have rejoined the Maoists in Bastar.

- Lanka Papi Reddy alias Ranganna, in his late forties now, surrendered to the police in February 2008. He said he surrendered due to ill-health and also because he was disillusioned. The Maoists later said that he was demoted because he had misbehaved with women comrades and that is why he surrendered.

Other senior leaders who are still underground include the chief of the Central Military Commission, Nambala Keshava Rao alias Ganganna, Varanasi Subramanium, Misir Besra, and Gudsa Usendi.

Some of the senior leaders killed in recent times (most of them in alleged fake encounters with the police) include Patel Sudhakar Reddy, K. Saketh Rajan, Cherukuri Rajkumar alias Azad, Sande Rajamouli, Sakhamuri Appa Rao, Solipeta Kondal Reddy, and Wadkapur Chandramouli. Almost all of them are from Andhra Pradesh. This is another criticism the CPI (Maoist) faces that the party leadership mainly consists of members from Andhra Pradesh and that there is little presence of women, Adivasis and Dalits in the Maoist leadership. Ganapathi contests this, saying, 'It is very natural for more comrades to be elected where our movement is strong.' He further goes on to say, 'Though we are striving to have more leadership from the oppressed classes, we had lost a majority of them in the enemy offensive and we want to clearly say that it is becoming a hindrance in achieving this goal. For example, in Andhra Pradesh more than 400 women comrades were killed by fascist governments. Most of them were from the background of oppressed classes and castes. Many educated women comrades who came from a middle-class background were killed too. Many martyred women comrades were quite capable of developing and were supposed to come into state committees and central committees of the party. Not just in the CC, but in the state committees too we have comrades from such backgrounds. It is obvious that it is these comrades who would be elected to the higher committees in the future.'

There also have been concerns about the senior Maoist leaders approaching old age and the subsequent question of whether there was a second-rung leadership in place and if it was capable of effective leadership. 'It is a fact that some of the party leaders at the central and state level could be described as senior citizens according to criteria used by the government, that is, those who have crossed the threshold of 60 years. You can start calling me too a senior citizen in a few months,' Ganapathi said in an interview with me in 2009. But he said that the party did not consider old age a serious problem. 'You can see the "senior citizens" in our party working for 16-18 hours a day and covering long distances on foot,' he said.

That reminded me of what a young PLGA commander told me in Jharkhand in 2009. 'We know we have faced severe losses in terms of leadership. But we are ready to don the mantle now. We are ready to take forward the legacy of GP sir,' (Ganapathi is referred as GP sir by many Maoist guerillas).

VII

THE GUERILLAS, THE REPUBLIC

Do not fear death so much but rather the inadequate life.
—Bertolt Brecht

How can you frighten a man whose hunger is not only in his own cramped stomach but in the wretched bellies of his children? You can't scare him—he has known a fear beyond every other.

—John Steinbeck

What is it that has attracted the young men and women of Dandakaranya into the Maoist fold? After all, apart from the hardcore 10,000 strength of the Maoist's People's Liberation Guerilla Army, there are hundreds of thousands of Adivasi youth who are associated with the Maoists in the form of civil militia and other base force (*see* the structure of the Maoists pp. 103–115). The Adivasis have no reference point to a better life. They have few aspirations apart from, perhaps, better food. Nothing has changed in these parts of the country for centuries except a sense of empowerment engendered by the Maoists.

It is the monsoon of 2010, and I am in a Maoist camp, set along an angry river, somewhere on the Maharashtra-Chhattisgarh border. The camp is big, and at any given point of time, squads of Maoist rebels are coming and going from the camp. There is a constant flurry of activity. Young men and women go about doing their duty with surgical precision. In one corner, men are helping in cooking food, two girls are chopping firewood, and in another, a cultural troupe is rehearsing for an evening show in a nearby village. In an open tent—essentially a thick sheet of plastic spread over a jute rope—a senior Maoist leader is conducting a strategy class for young recruits. Some girls are combing their hair and massaging it with coconut oil—their only indulgence. A small tape recorder plays Gondi songs.

The day begins very early in the camp. Those who are out on sentry duty at night will return, and another group will replace them. The security around the camp is multi-layered. If the police are spotted, the Maoists will get at least an hour to run away to safety. Though the last time police were seen in this area was when they passed through a neighbouring village around two years back. There are military drills and then the camp in-charge blows a whistle that means food is ready. Every guerilla carries a kit bag inside which is a uniform, a steel plate and a mug, a jhilli (thick plastic sheet) to sleep on, thread and needle, some medicines and books. There will also be a few things like a toothbrush and some kerosene oil to clean one's weapon, a knife and a torch. And there will be ammunition. Each one carries a weapon according to the training he or she has undergone. That means that the guerillas with advanced training may carry sophisticated weapons like an AK-47 or an INSAS rifle, while new recruits carry a .303 rifle. The food is very basic: rice, dal and some pickles. Occasionally, there will be eggs or the odd chicken, cooked with its guts intact. Food is precious and is not wasted at all though every guerilla can eat to his or her heart's content. During military classes, they might learn big words like comprador, bourgeoisie or imperialism, but the motto for an ordinary cadre is: *datt kar khao, datt kar chalo* (eat as much as you can, walk as much as you can). The Maoists walk a lot. No camp stays at one place for more than a few days. On an average, a Maoist squad walks anything between 25-50 km a day or even more depending on circumstances. A camp is dismantled within minutes. And then one moves on.

The rest of the day is spent in political and military classes. There are constant patrols around the area. In their free time, the guerillas read and write, and listen to the radio. In the evening, the senior cadres assemble at one place and listen to the Hindi service of the BBC on radio. That is their only way of keeping abreast of developments around the world.

The night that I am there, there is a small news item on All India Radio, Raipur, that the Chhattisgarh government has decided to give half a day's wages to labourers to enable them to collect the wages due to them under the National Rural Employment Guarantee Act (NREGA)—many NREGA beneficiaries live in far-flung villages and don't even have the money to go to the nearest post office to collect their dues, hence this populist decision. The guerillas laugh about it. 'You cannot expect looters to turn into saints. They will always remain looters,' says one of them.

I have arrived at the camp after walking for days through the forest. In the first hour of our arrival, two guerillas spot a poisonous snake with another snake in its mouth. It is killed immediately. 'If it bites you, you will die in twenty minutes flat,' one of them tells me, while another laughs. It is green everywhere, and it has been raining for days. While walking through the mud and slush, it almost feels as if one is in Vietnam.

The night before we arrived at the camp, we had halted at an Adivasi's hut, along with the Maoist squad. Under the influence of mahua or maybe in spite of the mahua, the Adivasi began to cry after some time as he forced a few morsels of rice down his throat.

'Why are you crying?' Maoist squad leader Samayya asked him in Gondi.

'I feel like crying,' he replied.

When the Maoists establish camps like these, villagers from around keep on trickling into its fringes. Here as well, a few villagers have arrived from the nearby village. Some of them have connections with the Maoists. An old man's daughter was a part of the Chetna Natya Manch—the Maoists' cultural troupe, and was killed in police action elsewhere a few months ago. Three other men from this village are also Maoist guerillas.

Vanessa, a French journalist who is with us, tries speaking to them in broken Hindi that a senior Maoist leader translates into Gondi. Vanessa is keen to know whether there is a school nearby and if a teacher ever takes classes there.

The leader translates it for them. There is silence for a few seconds. Then the one whose name is Dolu, laughs. His laughter doesn't stop for almost a minute. And when it does, it is almost as if he has applied brakes to it. 'Guruji!' he speaks with the same wonder with which he utters the word 'Dilli'. 'Guruji, he comes every year on 15 August, *jhanda phehraate hain* (unfurls the flag), and that is it. We never see him again,' he says, astonished that anybody should ask him about the schoolteacher, as if this is what schoolteachers are supposed to do. A young woman—a child suckling at her breast—walks over to the small group and kicks a mongrel. It runs away, whimpering, taking refuge beside two Maoists who sit on their haunches on one side.

In this part of the country, I think, there is hardly any difference between a mongrel and an Adivasi. Upon being kicked by the woman, the mongrel ran to the Maoists just as the Adivasis ran to them after being kicked by the State.

Two villagers have died of diarrhoea just a week before we arrive at the village next to the Maoist camp. The villagers grow paddy but in the absence of proper knowledge, the crop often falls victim to disease. To avoid this, the Adivasis can, at best, perform a dev puja through the vadde—the local witch doctor. The paddy they grow is not enough to fill their bellies. So their staple diet is rice gruel. The nearest ration shop is about 20 km away. 'But by the time we come to know the ration has arrived, it is already over,' says a villager. Many have run away, to work as labourers in Mumbai and Pune.

While senior guerillas like Tarakka can talk about their reasons for joining the Maoist fold, most of the younger lot shy away from the subject, often citing constraints of language as a reason. Even when leaders who can speak in Gondi and then translate it to us in Hindi or English offer to do so, it is difficult to get the younger guerillas to open up, especially the girls. It is futile to ask them why they joined just as it is futile to ask Adivasis in the villages what they would want in terms of a better life. The younger lot has no specific answer to the question about why they joined the rebellion. Only when one spends time with them does one understand that it is mostly because the uniform offers them a sense of who they are, makes them one large group, gives them some purpose in life.

It is also because in these parts the Maoists are the face

of governance rather than government officials. So for many Adivasis, joining a Maoist medical unit is like joining a government health centre.

The Maoist medical teams distribute medicines among the villagers and even anti-malaria or anti-venom vaccine. Eventually, some end up joining them. Take the case of 14-year-old Suresh who is now a part of Chetna Natya Manch. 'We dissuaded him from joining us at such a young age but he followed us for weeks,' says his team leader Raju. Suresh used to go a local paathshala run by the tribal affairs ministry. 'But the food there was so bad and erratic, I ran away,' he says. Suresh has returned to his village after months, since he travels with the troupe from one village to another. His mother has come to meet him. 'I ask him to come back,' she says, 'but he refuses.'

It is a sense of identity that prevents Suresh from leaving the Maoists. The work they do and the guns his senior comrades carry give him a purpose in life. It is the same sense of identity that prevents another young boy from removing his cap. It is olive green with a star. On its tip, he has scribbled the name given to him by the party: Viju. 'Some comrades who knew his original name would call him by that and he would get upset,' says another guerilla. 'That is why he wrote "Viju" on his cap.'

Some of the guerillas stay in touch with their families. They write letters, and sometimes get to visit them as well. A commander who is in charge of the camp security said he regularly sends letters to his mother. Commander Samayya joined the Maoists in 2003. He comes from a village on the Andhra Pradesh-Chhattisgarh border. 'There was a landlord in my village who had 200 acres of land. He would employ the rest of us as labourers and pay us Rs 30 for a hard day's labour,' he said. Samayya says he would often think of how a single man in his village owned so much land while others had a tough time even getting enough to eat. In early 2000, he remembers, a Maoist squad came to his village. 'They spoke to us, and said: "land to the tiller",' he said. Samayya joined them soon afterwards. A year later, the Maoists took away the landlord's land and distributed it among those who worked on it.

Samayya has taken part in many actions against the police. His first brush with death took place in the Dodai encounter in Chhattisgarh's Narayanpur area when his platoon attacked a police party. Eighteen policemen were injured but four Maoists lost their lives, including a close friend of Samayya, a young guerilla called Mangtu. 'He took a bullet in his chest. We took him away and tried to get him to a hospital but could not. Finally, after lingering on for two days he died,' said Samayya.

Samayya also took part in the October 2009 attack on police personnel in Gadchiroli's Laheri area in which 17 policemen lost their lives. It was led by the military head of the Maoists' Gadchiroli Division, Commander Eiatu.

Eiatu who is in his mid thirties is a lean man with a thick moustache. His brother was also a senior Maoist leader and was allegedly killed in a fake encounter along with his partner in 2008. 'They were members of the Maharashtra State Committee and were picked up by the Andhra Special Intelligence Branch men from Kolhapur, taken to the jungles of Andhra and then shot dead,' Eiatu says. His other brother is also a senior Maoist commander elsewhere, while Eiatu's partner works with the Maoists' doctor brigade. 'I meet her sometimes,' he says.

The Maoist leadership is quite open about relationships. The cadres can marry if both partners are willing, and in most cases, the leadership takes a lenient view by trying to place the couple close to each other's area of operation. There have been instances where two partners have held back in the wake of an encounter with the police and sacrificed their lives while letting other squad members escape. Bearing children is, however, not encouraged. Later that night, Eiatu offers us glimpses of the military planning that went into the Laheri attack he had led. 'Just before the Assembly election, the police had created fear in village after village to coerce people into submission,' he says. One day, a platoon of Maoists got information that a team of police commandos, led by their leader Rama, was moving in the area. For two days, the guerillas followed them, without as much as stopping for food. Finally, hostilities broke out at Laheri in Bhamragarh taluka, just 750 yards away from the Laheri police station. Some 42 policemen and 18 Maoist guerillas (who'd reached before their other exhausted comrades), found themselves locked in a fierce gun battle. 'The police have a lot of ammunition,' elaborates Eiatu, 'and they just lay on the ground, firing thousands of rounds all over. But since we have limited ammunition, we fire at specific targets.'

The policemen, Eiatu says, kept shouting that the guerillas would be mowed down since police reinforcements were coming, but they held their ground—and upped the ante. The police, he says, also fired mortar shells. But for the first thirty minutes, nobody was injured on either side. Then, in the next ten minutes, six policemen were killed. After that, Eiatu claims, most policemen fled, including their leader. Eight policemen who had taken positions at one particular spot were asked to surrender. 'But they let out another volley of bullets in which our senior comrade was killed,' says Eiatu. After that, the guerillas let their guns blaze—killing the eight of them and three others. In all, 19 weapons were seized in that encounter.

That the Maoist guerillas are more motivated and better trained than the security forces becomes clear in such incidents. In fact, a young Maoist guerilla who surrendered a few years back and now leads certain anti-Maoist operations in Chhattisgarh said it clearly. After he quit the movement he was sent by the police with dozens of other men to train with the army in Kashmir. Before that, he received training with the Naga battalion of the CRPF. 'But I tell you, the training was nothing in comparison with the training given by Naxals. They have a lot of *jazba* (motivation) . . . But look at the central forces. You just need to burst a cracker, and they will all roll over to one side. Naxals burst Laxmi crackers and the CRPF exhaust their ammunition in the return fire,' he said.[27]

'If they had surrendered, we would have let them go after snatching their weapons,' says Samayya of the eight policemen they killed in the last phase of the Laheri

---

[27]In an interview to *The Times of India*'s Supriya Sharma.

encounter. But have they ever done this? 'Many times,' he says. He cites the example of an encounter with the Special Task Force personnel in Kuddur-Narayanpur in 2007, where he claims they treated three injured jawans and sent them back. 'One of them had begged us not to kill him; he said he had children. We just talked to them about our party, bandaged their wounds, and dropped them at the nearest road head,' says Samayya.

But such occurrences are rare. Most encounters end in bloodshed. In the past eighteen months, says Eiatu, 77 guns—mostly AK-47 and INSAS rifles—have been snatched after such actions in Gadchiroli district alone.

Now, since the government is keen to flush out Maoists, it is inevitable that such encounters have increased. Sometimes, in their attempt to get at Maoists, the police forces end up further alienating the people.

A month before 76 soldiers were mowed down by Maoists in Dantewada, two things arrived in Gadchiroli's Pavarvel village, bordering Chhattisgarh. The first was a baby boy born to an Adivasi woman, Indu Bai. He died within an hour of his birth. The mother followed a day later. In Pavarvel and all other neighbouring villages, pregnancies are handled by elderly women. For everything else there is Devi puja since there is not even a primary health centre. There is no electricity but the villagers claim that a gram panchayat official comes every year to collect electricity tax. Water comes from a ramshackle bore-pump.

The other arrival was that of a police party. It had not come to apprehend Naxalites who the villagers say arrive at any hour every now and then, demand food, and slip back into the jungle. Pavarvel itself is in the thick of the forest. There is hardly any road, and if you don't have a local guide with you, it will probably take you weeks to figure out your location. In the forests full of mahua and other trees, there are memorials erected by the Naxalites in memory of their fallen comrades.

So, yes, the police arrived not for Naxals but to teach Bajirao Potawe, a simple tribal, a lesson. They went straight to his house and beat him up. 'With their boots and lathis,' Potawe says. 'They said bad things to my mother and sister, called me a bastard and said how dare my family accuse them of rape,' he recalls. Then they made him run errands like fetching water to cook a meal of dal and rice which they took away with them. Of course, Potawe hasn't been able to eat such meals for a long time. In fact, he has been living with his wife without a marriage ceremony. The ceremony demands a feast for the villagers, and until the villagers in turn collect some rice and give it to the family, the ceremony cannot happen. Now that is difficult since rice is a luxury for Potawe's neighbours as well.

The victim of the rape which the police party referred to was a 13-year-old girl, the sister-in-law of Bajirao Potawe's brother, Kaju Potawe. The girl, who lives in the neighbouring village of Tudmel, had come to his sister's house for treatment of her illness through Devi puja. She had stayed back, working as a labourer at a school construction site nearby.

It was on the evening of 4 March 2009, that a party of Maharashtra Police's C-60 Commando group came to

Pavarvel, led by a notorious commander Munna Thakur. The C-60 is a special anti-Naxal force mostly of policemen from the Adivasi regions (the police party ambushed in Laheri was also from this force). Reports suggest that the group saw a man running with a tribal water-flask made out of dried pumpkin. The police fired at him but he got away. It was the misfortune of the Potawe family that the man ran away towards the forest behind their house. In a minute, the police party entered their house and beat Kaju Potawe, who had just returned from the jungle after collecting wild berries. 'They kept asking me about Naxal whereabouts. When I said I didn't know they beat me more,' he says.

It was then that the police party saw Kaju's sister-in-law, the teenage girl. 'They dragged her by her hair and accused her of being a Naxal,' recalls Kaju. Later they asked another villager Dayaram Jangi and his family to vacate their house. Dayaram Jangi had also let the teacher of a nearby government school stay with him for free. He was also asked to leave. The girl was kept in Jangi's house along with a few men of the village who the police suspected of being Naxals. The next morning, the girl was taken to a nearby field, blindfolded, her hands tied, and raped several times.

A fact-finding team which visited her after the incident was told by the girl that the police did 'badmaash kaam' with her. She told them that the first person who raped her was Munna Thakur. 'He said I must have heard his name as he pushed himself over me,' the girl told the team. The girl said she fainted several times during her ordeal.

At about 10 a.m., a helicopter landed in Pavarvel to take the girl and other suspected men to Gadchiroli town. In an area where even a bullock cart is not available to take a sick person to the hospital, the state machinery spared a helicopter to ferry a teenage girl accused of being a Naxal. But nothing could be proven against her and she had to be released. As a damage-control exercise, Munna Thakur was transferred later to Nagpur.

But, after this incident, just how does the government expect the people of Pavarvel village to inform them about Naxal whereabouts? That too when this is not the only time when the police committed atrocities in this village. In 2006, 17-year-old Ramsay Jangi was picked up by C-60 commandos and beaten up severely. When his cousin Mathru Jangi went pleading that he was innocent, the police assured him that he would be freed after first-aid. In the night, the villagers saw Munna Thakur. They heard him shouting at his men, instructing them to 'finish off' the work. A moment later, the villagers heard several gunshots. The police had shot dead Ramsay Jangi. The body was taken to Dhanora taluka. After ten days, the police came back and asked Ramsay's father Manik Jhangi to come and collect his son's body. But nobody went, fearing arrest. The police disposed of the body.

Manik Jhangi has still kept the empty cartridges of the bullets that killed his son. 'My son's body must have rotted,' he whispers. 'No, they inject something inside the body to keep it fresh,' says a boy with some education. 'But he is gone, gone forever,' Manik Jhangi cries silently, his tears mixing with sweat. 'We fear going into the jungle now because if the police finds us they will kill us,' says another man.

The stark fact that the villagers live with is that these are not isolated incidents. Across Maoist-affected areas, the security forces have many a time ended up killing innocent tribals caught in the endless cycle of violence between the State and the Maoists. Sometimes these killings are intentional, just to show some results. And sometimes, innocent people just get caught in between.

In January 2009, 17 tribal youths were killed in Singaram village in Golappali area of Chhattisgarh's Dantewada. The police termed it a 'major breakthrough', but it was soon clear that the youths were taken to the forest behind the village by Special Police Officers (civilians employed by the police, who roam around with vigilante groups such as the Salwa Judum) and then shot dead in cold blood. The survivors of the attack later testified that the villagers were working in the fields when over 200 armed people stormed into Singaram and three other villages, accusing villagers of shielding Maoists. Some of them are believed to have paid whatever little money they had to avoid getting shot. But in the end, 17 youths lost their lives, including four women.

In September 2010, Border Security Force (BSF) personnel, accompanied by men from the Chhattisgarh police rounded up 40 Adivasis in their villages in the state's Kanker district. They were stripped naked, beaten up, and, according to their testimonies, five of them were reportedly raped with sticks. According to an Amnesty International report, 17 people from the two villages were also detained—blindfolded, split into batches and taken to the BSF camp in closed trucks. As per the report, at least two of those detained—Dhansu Khemra and Sarita Tulavi—were 16-year-old girls while another four were women and girls between 16 and 20. The report further states that during their detention, the BSF personnel beat the detainees in an attempt to force them to confess that they were Maoists involved in an ambush on security personnel on 29 August. The interrogators gave electric shocks to at least ten detainees and sexually assaulted two female detainees.

On 9 October 2010, soldiers of the Chhattisgarh police's Special Task Force, who were pursuing a woman Maoist, ended up shooting two innocent villagers in Lendigidipa village in Mahasamund area. One of them happened to be a deaf and dumb labourer. The family of the victim later said that one of the soldiers immediately realised his mistake and muttered: '*Hai Durga maiyya, pehli baar bekasur aadmi ko maar diya.*'[28] (Oh Mother Durga, for the first time I have killed an innocent man.)

The, Maoists, of course, kill their enemy with equal ruthlessness. In villages across Dandakaranya and in other areas of influence, villagers suspected of being police informers are often killed brutally by slitting their throats.

---

[28]Supriya Sharma, *The Times of India*, 12 October 2010.

In Lalgarh, hundreds of CPM workers have been killed either by slitting their throats or by just putting a bullet in their heads. In Jharkhand, a policeman, Francis Induwar was kidnapped by Maoists, and after the government refused to negotiate, he was beheaded.

But why is it that the Maoists end up killing people in such a gruesome fashion? A senior Maoist leader cites a story popular during the Chinese revolution as an explanation. A bonded labourer who is ill-treated by his landlord feels that the latter has no heart. So, when the peasants attack the landlord's house, the labourer says that he would like to kill his master himself and check whether he has a heart underneath his ribcage. It also serves a psychological purpose, say the Maoists. When a tribal guerilla kills the 'class enemy' in this fashion, it gives him immense satisfaction. His pent-up anger caused by suffering humiliation and exploitation, generation after generation, makes him act like this.

VIII

THE REBEL

Let me say, at the risk of seeming ridiculous, that the true revolutionary is guided by great feelings of love.

—Che Guevara

We cannot live only for ourselves. A thousand fibres connect us with our fellow men.

—Herman Melville

She had the best handwriting among her group. On a humid Bombay night, she would sit cross-legged on the floor at somebody's house and write political slogans on old newspapers. Yes, the world had to be changed, the world order had to be changed—she was so sure about it. So, ignoring the sweat gathering on her brow, she would create posters in her neat handwriting, in English, Hindi and Marathi. Then she and her friends would sneak out in the middle of the night. Someone would carry a pot of glue made of flour. At some intersection, or in some lane, the group would stick the posters on walls and electric poles.

It was a job fraught with danger in the early '70s. The police were on the lookout for adventurous youth—the Naxalbari types—who would talk of revolution and the plight of the poor. But the group didn't care. Tucking her pallu in at her waist, Anuradha Shanbag would address curious onlookers and talk to them about issues they hadn't even thought of. She would make them aware of what was happening around the world, and they would then realise what a wretched life they lived in the slums and chawls of Bombay while politicians and business tycoons slept peacefully, fanned by crisp currency notes and lulled to sleep by the buzz of air conditioners.

Though petite in appearance, Anu, as Anuradha was fondly called by her friends, was the most active and vivacious among them. She was very attractive as well and had many admirers. She was the natural leader of the group that consisted mostly of college students like herself. Among her admirers was a tall, lanky bespectacled man, who had returned from London, after serving a two-month sentence in a prison there. Kobad Ghandy had gone to London to pursue chartered accountancy, but had instead found himself one day in the thick of a violent attack on an anti-racism meeting. The meeting, held by left-leaning students and activists, to protest against the racism faced by Indians in the UK was attacked by a white fascist gang. The police had encouraged them and ultimately arrested three of the protestors including Kobad and a pregnant white woman. Inside the police station, Kobad was further beaten up.

After his release, Kobad happened to see a picture in a newspaper of Naxal rebels marching in single file through a vast field in Singhbhum in east India. He decided to return to India, wearing an overcoat that had 24 secret pockets, all stuffed with Maoist literature. He returned to Bombay (as it was then known), hoping to establish contact with Naxal rebels. In Bombay Kobad first got in touch with J.P. Dixit, his Hindi professor at St Xavier's college where he had studied. Dixit had been arrested briefly on charges of being a Naxalite. But Dixit was unable to help since he had no contact with the Naxal rebels. It was then that Kobad came in contact with PROYOM (Progressive Youth Movement), a student organisation inspired by the Naxal movement. PROYOM ran an 'alternative university', essentially a series of lectures that offered an alternate view (Marxist) of the subjects taught in colleges. The organisation was also quite active in the slums and other areas inhabited by the poor of Bombay. This is where Kobad met Anuradha for the first time.

Young people like Anuradha were inspired by the headiness of those times. A year before, Charu Mazumdar had died in Kolkata, and Naxal rebels were being hunted like mad dogs. Anuradha and Kobad came from different family backgrounds. Anuradha was born to Ganesh and Kumud Shanbag, both of them activists, who chose to marry in the office of the Communist Party of India (CPI). As a young boy, Ganesh Shanbag had run away from his home in Coorg to join Subhash Chandra Bose's army, and later, as a lawyer, he would fight the cases of communists arrested in the Telangana struggle. While his briefcase would be full of petitions filed on behalf of the arrested comrades, Kumud would be busy knitting and collecting sweaters to be sent for soldiers fighting the war with China. Kobad's father Adi Ghandy was the finance director of the pharmaceutical giant Glaxo while his mother Nargis played bridge and golf and was a regular at the elite Willingdon club. The family stayed in a 4000-square-feet Worli seaface house.

Even as a child, Kobad felt deeply for the poor, and a family friend describes an incident to illustrate this. Adi Ghandy's gold watch disappeared one day. Later, Kobad revealed that he had gifted it to a servant who, he said, needed it more than his father.

Anuradha's brother Sunil Shanbag, who is a progressive playwright, recalls her being good at studies as well as extra-curricular activities like dancing. But she was extremely aware of what was happening around her. Says Sunil: 'When I was in boarding school, she would send me letters, writing about issues like the nationalisation of banks. And she was only twelve then.' But beyond this awareness, Anuradha was like any other girl when she joined Bombay's prestigious Elphinstone college in 1972. 'She would come home and straighten her hair with the help of a warm iron as girls would do in those days,' recalls her mother. But in between straightening her hair, she also went on to do her M.A. in sociology and later an M.Phil.

Both Kobad and Anu took an instant liking to each other. Around that time, Kobad's parents had retired and shifted to Mahabaleshwar, a small hill station about 100 km from Pune. Kobad and his brother stayed on in Bombay in the Worli mansion. Kobad's brother was into making ice cream, and loved to experiment with new flavours. Kobad, Anuradha and their whole group would often assemble at the Worli house for discussions. Kobad's brother would seek the group's opinion on his experiments. Anuradha simply loved his ice cream. But he improved the quality to such an extent that, eventually, the cost of making it exceeded its selling price and he went bankrupt.

It is not clear whether Anu inspired Kobad more or the other way round but soon, as a friend puts it, both had turned into 'staunch activists'. In fact, Kobad organised the youth of Mayanagar slum near his house, and they stopped paying for water to the slumlord who was linked to the Congress and had connections in the municipality and the police. By the mid '70s, the two were at the centre of the Dalit Panther movement that organised groups to retaliate against any caste oppression. During those months, there were regular clashes with the militant Shiv Sena.

Kobad also took a liking to a song in *Namak Haraam*, a Hindi film set in the backdrop of the workers' movement in Bombay's textile mills: *Nadiya se dariya, dariya se sagar* . . . He took this film on VHS tapes to show it across various slums in the city. Around this time, Kobad and Anuradha fell in love, and Kumud vividly remembers the day Kobad came visiting their house. 'My husband was here on this chair,' she points out, 'and Kobad came and fell on his knees and said: "Can I marry your daughter?"'

The two got married on 5 November 1977 at Adi Ghandy's retreat in Mahabaleshwar. The Emergency had just been lifted, the Janata Party had come to power and all political prisoners including most Naxalite leaders were released. The two were very busy and only got a week off to celebrate their marriage. Anuradha's family drove down the day before. Kobad had gone earlier to help his parents with the marriage preparations.

On the morning of their marriage, Adi Ghandy drove down to neighbouring Satara to fetch the registrar of marriages. He wouldn't agree to come, and relented only after money and two bottles of whisky were passed on to him. For the wedding feast, Nargis Ghandy had prepared the choicest Parsi delicacies. The two families went on many outings together during the next two days. Anu and Kobad stayed on in Mahabaleshwar for another five days after the wedding, often taking long walks in the forest adjoining the house. It was the last time that they could enjoy such simple pleasures of life.

In Bombay, both Anu and Kobad became the shining lights of the civil liberties movement. Anuradha played a very important role in the formation of the Committee for the Protection of Democratic Rights (CPDR).

Meanwhile, by 1980, the Naxal squads had entered Gadchiroli. Some of the senior Naxal leaders who were active during the Telangana struggle came in contact with Kobad and Anuradha and their group in Mumbai. These leaders finally arranged a meeting between Kondapalli Seetharamaiah and Kobad during a conference of the Radical Students Union in 1981 in Guntur, Andhra Pradesh. After the session was inaugurated, KS sent a messenger to Kobad. But Kobad was not to be found there. Apparently, he had slipped out briefly with a friend. Varavara Rao remembers approaching Anuradha, enquiring about Kobad. In a memoir written after her death, VV describes those moments: 'Her (Anu's) anxiety was quite visible that Kobad was not present at a time when a great opportunity came in search for them. There were no cell phones at that time. Her lips were quivering, her face reddened and her eyes were filled with tears … She apologised several times. Meanwhile Kobad turned up. She pounced on him with anger like a child. Tears rolled down her face … she shouted at him, revealing her love, friendship and intimacy towards him.' Varavara Rao says the meeting between KS and Kobad paved the way for the foundation of the People's War Group in Maharashtra.

Soon afterwards, Anu and Kobad shifted to Nagpur

which has the second largest slum population in Maharashtra, and is also home to a significant number of Dalits (it was in Nagpur in October 1956 that B.R. Ambedkar accepted Buddhism). Kobad would be gone for long periods for party work and often Anu would be left alone. She first stayed in a barsati in the Lakshmi Nagar area. Kumud remembers visiting her there with her husband. 'When we saw where she stayed, we couldn't believe our eyes,' says Kumud. The roof leaked from many places. And it rained that night. 'Our helper who was with us crept under a table and slept there,' recalls Kumud.

By 1986, however, Anuradha had shifted to north Nagpur's Indora locality, the epicentre of Dalit politics. It is from here that an agitation broke out after the infamous Khairlanji case of 2006, the background being that four members of a Dalit family were lynched in Maharashtra's Bhandara district bordering Nagpur. In Indora, Anuradha rented two small rooms at the house of a postal department employee, Khushaal Chinchikhede. 'There was absolutely nothing in their house except two trunks of books and a mud pitcher,' he says. Anuradha also worked as part-time lecturer in Nagpur University. Later, Kobad would come to live there too. Both would be out till midnight. Anuradha used a rundown cycle to commute, and it was later at the insistence of other activists that Kobad bought a TVS Champ moped.

Anuradha was a fiercely independent person, and the couple had frequent fights on many issues. She would also be left fuming at Kobad's clumsiness while driving and later with his slow typing speed. A close associate remembers how she quarrelled with Kobad after she fell off the moped at a speed breaker as Kobad had not applied the brakes and did not even realise that she had toppled down! But these fights apart, the two had immense respect for each other. Whenever Kobad visited her, he would do most of the cleaning and washing to enable Anuradha to rest a bit.

Indora was notorious for its rowdies. 'No taxi or autorickshaw driver would dare venture inside Indora,' says Anil Borkar, who grew up in Indora. But Anuradha was unfazed. 'She would pass though the basti at midnight, all alone on a cycle,' remembers Borkar. He met Anuradha through a friend. 'She made me aware of so many things. It was like the whole world opened in front of me,' he says.

Because of Anuradha, Devanand Pantavne, a black belt in karate turned into a poet and the lead singer of a radical cultural troupe. Pantavne remembers her as a stickler for deadlines. 'She would get very angry if we took up a job and then didn't deliver on time,' he says. Another young man, Surendra Gadling was motivated by Anuradha to take up law. Today, he fights cases for various activists and alleged Naxals. 'She is my guiding light,' he says. It is not without reason. Anuradha led by example, living the life she wanted the basti boys to lead.

That life was tough though. One day, a friend recalls, Anuradha returned home late in the night totally exhausted. She was crying. That day, Anuradha had left home at 6.30 a.m. on her cycle to reach the university in time for her first lecture at 9 a.m., cycling part of the way and then taking a bus to the university which was 15 km away from her house. At 11.30 a.m., she had left for central Nagpur to attend a meeting on the reservation issue. At 4 p.m., she had to reach Kamptee, a handloom township, mostly inhabited by Muslim weavers, about 20 km from Nagpur. She had first made a detour to leave her cycle at home and had then taken a bus to Kamptee without even stopping for a glass of water. She returned late in the night and began to cry. She could not bear the plight of the poor weavers who were struggling hard to survive after the government stopped their quota of thread, which had enabled them to weave cloth. Many had not eaten for days, she said, and some women had to resort to prostitution to fend for themselves and their families.

In 1994, a Dalit woman, Manorama Kamble, who worked as a maid in an influential lawyer's house, was found dead. The lawyer's family claimed that she had accidently electrocuted herself. But the activists feared that she had been raped and then killed by the lawyer. Anuradha led an agitation, and it was due to her efforts that the case created ripples in the state assembly and in Parliament.

In Indora, one of Anuradha's trusted lieutenants was Biwaji Badke, a four-foot-tall Dalit activist. 'Every morning Badke would come to her house and share all the news with Anuradha over tea,' recall friends. Later, when he was diagnosed with throat cancer, Anuradha brought him to her house and nursed him for months. Another associate, Shoma Sen remembers her being very sensitive to the concerns of others. 'Her house in Indora was open to everyone. Every time someone would come and one more cup of water would be added to the tea that was constantly brewing on the stove,' she says.

Because of her, many others from well-to-do families were inspired to become activists. Says her old friend and associate of her activist days, Susan Abraham: 'When I became an activist it was always heartening to see someone from Anu's background working along with you.'

In the mid '90s, because of police pressure, it had become impossible to work 'overground'. Anuradha's name had prominently figured in two important programmes she had organised in the Vidarbha region. One was the Kamlapur Conference of 1984, held at the small hamlet deep inside the forests of Gadchiroli. There was a huge mobilisation of people, including various intellectuals and activists. But it was crushed by the police. In 1992, Anuradha organised a cultural programme of the revolutionary balladeer Gaddar in Nagpur. Despite court orders, the police prevented people from attending the programme. The police had also intended to prevent Gaddar from reaching the venue but he appeared in disguise. No sooner had he reached the venue than the police resorted to a lathi charge and did not let the programme happen.

It was in the mid '90s that both Kobad and Anu finally went completely underground.

From 1996-98, Anuradha was in Bastar. Kobad was elsewhere and the two got to see very little of each other. But right from day one, Anuradha set an example in Bastar. Maina, a member of the CPI-Maoist's Special

Zone Committee in Dandakaranya, remembers her efforts to mingle with the local Gond tribals: 'Many people used to question us about her, saying didi (Anuradha) is not from this country, she does not know our language. Didi would smilingly approach them saying: "I know what you are asking; please teach me your language; I will learn everything from you."'

Life in the jungle is very harsh. The guerillas are always on the move, from one village to another, carrying heavy kit bags. Even there, Anuradha wouldn't shy away from hardships; she did everything that other guerillas would do. A Naxal leader, who was in Bastar when she first came there, remembers her not sparing herself any of the regular military drill: running, crawling, push-ups, the works. Says Maina, 'She would slip and fall many times while walking in the slushy mud, but she would get up and laugh.'

In 1999, Anuradha was camping along with other guerillas in Chhattisgarh's Sarkengudem village when the police surrounded them. An encounter ensued. Lahar, a senior guerilla remembers Anuradha taking cover and aiming her gun at the 'enemy'. Later, she would always recollect that incident, urging the youth to learn the skills of guerilla warfare. But her brother Sunil remembers her speaking about the 'awkwardness of carrying a gun'.

The hard life of the jungle took its toll on her body—she suffered frequent bouts of malaria. During the same summer, after she had been walking for hours one day she lost consciousness. Her comrades revived her and made her drink glucose water. Apparently, she had suffered a sunstroke. Even then, after she recovered, she refused to hand over her kit bag to others, says Lahar.

When south Bastar was affected by severe drought in 1998-99, the tribals were forced to eat rice which, Maina says, 'had more stones than grain in it'. The same rice was offered to the guerillas as well, which they would eat with tamarind paste. 'Taking one fistful after another and then gulping water in between, she used to take a lot of time to finish her meal,' recalls Maina. She also developed ulcers in her stomach. 'She would relieve the pain by eating one or two biscuits with a glass of water,' she says.

Sometimes, Kobad came to Bastar and the two would have a reunion of sorts. A senior guerilla remembers that Anuradha didn't know how to use a computer and save or open files on it. But since she had good speed on a manual typewriter, she would type furiously. Kobad knew how to use the computer but could not type as fast as Anuradha, and she would tease him about this. To lessen her load, Anuradha also decided to do away with the heavy blanket guerillas carry, opting instead for a thin bedsheet.

No matter what the Centre claims, the Naxals often fill the void created by the government in their areas of influence. In Basaguda in Chhattisgarh, an embankment needed to be built around a tank called Kota Chervu; some ten villages were counting on the water from this tank. The government had ignored the villagers' pleas for years. It was under Anuradha's guidance that people from 30 villages undertook this work. Those who worked were given a kilo of rice a day. The government panicked and sanctioned 20 lakh rupees; it was refused. By 1998, more than a hundred tanks had been constructed by the Naxals in Dandakaranya.

Anuradha also took on the responsibility of crafting study modules to educate women. She regularly took classes on the problems faced by women guerillas, and wrote and translated Naxal propaganda material. She would prepare charts with photos of political leaders and explain world affairs to the locals who were illiterate. Sometimes, she would conduct classes on health issues. Aman, a senior member of the Maoists' Dandakaranya Special Zone Committee recalls how discussions with her would range from the Salwa Judum to films like *Rang de Basanti*.

But her health was in bad shape. By 2000, she had developed serious health issues. She would feel exhausted quickly and her knees gave way while her fingers would not bend. At the end of 2002, the diagnosis turned out to be shocking: Anu was suffering from the deadly systemic sclerosis that would ultimately lead to multiple organ failure. The news was broken to Kobad in an internet chatroom. Kobad could meet her only two months later, and he saw that in a little time, Anu had aged a lot. But undeterred by all this, Anuradha continued making secret trips to Mumbai. 'She would come, and I would apply oil in her hair and massage her body. I wanted to pamper her as much as I could,' says Kumud.

'The most amazing thing was that she would always know much more than us about films and other popular culture,' says Sunil. During the staging of one of his plays, *Cotton 56, Polyester 84* (depicting the plight of textile mill workers) in Mumbai, Anuradha slipped in quietly, watched the play, and left as quietly as she had come. 'I only came to know later that she was there,' says Sunil. As Kobad says: 'She enjoyed plays, novels, good films, good food, whenever she got a chance. But she never craved after anything. I have seen her selflessness living sometimes in the most horrible conditions—in slum-like places. There would be never any complaints. She always adjusted. She would bear the worst sort of hardships as part of normal tasks. She would always spend the least on herself.'

At the ninth Congress of the CPI (Maoist) in 2007, Anuradha was made a member of the Central Committee. A picture of that time shows her wearing the uniform of the PLGA, a rifle slung across her shoulder. She is smiling in the picture, very conscious of the gun she is carrying. By this time, Kobad had also become a senior ideologue writing articles under the pen name Arvind.

It was on the basis of Anuradha's work that the Naxals prepared the first-ever caste policy paper within the Marxist movement in India. She also drafted papers on Marxism and feminism, of which the top Naxal leadership took note. During the time spent in Dandakaranya, Anuradha helped the guerillas overcome the limitations of collective work by making them understand what roles cooperatives could play in increasing agricultural production. In Bastar, Anuradha raised questions on the patriarchal ideas prevalent in the party. She had also been working with the women's cadre, to devise plans that would help them take greater leadership responsibilities.

Towards the end of March 2008, Anu had travelled to Jharkhand to conduct classes for the women's cadre. She spent about a week among these women, mostly tribal, and her lectures were taped for use elsewhere. At the end of the classes, she had become such a hit among the women that they refused to let her go, and she had to delay her departure by two days. As she prepared to leave, all the women whom she had taught followed her for a few kilometres inside the thick forest before she persuaded them to return. One Maoist guerilla who took those classes said that there were tears in everyone's eyes. From there, it seems, she travelled to Mumbai where she developed high fever. She went to a doctor who advised some tests. By evening the tests had reached the doctor, and on looking at them, the doctor started making frantic calls to the phone number the patient had scribbled in her nearly illegible handwriting. The number, he soon realised, did not exist. The reports indicated the presence of two deadly strains of malaria in Anuradha's bloodstream—she had to be admitted to a hospital without delay. Time was racing by and there was no trace of her.

By the time Anuradha contacted the doctor again, a few days had passed. The doctor wanted her placed under intensive care immediately. But it was too late. The next morning, on 12 April 2008, Anuradha Ghandy was dead. She had suffered multiple organ failure, her immune system already weakened by systemic sclerosis, which was responsible for, among other things, her bad handwriting.

Writing to me from Tihar jail, two years after Anu's death, Kobad recollects his thoughts: 'Two years is a long time, yet the fragrance lingers on. The sweet scent, like from an eternal blossom, intoxicates the mind with memories of her vivacious and loving spirit. Even here, in the High Risk ward of Tihar jail, the five sets of bars that incarcerate us cannot extinguish the aroma that Anu radiates in one's memories. The pain one suffers here seems so insignificant compared to what she must have faced on that fateful day.'

How did a girl like Anuradha, born into privilege, come to choose a life of struggle and hardship in the treacherous jungles of Bastar, a rifle by her side and a tarpaulin sheet for her bedding? The answer perhaps lies in the times she lived in. Or the kind of person she was. Or, maybe, a bit of both.

In Nagpur, a year after her death, I requested her former landlord in Indora, Chinchikhede to open the rooms once occupied by Anuradha. All that remained of the old days was a sticker of Bhagat Singh on the door. It was sunset and the sky had turned crimson. A comrade who accompanied me lay on the floor, a floor he was too familiar with. And he recited a poem by revolutionary poet Gorakh Pandey:

> *It's thousands of years old*
> *their anger*
> *thousands of years old*
> *is their bitterness*
> *I am only returning their scattered words*
> *with rhyme and rhythm*
> *and you fear that*
> *I am spreading fire.*

IX

THE URBAN AGENDA

The final objective of the revolution is the capture of the cities, the enemy's main bases, and this objective cannot be achieved without adequate work in the cities.

—Mao Tse-tung

If you are far from the enemy, make him believe you are near.

—SunTzu

The sleuths of the Intelligence Bureau were waiting for him. The moment Anthony Shimray crossed the entry gate of the Patna railway station on the morning of 2 October 2010, he was nabbed and immediately whisked away. Shimray was under surveillance for quite some time. Though the insurgent group NSCN-IM [National Socialist Council of Nagaland (Isak-Muivah)]—active in north-east India—had a ceasefire agreement with the Indian government, interrogating Shimray had become quite necessary for the intelligence agency. Apart from being the 'foreign minister' of the outfit (and the nephew of its general secretary, T. Muivah), Shimray was also its chief arms procurer, and he had recently travelled to Beijing, paying an advance of 800,000 dollars to a Chinese firm. He was based in Bangkok and had travelled to Kathmandu from where he slipped into the Indian territory to return to Nagaland. During sustained interrogation, Shimray finally opened up. He confessed that this amount was paid to book a huge consignment of arms that included sophisticated guns, rocket launchers, explosive devices and communication gadgets. He told the Indian authorities that he was to make a payment of another 200,000 dollars to the Chinese firm before they would dispatch the consignment to India either through Bangladesh or Myanmar. According to Shimray, this was to reach India in three batches and the consignment was meant for Maoists and insurgent outfits in the north-east. Intelligence agencies believed that the first batch had already reached the Maoists.

This was confirmed on 3 December 2010, when a special unit of the Kolkata Police nabbed the state secretary of the CPI (Maoist) Kanchan alias Sudip Chongdar and his two other associates from a city suburb. Intelligence sources say that the arrests were made after Shimray provided important leads to the leader's whereabouts. The police now believe that some of the modern communication equipment seized from the Maoist leaders was a part of the first batch of the Chinese consignment. The Maoist leaders were planning their strategy to be a part of the agitation in the Rajarhat area where 7,000 acres of land had allegedly been forcibly acquired from farmers. The Maoists had earlier participated in similar agitations in Singur and Nandigram, where the protests had turned violent.

Participating in such agitations is a part of the urban agenda of the CPI (Maoist).

In February 2010, the Uttar Pradesh police arrested a scholar Chintan alias Bansidhar Singh from a hideout in the industrial town of Kanpur. Chintan held a doctoral degree in social science from Delhi's Jawaharlal Nehru University, and, according to the police, the 64-year-old man was a senior Maoist leader working towards spreading his party's area of influence. In all, the police arrested 11 people, which included, apart from Chintan, another senior leader, Balraj. Balraj, the police said, had been active in socialist leader Jayaprakash Narain's movement in the '70s in Bihar, and both he and Chintan were assigned the task of spreading the Maoist network to Uttarakhand and Bundelkhand regions. It is believed that Chintan had been in touch with people in the poverty-stricken areas of Bundelkhand where a void had been created due to the elimination of various dacoits. In Uttarakhand, the Maoist cadre hoped to spread their movement by backing protests and agitations against big dams, which had rendered many homeless in the state. The Maoists have been active in the anti-dam agitation in Polavaram in Andhra Pradesh. In March 2010, senior Maoist leader Venkateshwar Reddy alias Telugu Deepak was arrested from West Bengal in Haripur where a resistance movement had been building up against the proposed construction of a nuclear reactor.[29] Similarly, in recent years, police have arrested other alleged Maoist sympathisers from Delhi who, the police claim, have been trying to influence jobless labourers and other displaced people in the city.

In fact, the Maoists regard the urban movement as very important since they believe that revolution will occur only when cities are finally taken over. Also, it is from urban areas that the Maoists hope to draw their leaders, and it is here that they plan to shift some of the senior leaders in the wake of sustained military operations in their strongholds like Bastar. A Maoist document prepared in 2007 makes clear the significance of Maoist influence in urban areas: 'We should not forget the dialectical

---

[29]*The Telegraph*, 4 March 2010.

relationship between the development of the urban movement and the development of the people's war. In the absence of a strong revolutionary urban movement, the people's war will face difficulties.' Stressing upon the need to recruit people from urban areas, it says: 'A steady supply of urban cadre is necessary to fulfil the needs of the rural movement and the people's war. This is necessary for providing working class leadership, as well as technical skills to the people's war.'

The Strategy and Tactics document adopted at the last Party Congress (held in 2007) further says: 'However, we should not belittle the importance of the fact that the urban areas are the strong centres of the enemy. Building up of a strong urban revolutionary movement means that our party should build a struggle network capable of waging struggle consistently by sustaining itself until the protracted people's war reaches the stage of the strategic offensive. With this long-term perspective, we should develop a secret party, a united front and people's armed elements; intensify the class struggle in urban areas and mobilise the support of millions of urban masses for the people's war.'

The Maoist leadership believes that India's urban population today is significantly larger in numbers in proportion to the total population, as also in economic weight, when compared to China's urban population at the time of the revolution there. The leadership says that this would mean that India's urban areas would have to play a relatively more important role than the cities in China during the revolution. The document specifies that with the exception of Delhi and its suburbs, much of the north, the east and central India have been by-passed by new India. This vast area covering the eastern half of UP and stretching across Bihar, West Bengal, the north-eastern states, Orissa, Madhya Pradesh and the eastern part of Maharashtra remains an area of urban backwardness with old industrial bases and high unemployment.

According to the document, India's liberalisation policies mean that investment is not regulated and only goes to the areas promising the greatest profits. Such areas identified by the Maoist leadership are:

- Ahmedabad-Pune Corridor which includes the top ten cities of Mumbai, Ahmedabad, Pune and Surat, Vadodara and Nashik. The Maoists believe that these cities and adjoining districts attract the largest amount of new investment in the whole country. The working class is the most diverse, having migrated from all parts of the country.
- Delhi region which includes the areas of Gurgaon, Faridabad, Ghaziabad and NOIDA.
- Bangalore which the Maoist leadership identifies as a fast-growing centre.
- Chennai which is the industrial hub of the south.
- Coimbatore-Erode belt which has experienced the fastest growing urbanisation in the country hinging on textile mills, power looms, knitwear, etc.
- Hyderabad where the new investments are mainly in electronics and information technology.
- Kolkata where due to slow industrial growth the unemployment rate is relatively higher.

It also points to the cities of the Gangetic plain, cities like Kanpur that are not receiving much new investment and are thus stagnating.

The document says that with closures of industries and the accompanying loss of jobs, many workers are forced to take up casual work or earn on their own through hawking their wares, plying rickshaws, operating roadside thelas. It points out that at the same time new youth entering the work force do not get regular jobs and that the unemployment rate is the highest in the 15 to 24 age group.

'In the liberalisation-globalisation period, however, the ruling classes in most major cities aspiring to make them "global cities" have in a coordinated and planned manner launched numerous measures to push the poor out of the core of the cities like Delhi, Mumbai, Hyderabad, Bangalore, Chennai. These measures extend from the old measures of slum demolition and hawker eviction to new forms like closure of polluting factories, banning of protests in central areas, regulations encouraging concentration of development in the richer zones,' says the document.

The document also states that caste violence and caste riots are more numerous, with some towns and cities repeatedly witnessing attacks on Dalits. Such upper-caste violence, it says, has further sharpened the division of many towns by forcing all Dalits to live in separate areas to better organise their self-defence. The Maoists are believed to have taken part in the Khairlanji agitation of 2006 against the lynching of four members of a Dalit family. Some of these protests had turned violent with Maoists at one time even threatening to kill the people behind the killings.

The document also takes into account the plight of Muslims in India. 'Our party in the urban areas has to seriously take the ghettoisation process into account in all plans. Sharp ghettoisation leads to lack of jobs for Muslims and pushes larger sections of them into semi-proletariat. Thus merely organising within industry will not enable us to enter this oppressed community. Unless we base ourselves in the middle of the ghetto, we will not be able to gain entry into organising the community (sic),' the document advises the Maoist cadre.

In the document, the main objectives of the urban work have been categorised under three broad heads:

- Mobilising and organising the masses which involves organising the working class and students, middle-class employees and intellectuals. It must also undertake the task of dealing with the problems of special groups like women, Dalits and religious minorities and mobilise them for the revolutionary movement.
- Building a united front, which involves the task of unifying the working class, building worker-peasant solidarity and alliances and building fronts against globalisation.
- Military tasks which involve sending cadres to the countryside, infiltration of enemy ranks, organising people in key industries, acts of sabotage in coordination with the rural armed struggle, logistical support, etc.

The Maoist leadership also lays emphasis on forming cover mass organisations which may not disclose their link with the party. An example it specifies is the case of unorganised workers where the established trade unions have a limited presence and the party has no option but to set up its own trade union organisation. The document warns that the cadres should be very careful not to attract attention by exceeding the socially acceptable limits of militancy for that area. So if knives and swords are used, the cadres should not resort to firearms or they should not normally resort to annihilation in a new area where there has been no history of such actions.

The Maoist cadres are also advised to form legal democratic organisations such as those catering to a particular section like students, lawyers, teachers and cultural bodies. It says that other groups may be formed with issue-oriented programmes focusing on core questions like communalism, violence against women, corruption, regional backwardness and statehood, etc. 'It is necessary that the party in the urban areas should give considerable importance to the task of participating in and building up a strong and broad legal democratic movement,' it says.

Expanding into urban areas has, so far, proved to be tough. In recent years, many of the senior Maoist leaders have either been arrested or killed in urban areas. In March 2010, two senior leaders, Solipeta Kondal Reddy and Sakhamuri Appa Rao were picked up by the Andhra SIB from Pune and Chennai, respectively, and later allegedly killed in fake encounters. The Maoist chief spokesperson Azad was allegedly picked up from Nagpur railway station in July 2010 and killed, as the activists allege, in cold blood.

Despite the perceived difficulties, the Maoists are keen to spread out to urban areas. The urban agenda document urges Maoist cadres to pay attention to organising the workers within the slums and such localities. 'Through this we can get in touch with new workers from various industries, we can draw the families of the workers into the movement, and we can organise the semi-proletariat and other sections of the urban poor living in the slums and poor localities,' it explains.

The document advises cadres to cover themselves by building or joining traditional organisations like chawl committees, sports clubs, cultural bodies and mandalis for Ganesh and Durga puja, for Ambedkar jayanti, etc. The Maoist leadership also points out what it calls the 'problem of imperialist funded NGOs'. It says that such NGOs are in existence in almost all the slums of the major cities and that it is the duty of the Maoist cadre to educate the slum masses and particularly the activists about the sinister role of such organisations and the agencies financing them. 'We should particularly expose them when they stand in the path of people's struggles.' However, the cadres are told that in times of repression they can work within them. Citing the example of the Peru Communist Party's success in creating strongholds in the shanty towns of its capital Lima, the document says that the Maoists should also work at creating such strongholds in India's major cities. It says that the situation of the urban poor in the slums and poor localities is worsening continuously: 'The slum population of India is over four crores, spread in more than 600 towns. The largest mega city, Mumbai has 49 per cent of its population in slums.'

'Propaganda and agitation on issues and incidents of repression on various other urban classes are the main means by which the working class and the party expresses solidarity with the affected sections—issues such as the eviction of hawkers, demolition of slums, suppression of students' rights, funds for teachers' salaries. While it may not be possible to hold a solidarity action on every such issue, the party should be ever alive and respond in whatever manner possible—propaganda pamphlet, press statement, dharna, demonstration, or some more militant action,' the document explains.

The document also says that the Maoist cadres working in urban areas should also try to forge a unity between blue-collar (workers, labourers) and white-collar employees (like bank workers, insurance workers, teachers and other government employees). It says that efforts should be made to oppose the creation of separate 'workers' and 'employees' unions. However, where such separate unions exist already, forces should be allocated for fractional work within them. 'Some industries like transport, communications, power, oil and natural gas, defence production can play a crucial role in the people's war. Disruption of production in these industries has an immediate impact on the enemy's ability to fight the war. If struggles in such industries are coordinated with developments in the people's war they can provide direct assistance to the People's Guerilla Army. Party-led units within such industries can also perform industrial sabotage actions which would provide effective assistance during certain points in the war.' The document says such operations normally will be necessary at later stages in the war. 'But we have to give importance to allocation of cadre for such industries right from the beginning.'

The document also instructs the cadres to focus on workers in industries and try and influence them: 'At level one we can influence the workers in these industries from outside through various forms of propaganda, particularly during the struggles of these industries. This can be done through legal democratic workers' organisations, workers' magazines, and secret pamphleteering and even through party statements.

'At another level we should send comrades to secretly develop fractional work from within the industry. This work should be done with a long-term approach taking care to avoid exposure. The comrades doing propaganda and extending solidarity from outside need not know about the existence of the work being conducted from within. It is also not necessary to do work at both levels at the same unit.

'Due to the critical character of these industries the enemy too is very conscious of the need to prevent any revolutionary or other genuine struggling forces from entering such industries. We therefore have to be very guarded and careful while entering and working within such enterprises. All work in such places should be under cover of some sort.'

The Intelligence Bureau (IB) believes that the Maoists have more than 50 bodies working for them as frontal organisations.[30] In March 2010, the Home Minister

---

[30]Raman Kirpal, 'The Crimson Brief', *Tehelka*, 22 May 2010.

P. Chidambaram made a statement in the Parliament on this issue. He said: 'Available inputs indicate that organisations such as PUDR, PUCL and APDR take up issues of the CPI (Maoist). Both the central and state governments keep a close watch on the activities of these organisations.' The IB list includes RSU and RYL and organisations like Naujawan Bharat Sabha and Jan Chetna Manch. The IB dossier accuses two organisations based in Delhi, Revolutionary Democratic Front (RDF) and Delhi General Mazdoor Front of being front offices of Maoists. The same report says that the Maoists have formed a committee for Delhi to concentrate on mobilisation and recruitment and protests against the arrest of Maoists.

The Maoist document also lays emphasis on the need for what it calls 'infiltration into the enemy camp': 'It is very important to penetrate into the military, paramilitary forces, police and higher levels of the administrative machinery of the state. It is necessary to obtain information regarding the enemy, to build support for the revolution within these organs, and even to incite revolt when the time is ripe.'

In May 2010, the UP Special Task Force (STF) arrested six persons, including three CRPF personnel for supplying arms and ammunition to Maoists from the CRPF armoury in Rampur, UP. The police recovered a huge cache of arms from the arrested persons, including thousands of live cartridges. Investigations revealed that some of this ammunition had been used by the Maoists even in the 6 April ambush in Dantewada that killed 76 security personnel. In January 2011, a CRPF jawan, Satyaban Bhoi was arrested for allegedly helping Maoists by giving them information about the troop movement in Orissa's Sundargarh district.

The home ministry believes that while the centre has been successful in containing Maoists in certain places, there are other areas where they are expanding. 'I can tell you that so far we have reclaimed about 10,000 sq km area (from Maoists). Of course, in certain areas, like Orissa, the Maoists have expanded as well,' says Union Home Secretary G.K. Pillai.[31] Recently, the Punjab police chief revealed that the Maoists had made deep inroads in the state. He said that the rebels had penetrated into villages and mohallas and were running recruitment drives across Punjab.

The Maoist document also speaks of building city action teams—small secret teams of disciplined and trained soldiers of the Maoist army who are permanently based in the cities or towns to hit at important, selected enemy targets. It may be the annihilation of individuals of military importance or sabotage actions like the blowing up of ammunition depots, destroying communication networks, damaging oil installations, etc. The Central Military Commission of the CPI (Maoist) is supposed to undertake such tasks and provide training and education to city action teams.

'Since the enemy is centred in the big cities, it is very important that our party develops a network to obtain and analyse political and military intelligence at higher levels. Besides human intelligence, use of internet and other

---

[31]Interview to the author.

modern electronic means for gathering information by entering the enemy's networks should also be utilised,' the document says. The internet is increasingly becoming an important tool for the Maoists in their fight against the state. The Maoists use the internet for propaganda and also to be in touch with each other. Messages from one place to another, from one senior leader to another in urban areas are often delivered as encrypted messages using data cards. The internet is also used to send press releases and other information to journalists and activists.

The document accepts that throughout the past 30 years there has been a disregard towards the tasks of the urban movement. 'Having understood the formulation that rural work is primary and urban work is secondary in a mechanical way we concentrated most of our leadership forces only in rural work,' the Maoist leadership felt during discussions at the Party Congress. The document says: 'Therefore a culture was created in the organisation where only the rural work was seen as fieldwork or struggle area work, whereas the urban areas were seen to be out of the field, and non-struggle area work. All the best and most committed cadre would therefore opt for (rural work) and be transferred out of the urban field . . . All this took place despite our understanding that the importance of the urban areas in India is growing and that the urban areas and the working class in India will have a relatively more important role to play in the revolution.'

But, how do the Maoists expect the middle class in cities to be sympathetic to their cause? In fact, the middle class fears that if the Maoists come to power, they would be annihilated and their properties confiscated. Ganapathi tried to address this issue in his interview. He said: 'Only a very small percentage of the upper crust in the middle classes join the upper classes (elite) and turn anti-people. But the entire middle class, the majority of the intellectuals and democrats who belong to the middle class would either join the movement or would stand in support of the movement. Not only during the revolution but in a post-revolutionary society too, the role of the intellectuals in building a new society would be excellent. When they join their hands with the working people, we will be able to complete the revolution sooner and also build the new society at a rapid pace. Due to the prejudices propagated by the ruling classes and some of their stooges, who lick their boots, a negligible number of them may have some fears but we want to clearly say that it is not at all the truth.'

The Maoists are currently facing problems on account of very little recruitment from the urban areas. The Maoist movement is not attracting youth from universities and other academic institutions the way it did in the '70s and '80s. Ganapathi accepts that this indeed is a problem. 'It is true that at present we are not able to mobilise workers, students and intellectuals as we had done in the '70s and '80s. There have been some considerable changes and phenomena in those conditions. It has become very complex to work in areas where the enemy is strong and in the trade union movement where the revisionists have entrenched themselves. This is not just the case in India. This condition is prevailing in the whole world,' he says.

But he is sure that their movement would be able to overcome this. 'In order to liberate this country we have to concentrate on organising the peasantry. At present we would strengthen our movement among the peasantry and definitely extend it to the urban areas. On the other hand, this peasant movement is inspiring the urban people and is having a great impact on them. So, the days when we would vastly organise peasantry of plain areas, the suburban people and urban people are not that far off,' he says.

In the meantime, the Maoists are trying their best to increase recruitment, and, according to intelligence sources, they have cadres in students' hostels and slums from where they try to recruit youth, especially targeting Dalit and tribal youth. Recently, the Maoists have been on a recruitment drive in their erstwhile bastions of Andhra Pradesh as well.

The Maoist leadership believes that due to the government's 'pro-imperialist' policies, more and more people are getting affected and isolated. I had asked Ganapathi whether he thinks the Maoist movement will ever be as successful in Guragon, Haryana, as in Giridih (a Maoist stronghold in Jharkhand). He replied: 'All the riches between Giridih and Gurgaon have been produced by people from poor areas like Giridih. It is the poor Dalit and Adivasi labourers who are spilling their sweat and blood for the construction of huge mansions and infrastructure by Indian and foreign corporate lords. The majority of the workers and employees who work in the shopping malls and companies are from these areas. In terms of social, economic and cultural ties or in terms of movement relations Gurgaons and Giridihs are not two unconnected islands as such. They both are influencing each other. This is creating a strong base for our extension. If Giridih is liberated first, then basing on its strength and on the struggles of the working class in Gurgaon, Gurgaon would be liberated later.'

That may be a far cry, but not as far as it may sound to the government.

Postscript

THE DEATH OF A BALLOON SELLER

On New Year's Eve 2011, when thousands of revellers were celebrating across Delhi's numerous clubs and hotels, a 35-year-old balloon seller Bhima died on a roundabout outside the illustrious Indian Agricultural Research Institute. Even his name could not save him from the biting cold after a temporary shelter he used to take refuge in was demolished by the Municipal Corporation of Delhi. About a month later, in a park near the same roundabout, a pregnant homeless woman delivered her child in shock after a policeman chasing beggars hit her with a lathi. After her husband was sentenced to life imprisonment, Binayak Sen's wife Ilina Sen said she feared for her security following her husband's imprisonment, and that the only recourse she could think of was to walk into some embassy and seek political asylum. In its new avatar, the Salwa Judum in Chhattisgarh, now called the Maa Danteshwari Adivasi Swabhimani Manch, called for the deaths of three local journalists who had been trying to expose the facts about everyday atrocities and human rights violations. In a statement the group said that whoever worked against its interests would have to leave Bastar otherwise 'you will die like a dog'. In Gurgaon, meanwhile, a textile trader and his family were busy setting their dog upon their eight-year-old domestic help Usman (not his real name). He was rescued after facing two months of torture at the hands of his employers that included regular beatings with shoes. A neighbour who reported the case said later that he hadn't seen anybody even treat an animal the way Usman was being treated. Metres away from where Usman was rescued, a Citibank employee, Shivraj Puri was arrested on charges of fraudulently collecting 400 crore rupees from high net worth individuals. Also in the month of January, a UK-based art gallery brought a sculpture titled 'Eternal Spring' worth Rs 62,000,000 to Delhi, hoping to sell it during an art summit.

But there is another Delhi—unknown, unseen—which the government does not pay heed to but the Maoists are well aware of. One such area is north-west Delhi's Bawana that the TV journalist Ravish Kumar calls the Bastar of Delhi. In a medium obsessed with pretty faces and glam news, Ravish does something that the big bosses of TV journalism term as 'downmarket': he visits areas like Bawana, inhabited by the poor, and chronicles the life of people living in such areas in his weekly show. What Ravish has seen has left him shocked. He speaks of meeting women who earn 60 paise a day after a day's hard labour. 'I couldn't show that in my show because no one would believe me,' he says. But such women do exist, he says, here in the national capital. These are women who sift through mountains of paper waste out of which about a kilo of cardboard is prepared for which they are paid an amount ranging from 60 paise to Rs 1.25 a day. He has met women who glue together key chains commemorating the Commonwealth Games, and after putting together 144 such keychains, the women are paid three rupees. Out of this, 50 paise is taken as commission by the contractor. Not only this, they have to collect the material from the contractor and bring it back on a cycle rickshaw that costs them two days' labour. He speaks of women who stitch 144 socks that takes them three hours for which they are paid two to five rupees. He says 80 per cent of such women have just started working three to four years ago when the little incomes their husbands brought home would not suffice. 'With their own little income, they buy small things—like a pack of cheap glucose biscuits or a pouch of milk for their children,' Ravish says. These women, he says, cannot even work as domestic servants since they live very far away from homes where demand for such maids exists. These people now cook their food in zeera instead of onions and eat potatoes instead of dal since both onion and dal are beyond their reach.

In January, the Supreme Court issued a notice to the Centre and the Andhra Pradesh government on a petition seeking a judicial probe into the killings of Maoist leader Azad, 58, and journalist Hemchandra Pandey, 32. 'We cannot allow the Republic killing its own children,' a court bench observed. The two were shot dead together in July 2010 by security forces in an alleged fake encounter. Azad had on him a letter written by Swami Agnivesh, the mediator appointed by the Centre for talks with Maoist insurgents. The police said that Hemchandra was a Maoist as well and that both were killed in an armed engagement in Adilabad district of Andhra Pradesh, close to the Maharashtra border. Civil rights activists, however, allege that both of them were picked up from a hotel in Nagpur, flown in a helicopter to the jungles of Adilabad, and then executed in cold blood. Azad was supposed to travel to Bastar from Nagpur to seek the opinion of a section of the Maoist leadership on talks with the Centre. The post-mortem reports of both Azad and Hemchandra suggest that they were shot from very close range, even as an independent probe carried out by human rights groups, tears apart the police version of events in Adilabad's jungles. Activists allege that Hemchandra was killed alongside Azad because the police did not want an eyewitness to survive.

On 23 March 2010, the death anniversary of Bhagat Singh, Naxalbari's leading light Kanu Sanyal committed suicide at his residence in West Bengal by hanging himself. Over the years, he had become a staunch opponent of the current Maoist movement, and he would express this by saying that killing a traffic constable on a busy street could not bring about a revolution. The Maoist leadership called him an opportunist. During the Lalgarh siege, Maoist leader Kishenji even called him a pheriwala, a hawker. In October 2010, forty years after the encounter death of Kerala's Naxal leader A. Varghese, a court sentenced to life imprisonment a former inspector general of police in his murder.

On 10 September 2008, Raghuram Rajan, noted economist and honorary advisor to Prime Minister Manmohan Singh, delivered a speech at the Bombay Chamber of Commerce where he spoke about how most of India's billionaires did not derive their wealth from IT or software but from land, natural resources, and government contracts or licences. He spoke of India being second only to Russia in terms of wealth concentration (the number of billionaires per trillion dollars of GDP). To show how extraordinary this number was he quoted the case of Brazil which had only 18 billionaires despite a greater GDP than India. Or Germany, which had three times India's GDP and a per capita income 40 times India's but had the same number of billionaires. 'If Russia is an oligarchy, how long can we resist calling India one?' he wondered.

What Rajan said is complete truth. One such case to prove this point is the bizarre manner in which the Orissa government bent over backwards to give clearance to Vedanta University, floated by Anil Agarwal, the chairman of the London-based Vedanta Group, now venturing into oil and gas. *Forbes* magazine's 2010 list of billionaires ranks him the world's thirteenth richest Indian, his net worth estimated at $5.5 billion. Investigations showed that the state government had flouted norms to let Vedanta acquire more than 6,000 acres of land even as the Atomic Minerals Directorate for Exploration and Research had identified 1.82 million tonnes of thorium-bearing monazite resources along the Orissa coast—the same area, coincidentally, where Agarwal wants his world-class university. Those opposed to the deal called it 'India's biggest land grab', and alleged that Vedanta was being favoured because it had funded the 2004 and 2009 Lok Sabha election campaigns of the state's ruling party, the Biju Janata Dal (BJD). They contended that when some of the world's top universities such as Harvard or MIT had main campuses under 400 acres, why did Vedanta require so much land? (They had initially asked for more than 10,000 acres). In Delhi's Tees Hazari court, meanwhile, inside room number 308, Kobad Ghandy sits on a chair, wearing a striped formal shirt and worn-out sandals, flanked by uniformed men of the Delhi Police. His sister sits next to him. After about ten minutes, he is to be produced in front of the judge. They make him get up. He walks straight, keeping his head high. He listens to his lawyer's arguments and then that of the government's. In a few minutes, the hearing is over. Another date. Kobad's sister wants to buy him a pair of shoes. She asks him to put his foot on a piece of paper. She marks the outline of his foot with a pen. And then he is taken away.

Like all his comrades in the jungles of Bastar, and elsewhere, Kobad Ghandy believes too much in the cause he has taken up. He has too much belief in the idea of revolution. He may be condemned, it will not matter to him. He would say, as Fidel Castro said in his famous 1953 speech: 'History will absolve me.'

That is about him. To us, Kobad may not matter. Or Ganapathi. But what does Nobel laureate Amartya Sen have to say about what the pink newspapers often term as India's elephant-sized growth opportunities? 'India cannot be seen as doing splendidly if a great many Indians— sometimes most Indians—are having very little improvement in their deprived lives,' he said in a recent newspaper article.

Now, let us translate this into one particular image. For a moment, think: what if Usman ever gets to go to Giridih? Or what if Giridih visits him in Gurgaon?

Afterword

COMRADE ANURADHA GHANDY AND THE IDEA OF INDIA

On 5 February this year, in a village in Uttar Pradesh, a 16-year-old Dalit girl was attacked by three upper-caste youth. While she was returning from the fields, they dragged her away in an attempt to rape her. When she resisted and shouted for help, they fled. But before running away they chopped off her ears and part of her hand with an axe and badly injured her face. The inhumanity of this action would be unthinkable in any civilised society. But here, in India, it is hardly noticed. This is routine. In our highly patriarchal system, a girl's life is cheap; a poor Dalit girl is less than a chattel in the prevailing upper-caste/upper-class social thinking.

This single incident brings out three factors. First: the intolerance to any form of Dalit assertion, even if it is an assertion to resist rape. Second: the impunity with which Dalits can be attacked even in a state ruled by a Dalit leader that comes from the knowledge that the establishment will not touch the culprits. Third: it brings out the arrogance of the upper-caste youth, a superiority complex instilled since birth.

Rahul Pandita's *Hello, Bastar* coincides with the third death anniversary of Anuradha Ghandy. It is an occasion to remember her monumental contribution to the understanding of the caste/Dalit question in India and the significance of its resolution for the democratization of the individuals, and with it, the society. In a society where a small percentage of people consider themselves superior to all others merely due to birth, there can be no democratic consciousness. Where major sections of society are seen as inferior (and nearly 20 percent treated as untouchable) merely due to their birth, what results is a society that is hierarchical and not democratic. Even nation building and national consciousness get sacrificed at the altar of caste. Caste consciousness supercedes national consciousness, identity, loyalty—everything.

Anuradha's pure simplicity, her total lack of any ego or arrogance and her innate attitude to see all others as her equal drew her to the issue of caste in her early college days itself. The outbreak of the Dalit Panther movement in Mumbai (1974) further helped fuel thought on this question. She began studying the caste/Dalit question at a time when the issue was anathema to most shades of Communists. And by 1980 itself she had presented extensive analytical articles on the issue. The Dalit question and Ambedkar's role in taking it up was not in fashion amongst the Left then, and Anuradha's writings resulted in hostile reactions from many of these circles. But Anuradha stood her ground. Even as a lecturer later in Nagpur, she lived in a Dalit basti and worked among them thereby getting a practical experience of their lives—the horrific humiliation they face, and their struggles for self-respect much before their desperate struggles for livelihood.

Anuradha was one of the few in the 1970s to understand the negative impact of casteism on genuine democratization of society—a disease worse than the apartheid in South

Africa. Anuradha's creativity and intellect was a product of the fact that her mind was not fettered by hundreds of ego complexes. She was modesty personified. Her child-like simplicity with no element of pretence, trickery, or cunning allowed her to focus fully on whatever issue she took up. Her mind was not dissipated in varied futile directions to create impressions, appearances and images. As a result, her mental sharpness and intellectual capacity continued to flower and grow even towards the last years of her life, even after she was afflicted with the deadly disease, systemic sclerosis. In the 35 years that I knew her—from a simple student leader to a mass leader—she never lost her straightforwardness and pristine honesty. I never saw her struggle to achieve this; it all came very naturally to her. One tends to see these values amongst the simple tribal folk who live with nature and have not as yet been corrupted by the system and are also outside of the caste framework.

Through all our ups and downs we were often apart for months. But the times we were together are the most cherished periods of my life. Her fiercely independent thinking acted as a great help to rational understanding of events, people and issues. There was no other person with whom I have had as vehement debates. This normally brought a balance to my often one-sided views.

Back to *Hello, Bastar*. This book by Rahul Pandita is an authentic introduction to a subject that is being much debated in the media. There have been other books on this subject, but they have primarily been based on secondary sources. But Rahul has personally investigated the issue, traversing difficult and often risky terrain. Such investigative journalism is a refreshing breeze in the stagnant air of superficiality that dominates reporting today. Having personally studied the developments in Chhattisgarh and having interacted with many revolutionaries and their sympathisers, the author has no doubt added to the reliability of the information. One may agree or disagree with the views presented, but the facts of the Maoist movement seem well elucidated. So, this book becomes an important source material for anyone seeking to study the particular model of development. For even if one does not agree, it is necessary to know the efforts and viewpoints going on in the country today. This is important in order to seek effective solutions to the problems—problems that are serious.

Generally, to the ordinary reader of the mainstream media, the issue is just that of violence. This book brings out that the question of violence is secondary; the key question is how to develop the country and its people. The Maoists have one method as reflected in their policies as elaborated in this book while the established government has another, seen in their economic and political policies over the past years.

Let us now address the larger question of India's real growth. The government's Economic Survey 2009-10 has rightly commented: 'A nation interested in inclusive growth views the same growth indifferently depending on whether the gains of the growth are heaped primarily on a small segment or shared widely by the population. The latter is cause for celebration but not the former. In other words, growth must not be treated as an end in itself, but as an instrument of spreading prosperity to all.' Then it goes on to show how inclusive growth has taken place in the country, by showing a growth in the per capita GDP and the per capita consumption expenditure of the country. But these figures, I am afraid, do not give an accurate picture as it averages out the billionaire's income and wealth with that of a pauper and puts them in a common category. This is particularly skewed in India where just a few families have a wealth equivalent to 25 percent of our GDP. All official indicators in fact show a terrifying situation within the country that is quite contrary to the rosy picture painted by the government. In the Global Hunger Index 2010, India ranks 67th among 88 countries— it was 65 in 2009. And if we turn to the recently-developed UNDP Multidimensional Poverty Index (MPI), which more accurately measures income on the basis of income, health, education etc., we find the situation even worse. India, it says, has 65 crore people who are poor on this index. It amounts to 55 percent population. Eight states of India (Bihar, Chhattisgarh, Jharkhand, Madhya Pradesh, Rajasthan, Uttar Pradesh and West Bengal) account for more people than those present in the 26 poorest countries of Africa.

According to the United Nations Children's Fund (UNICEF), India ranks better only than Ethiopia in the number of malnourished children (under five). In 2008, the percentage of malnourished children was 51 percent in Ethiopia, 48 in India, 46 in Congo, 44 in Tanzania, 43 in Bangladesh, 42 in Pakistan, 41 in Nigeria and 37 in Indonesia.

The Right to Food Campaign says that two-thirds of our women are anaemic. India is also at the very bottom of the recently-compiled 'Quality of Death' index. This new study, on the provision of end-of-life care, takes a look at the quality of life and care made available to the old and the dying in developed and 'emerging' economies of 40 countries. In a scale of ten, the US was at 6.2 while India figured last at 1.9. So pathetic is the situation that even a country like South Africa that got independence after India has an index that is double that of India's.

The water in our country is so badly polluted that it has turned into one of the major killers. According to the United Nations (UN), one lakh people die each year of waterborne diseases in India. A Planning Commission report adds that out of over 600 districts, one-third (203) have high fluoride content in drinking water that causes flourisis among 6.5 crore people. Thirty-five districts have high arsenic content that results in 50 lakh people suffering from poisoning; 206 districts have high iron content and 109 districts have high nitrate content. Then, according to a study led by the Registrar-General of India, 14 lakh infants die every year of five major preventable diseases. This includes eight lakh children who die within one month of their birth. The study said 23 lakh children died before completing five years of age in 2005 alone, and of these 14 lakh children died from preventable causes like pneumonia, diarrohea etc. Even as one can clearly see that India is a 'sick' nation, national expenditure on healthcare is amongst the lowest in the world. State governments now barely spend 0.5 percent of their GDP on healthcare and hygiene as compared to one percent in the 1970s. Only 34 percent of India's population has access to government hospitals.

If one looks at the issue of food, the situation appears equally grim. Per capita food grain consumption has fallen from 177 kilos per year in 1991 to 151 kilos in 1998 (it has dropped even further now). Compare this to 182 kilos recorded by the LDCs (Least Developed Countries) and 196 kilos in Africa.

Such then is the horrific condition of the people of our country—that too after six decades of independence. This surely is a matter of grave concern. And, add to this the massive destruction of our land, forest and water resources, together with the total degradation of the moral fabric (corruption, greed, nepotism), is it not time to discuss various alternate models to better the policies of governance?

For those serious about our country and its future, there is an urgent need for discussion of various models and policies being put forward—like those of the National Advisory Council (NAC), various commission reports, Maoist views and from civil society. As far as the Maoist viewpoint goes, this book offers excellent information. Besides general reading, this book could be useful for any future dialogue between the government and the Maoists which is an urgent necessity.

Overall, this book will be a very useful read for varied sections of people to understand the root causes of the four decade-old Maoist movement in India and their alternatives in the spheres of economy and social life. Rahul has put in enormous effort to produce a work based

on an important phenomena in today's India. This will
only help any discourse to evolve a better future.

April 2011   KOBAD GHANDY
                                          Tihar Jail, New Delhi

Index

Scan QR code to access the
Penguin Random House India website